SOUTH *of* BIXBY BRIDGE

Ryan Winfield

BIRCH
PAPER
PRESS

South of Bixby Bridge
By Ryan Winfield

ISBN:
ISBN-13: 978-0615511603
ISBN-10: 0615511600

Cover design: Ryan Winfield
Cover image of women: Aldra / Vetta / Getty Images
Cover image of booze: Mark Wragg / Vetta / Getty Images
The Licensed Material is being used for illustrative purposes only; and any person depicted in
the Licensed Material, if any, is a model.
Back cover photo of author: Mike Chard

Printed in the United States of America.

BIRCH PAPER PRESS
Post Office Box 4252
Seattle, Washington 98194

For Bridget

ACKNOWLEDGMENTS

Stewart Stern is my best friend and mentor. He taught me everything I know about drama. This story was born on the Congress Avenue Bridge on the wings of a million Mexican free-tailed bats as Stewart and I watched the hot Austin sun slip behind Lady Bird Lake.

Jack Remick, the fighting bishop of science, the novelist, the poet, and the teacher, invested countless hours instructing me on language, style, and rhythm. I owe him a great debt—a debt I can only pay by promising to pay it forward.

Robert J. Ray taught me to discover the myths and rituals buried in my prose and his rewriting course moved me deeper into my story. His quiet laugh when I hit the mark was a balm that kept me writing.

Joel Chafetz's keen ear always heard what I was trying to write even when I didn't. His feedback on my pages was invaluable.

To the poets, painters, and polymaths who welcomed me into their third Sunday sanctuary, I thank you all—Don Harmon, Geri Gale, M. Anne Sweet, Gordon Wood, Jack Remick, and Priscilla Long.

A special thanks to Geri Gale whose proofreading pen plucked my errors from the following pages.

"Loneliness is the most terrible poverty."

—Mother Teresa

SOUTH *of* BIXBY BRIDGE

1 *Afraid of What?*

Y ou gotta hit rock bottom to get sober. Some of the people in here must've bounced and hit twice. I hit 30 in March and no way can I picture the rest of my life without a drink. But they got a saying for that here too.

It's the day before Thanksgiving and I'm standing at the Brave Ascent treatment center window watching a man in a trench coat stumble up the street. He stops at the gate, fumbles the latch, climbs the steps, and slumps down in the doorway. Then he reaches into his coat—nothing looks more like booze than a bottle in a brown-paper bag. Poor bastard. Maybe he can have my bed.

I only agreed to treatment because Stephanie left me.

~~~

I remember the day, 28 days ago, when she walked in the door from a Halloween party and cut a beeline to the refrigerator. The refrigerator was gone, a blue Igloo ice chest on the floor in its empty nook. Stephanie winged into the living room wearing high heels and a halo, white panties, and a push-up bra. She stood in front of me, hooked her hands on her hips and said, What the fuck, Trevor?

I just sat there on the couch, an empty pizza box on my lap, and three empty wine bottles on the coffee table. What? I said.

Where's the refrigerator?

I started selling stuff when they fired me at Edward & Bliss where I was selling stocks. I told Stephanie they made a big mistake, said I had my broker by the balls, swore the regional boss would call when he got my message. Then I sat around drinking what was left of my wine collection. The recycle bins bulged with bottles, the neighbors whispered, and the only calls were from my mortgage servicer threatening me about payments past due.

Where is it? Stephanie said again.

I sold it.

Stephanie dug her heels into the carpet and, with her halo shaking, stood there in her angel costume lingerie whipping me with a year's worth of contempt. She said I was a lousy lover. She said I was a drunk. She said we were over. I walked out when she started whipping me for real with a wine bottle.

Driving into the city that night, I washed down three caps of GHB with a six-pack of silver bullets. Alcohol made me feel. Alcohol and GHB together made me feel better.

At Clift's historic Redwood Room I met a beautiful Brazilian highballing on Johnnie Walker and sodas and then the GHB kicked in and I don't know how she did it, but the Brazilian turned herself into a Russian or at least it sounded like Russian that chick was yelling when I came to, pissing on her cold apartment floor and she kicked me to the community bathroom in the flophouse hall, but I was creeped out so I cut out into the bright swirling afternoon street with no idea where to find my Porsche, the Porsche my mom gave me just before she died. I never used to drive it drunk.

Laying shoe leather over half of San Francisco until sunset, I found the Porsche with three parking tickets under the wiper.

I was still stoned when I pulled up to my dark house and I found a bright-red notice taped to the front door advertising the foreclosure sale to our entire neighborhood. Stephanie was gone and so were her things. I lost Stephanie. I lost my job. I lost my house.

I found a half-dozen Vicodin and washed them down with the last of my GHB. Then I climbed into the backyard hot tub gazebo, pulled the privacy doors closed, and melted into the 106-degree water letting the drugs sponge up my second thoughts.

When I woke, I was flat on a gurney parked in the crowded emergency room hallway and Stephanie was leaning over me crying. Her mother Barbara was there too. My throat was sore, my tongue swollen. Stephanie handed me a plane ticket to this Brave Ascent bed they were holding for me and Barbara drove me to the airport.

From the air, the Central Valley spread beneath me, green and gold, and when the sun hit just right, I saw a thousand miles of rivers and sloughs crawling through it like silver veins until they met in the delta and bled into San Francisco Bay. The flight south was short. I sobered up just enough to remember what I had agreed to when the city of Fresno rose out my window like an oil rig on a dead sea.

~~~

That was 28 days ago. I missed an entire fucking month and I have a green graduation chip from yesterday's bullshit Brave Ascent punch party in my pocket to prove it. But I'm getting out of this treatment center hell house, here—today—now.

The yellow cab pulls up and honks. I sling my duffel over my shoulder and turn for the door. My roommate Jared rolls over in bed. His thick, mussed hair sticks up on one side and he rubs his eyes and blinks up at me even though he was pretending to sleep. He says,

You afraid?

Afraid of what? I ask.

Afraid of leaving, bro. Before my mom left us, she asked me what I would do if I weren't afraid.

I'm not afraid of anything.

Everybody's afraid of something, he says.

I sit next to him on his bed. He looks at me like a puppy in the pound. I never had a little brother, but Jared makes me wish I did.

I remember when Jared showed up to Brave Ascent, a week after I did. He was coming down off crystal—the bathtub rocket-fuel meth that launches you into orbit, sleepless week after sleepless week of real nightmares—and he crouched in the corner snapping at the air trying to eat his own head. When he landed, he slept for a week. When he woke, he shambled into group and sat right next to Rooster.

Rooster is an asshole. He's here on a nudge from the judge because he had a bad trip, wandered away from a pool party and stumbled three blocks buck-ass naked into a sleeping family's kitchen to make himself a sandwich. Turns out Rooster is an unlucky asshole because the father in the house just happened to want a sandwich too. The police followed the ambulance to the hospital.

Rooster got his name because he corners new patients and makes them promise to give him a blowjob if he has a cock hanging below his knees. Then he hikes up his pant leg and shows them the rooster-in-a-noose tattoo on his calf. He laughs at his own joke and struts around crowing for an hour every time.

When Jared slumped into the chair next to Rooster, we all knew what was coming. Jared had been chasing the white dragon under the knives of dealers in their icehouses for so long that he thought Rooster was serious and he dropped to his knees in Rooster's lap to give him the blowjob he was asking for. Rooster freaked out. Floored Jared. Kicked him in the ribs. Called him a faggot. I yanked Rooster off Jared, walked him across the room, and put a hole in the Sheetrock with the back of his head. The main counselor Mr. Shaw limped in and broke up the fight before I could put the rest of Rooster through the wall.

Mr. Shaw pointed his finger at Rooster. Sit down and shut up, he said. Addiction is a deadly disease. Save your grab-ass games and hateful name calling for civilian life.

Rooster got defensive. Swelled up. Said he was going to sue. Accused Mr. Shaw of exaggerating the consequences of an occasional binge, a little recreational drug use. He said Mr. Shaw was part of the treatment business and that the treatment business is big business.

That's when Mr. Shaw unstrapped his prosthetic leg and hurled it into the middle of the room. His plastic skin-colored leg lay on the floor bent at the knee joint, his sock and rubber-sole wingtip shoe still attached. He stood there on one leg and waved his amputated stub at Rooster. That's your exaggerated consequence, he said. Me? I passed out drunk in front of the TV—legs crossed for 13 hours—diabetes—no circulation—no leg. And you tell me I'm exaggerating, you asshole.

It was a sad thing to see. I just stared at the leg and wondered who would carry it back to Mr. Shaw.

~~~

With Rooster still here, I know Jared doesn't want me to leave. I jab a finger in his ribs, tickling him. I say,

You're not afraid of old Rooster are ya?

Jared laughs. No, he says. I'm not afraid of that jerk. I'll punch and hunch him just like you showed me.

Well, what are you afraid of?

Leaving my dad all alone.

And if you weren't afraid, what would you do?

Jared drops his head. I'd go be with my mom, he says.

The cabbie lays on his horn. I rub Jared's shaggy head. I say,

I'm still not afraid of anything, pal.

Well whatcha gonna do then?

I guess just get my Porsche and drive south—get out of this damn valley.

Can I come with?

You mean fuck the treatment?

No! Jared says, I graduate next week. How cool would that be, you and me taking the 13th step together?

All right, Jared. Look me up when you get out.

You promise?

I don't want to promise him. Everyone always says they'll get together and do this and do that but they never do. Jared will never learn that. He's too innocent to be an addict. But he is an addict.

I reach in my duffel and grab my big blue sobriety book, the book Mr. Shaw gave to me yesterday at graduation. I open the cover and write Barbara's number inside. I toss the book to Jared. I say,

You can get me a message at the number inside.

As I open the door to leave, Jared says,

Hey, Trevor.

I turn back. He lowers his eyes to the book. He says,

I've only known you three weeks, but you're the best friend that I ever had.

2 Yes, I've Changed

Across town, at the Santa Fe Railroad Depot, I slide two 20s beneath the scratched Plexiglas window and point to SACRAMENTO on the dingy sign. The sweaty attendant looks like a chicken in a battery cage. He pushes the ticket and 14 dollars out. You'll hafta hustle, he says.

Jogging to the waiting train, I pass an old woman tugging a pile of faded luggage on a roller with a broken wheel. She won't make it in time. I turn back and scoop up her bags. We board just as the final whistle blows.

After I stow her bags with mine in an overhead compartment, she points to the window seat. Would you mind taking the window? she says. I get claustrophobic. I never used to.

The train is almost empty but her eyes plead for company so I squeeze past her into the seat and then she settles in beside me, fussing with everything, her white ball of permed hair waving the suffocating smell of Avon perfume and I'm about to move when the train jerks forward and she falls back into her seat and says,

Oh, heh! Everybody's always in such a rush nowadays.

Then she smiles at me and I don't mind her smell any longer.

Well now, here we are then, she says. Thank you, dear. My name is Evelyn.

Nice to meet you, Evelyn. I'm Trevor.

Are you going home for Thanksgiving, Trevor?

Yes—well, sort of I guess. My girlfriend is meeting the train in Sacramento. After that, it's one minute at a time.

Are you in Fresno for University?

I laugh. Something like that.

~~~

I don't tell her about treatment, or that I graduated six years ago from Sac State with a BA in political science because my teachers said I would make a good attorney, but then I discovered alcohol and switched my real major to drinking. I never drank because of my dad. Nineteen years old and never even a drop but when I pledged the fraternity, they made me down a full 40 of Old English 800 High Gravity. I felt like I would puke. Then a strange thing happened—a key turned in a lock and chains that had tangled in my guts for 20 years slipped away. I felt invincible.

I met Stephanie my senior year. I was three years ahead of her—she was a decade ahead of me. I reread the same paragraph about Pinochet and Chile's legacy of torture for two hours before I found the courage to ask her name. What took you so long? she said.

~~~

Evelyn is still talking. I haven't been listening. I say,

I'm sorry, come again.

Your parents, she says. Are they in Sacramento also?

No. They're not.

I'm sorry. I didn't—

It's okay, I say. How about you? Where are you going?

Oh, yes, she says, I'm just going as far as Stockton. My daughter and her husband live there. You look like their son, my grandson. In fact, you remind me of him—older, but I would bet my teeth you looked just like him as a boy. You have the same blue eyes. He's 10. Here, I have a picture.

Evelyn unsnaps her wallet and passes me a photo. Her grandson has a shaggy head of curly blond hair falling into his blue eyes like I did, but he doesn't look like me at 10—he's smiling.

Evelyn taps her finger on the photo. I'll bet you looked just like him at this age, she says.

I don't have any pictures of myself so I really wouldn't know, I say, passing her back the photo. My eyes are wet. It just happens sometimes. I turn away and watch power poles pass out the window. The train doesn't seem to be moving very fast unless you look right at the poles. My eyes range east looking for something to focus on before a memory can slip in—green tufts in the shallows of dry hills, I wonder if they're ash trees—I think Fresno means "ash tree" in Spanish. My mind flies out farther into the haze, out to where the distant Sierra Nevada bites into the sky.

The power poles rush by, the rocking rhythm of the rails keeps time, and fading in the background, Evelyn drones sweetly on—

My daughter—her name's Ginger—she wanted to pick me up—insisted on it—but I like to ride the train—she says I'm getting too old to travel alone—oh, heh!—everyone's too old, or too young, to travel alone—

My defenses droop with my eyes and the memory slips in.

~~~

My grandfather had one dream—to drive the Autobahn in a new Porsche. When breast cancer killed my grandmother, he ordered a 1983 Porsche 911SC convertible with the life insurance. He flew to Stuttgart, met his Porsche at the factory and drove the Autobahn before shipping it home. Grandpa loved that Porsche. Four years later, he died on Christmas and left it to my mom.

Grandpa also left Mom his money but it wasn't much money because my dad used it to open his bar and then drank through every penny before they even shipped the bar sign.

I remember it was March, my 10th birthday, and my mom made

me a crocodile birthday cake with 10 candles on its tail. I had a neighbor friend over and we were finishing dinner when my dad stormed in drunk. He paced the kitchen yelling. He said we didn't respect him. He said we didn't wait for him to eat supper. He said we didn't even tell him there was a party. Then he threw the crocodile cake in the trash where it mangled into a mush of green frosting.

Mom collected the dishes and washed them in the sink. She was always calm. Dad paced faster, yelled louder. My friend ran home and I crawled beneath the table to listen. Dad said,

Why in God's name do you need to parade around town in a sports car? We're struggling to just get by.

Sometimes Mom yelled back, sometimes she should not have. Getting by? she said. If you didn't drink your register every week, we'd do a whole hell of a lot better than just get by.

Dad stopped pacing. His eyes turned serious. He said,

I'm selling that damn car tomorrow.

Mom pulled her soapy hands from the sink and stripped off her wedding ring. She held the ring out to Dad and said,

If you want something to sell, sell this!

Dad slapped Mom's face. The ring bounced on the linoleum floor. I watched it roll behind the refrigerator. Mom turned back to the dishes. She said,

Oh, go to hell.

She yelped when he wrapped his hands around her neck. Then she went quiet. I wanted to pull him off Mom—choke him—stab him—kill him. But all I could do was beat my fists against his back.

Mom gasped for air when he let go of her neck to punch me in the face. I bounced on the linoleum too. I wished I could roll behind the refrigerator.

WHEN I WAKE, Evelyn is gone. The photo of her grandson sits propped beside me in her empty seat—she must have thought I needed the company. As the train hisses to a stop at the Sacramento station, I tuck the photo in my pocket.

The doors pop open. The train is fuller now and I wait for the other passengers to spill out and then I step off, sling my duffel over my shoulder, and scan the crowd for Stephanie. As the people wash past, I spot Stephanie's mother Barbara standing alone, her slender arms wrapped around her shoulders even though the sun has already warmed the air. I approach Barbara. She hugs me. I pull away.

Where's Stephanie, Barbara? I say.

She needs more time, Trevor. She didn't want to come.

So she sends her mother?

I wanted someone to be here for you.

Why didn't Stephanie want to be here?

She's not sure you've changed.

Not sure I've changed?

Have you?

Yes, I've changed.

~~~

I'm not really surprised that Stephanie isn't here. They only allowed us one hour of evening phone access in treatment and even then, I had to line-jump by trading dessert from my dinner tray and Stephanie's cell wouldn't accept collect calls and whenever I dialed Barbara, she would never say if Stephanie was there or not, but I made her promise to tell Stephanie what time the train got in—I even prayed that Stephanie would be here—so I'm not surprised she isn't.

~~~

Have you eaten yet? Barbara says. You must be starving.

Barbara drives us east in her Pontiac sedan and I watch the brown, dead November highway roll past. The palm trees here aren't the ones you see on postcards because nobody bothers to trim them and the new growth folds over and dies until they resemble giant shaggy-headed monsters leaning over broken freeway fences.

Barbara passes by the Folsom exit—the exit to my house, my house that the bank auctioned on the Sacramento courthouse steps two weeks into treatment. High bidder won my house and everything left inside because I had no money and no way to move things into a pricey Public Storage unit.

Exiting in Eldorado Hills, Barbara turns up her street and the lawns we pass are all dead-brown but Barbara's lawn is green as a golf course and her porch swings with baskets of color. Her house is a cozy mid-century rambler with a red terracotta-tile roof and white-painted bricks. She pulls beneath the carport and parks next to my car and I'm glad she remembered to cover it.

I get out and circle my car tossing the bricks aside that hold the mildewed cover in place and then grabbing the canvas with both hands, I uncover my mother's white 1983 Porsche convertible.

Please stay and have lunch, Barbara says.

I'm tempted to go inside for lunch and see if Stephanie is staying here but I throw my duffel behind the seat and climb into the Porsche. The interior smells like damp leather and vanilla—Barbara hung a vanilla tree car-freshener from the mirror. I rip it free and toss it beneath my seat.

Where are you staying, Trevor? Barbara says.

I don't know yet.

She drops her head. I wish you could stay here for a while, she says. Maybe after the holidays then, when Stephanie goes back to the dorms—if you're not already settled.

Don't worry about me.

You need a peaceful place to repair yourself.

I am repaired, I say.

Pushing in the clutch, I slide the key in the ignition and turn it—Click—click—click. The battery is dead.

I pop the boot, rummage through my dirty clothes, and pull out the cables. I can feel Barbara watching me. She says,

What are your plans for Thanksgiving tomorrow?

I drag the cables around to Barbara's car. I say,

Pop your hood, will you?

Barbara gets in her Pontiac, pulls the hood release latch, and starts the engine. I lift her hood and connect our batteries. The Porsche turns over slow and weak. I lean out and give Barbara a thumbs-up. Give me some juice, I say. She revs her engine and the Porsche starts. I close the hoods and put the cables away.

Barbara stands next to me with her arms wrapped around her shoulders again. She says,

I feel just awful about this, Trevor.

Don't feel bad.

I just wish I could help, she says.

Maybe I could use your phone number on my résumé? I'll call you and check for messages. And you know—check in.

Barbara nods fast and I see she's choked up so I kiss her on the forehead. Stephanie's wrong, you know, I say. I have changed.

She'll come around, she says. She loves you.

I love her too, Barb.

I know you do, Trevor.

I climb in, shut the car door, and wave goodbye. I back the Porsche into the street and the engine dies. I jump out, push it rolling downhill, jump in, and pop the clutch—the engine fires back to life.

I turn around at the intersection and drive back to reassure Barbara still standing in her driveway with her arms wrapped around her shoulders. I press the clutch, rev the engine, toot the horn twice, and then speed away.

3 God Always Provides

ighway 99 runs south from Sacramento on the eastern edge of the valley. In summer, rotten tomatoes pile up in the ditches bounced from a parade of tomato trucks and when a truck turns over the road turns slick as oil. In winter, the tule fog rolls in a thousand feet deep, fog so thick you can't see the cars piling up in front of you and the cleanup crews bring floodlights to find the bodies flung in ditches.

My mother's car points for home like a whipped horse returning to its stable even though the barn has burned down. It's been a dry fall. No fog yet. Out my window, a sea of silver tassels flutters in the breeze, tassels tied to grape vines to scare the starlings away.

On the grape farm near our house, the farmer draped netting over the vines and when I was a boy, I would duck beneath the netting, crawl beneath the vines, and imagine a labyrinth of secret caves leading to a new world. It was my favorite thing to do until I came face-to-face with a hissing rat snake.

It feels good to be back behind the wheel, to be moving. Moving steadies my mind. Driving, I let my thoughts slide along with soft edges and if I grasp at them for a closer look, they bob and disappear like apples in a barrel of water. I like it that way.

I exit the highway.

Passing beneath the famous Modesto Arch, I read the town slogan and laugh—WATER, WEALTH, CONTENTMENT, HEALTH.

I park in front of the bar. After all these years, the neon-yellow CARL'S BAR sign still glows in the window. Someone added a smaller neon-red sign beneath it, and at least that sign is honest—ENTER AT YOUR OWN RISK.

~~~

I remember when the call came—Mom's breast cancer was back. A recurrence she called it. The cancer ate through her body like a pack of hungry dogs in a butcher shop and when I wasn't at the hospital with Mom, I was here at this bar sucking down whiskey and Cokes with Dad. I hated my dad but I wasn't 21 yet and drinking with him was the only way to be served.

THE CLICK OF POOL BALLS mingles with the mindless sound of TV as I step in the door. Across from the pool table, the antique jukebox still bubbles like a lava lamp. The unfinished wood floors still reek of stale beer, and the long bar top has been shellacked so many times beer glasses still float two inches above the wood. This bar is a world between worlds—it never changes.

As I approach the bar, peanut shells crunch beneath my feet and Hank looks up from his romance novel with moist eyes beneath his scarred brow. He recognizes me and smiles. He says,

Hey, Trev! Goddamn it's been a long time. How are ya?

Fair to midland, Hank.

You mean middlin'?

You're awfully learned for a fella who names his bar Carl's Bar when he himself is named Hank.

He laughs and sets his book down on the bar.

You know better'n anyone it had that goddamn name when I bought it, he says, grabbing a glass. Whiskey and Coke, right?

No, I say, not today, Hank.

Shame on me for assuming, he says, putting the glass back.

I nod to his romance novel and say,

Still reading the classics, I see.

Ah shit, who knows anything about anything anyways?

Well do you know where Carl is?

Down at the old Carver Road Church.

I thought this was his church.

Well, you know how these damn Christ-ers have a day before Thanksgiving sermon—bad for business. Shit. But you can probably just catch him.

I know Hank wants to tell me not to bother, to leave and not come back. But I dismiss the concern in his eyes with a smile. I say,

It's good to see you, Hank.

I SLIP UNNOTICED inside the cramped Carver Road Church. It looks like every nondenominational church I've ever seen. Tight weave red carpet and cheap wooden pews with Hymnbook holders in their backs and tiny yellow pencils stuck in holes. And flocked in the pews are rows of heads with shorn, farmboy haircuts. They look like bobble heads lapping up the sweaty sermon of the young, wild-eyed preacher. I stand quiet and listen.

For the times past may have sufficed to have wrought the desire of the Gentiles to have walked in lasciviousness, lusts, winebibbings, revelings, carousings, and abominable idolatries. Here Peter admonishes us as being now called and ordained to contend against the devil by faith and prayer. Later on he brings in the same warning in clearer phrase, exhorting Christians to be sober and watchful. He says—Your adversary the devil, as a roaring lion in the midst of a flock of sheep, walketh about, seeking whom he may devour!

The preacher pauses to wipe his brow and drink from his glass of water before continuing in a calmer tone.

As we give thanks tomorrow, let us resolve to be sober and watchful. God bless and keep you my striving lambs. Keep coming back!

In the corner behind the preacher, at the wood bench of an old melodeon, a woman's tower of gray hair, sprayed up and cropped flat like a garden hedge, moves up and down as she pumps the pedal and organ music rides the stale air like screeching cats screwing on a roof.

The congregation shuffles past me. I spot him at the back of the crowd. He looks much older than I remember. His shoulders are still wide, his barrel chest still hangs over his waist, but his legs are thin and he's dragging a crooked foot. How long has it been, almost 10 years now?

He limps by without noticing me.

I reach out and touch his shoulder. Dad.

He turns around with no expression and stares at me silent until I wonder if he hasn't soaked his brain for good. Then he coughs into his hand and says,

Well, well—if it ain't the Prodigal Son.

WE WALK TOGETHER down the street to a greasy-spoon diner called the Hangtown Fry. Dad carries an enormous Bible that he has highlighted and underlined so many times it springs from its binding like an accordion. We sit on cracked vinyl stools. Dad flops his Bible on the counter. On the other side of Dad, a skinny punk with a ring through his eyebrow leans over to his buck-toothed friend and mutters, Great—fucking church crowd.

A tired waitress appears behind the counter. Her eyes seem to apologize for having to work here. She folds her hands in front of her apron and sighs.

What'll it be boys? she says.

Dad smiles. Doll, could I get just a drop of whiskey if you have it? For medicinal purposes, you know.

Don't push it, Carl, she says.

Figures, he says. Coffee and apple juice in front of my son—but make it organic!

Then he turns to me saying,

I know damn well she's got a bottle back there.

You ever try to quit?

You want to reform me?

I open my menu and say,

Dinner's on me, Dad.

~~~

My dad bankrupted his bar, almost before he opened the doors. The neon CARL'S BAR sign arrived the same day he closed the sale with Hank. Hank felt bad so he hung the sign. The name stuck and so did Dad. He picked out a barstool where he could see his name in the window and then he spent the next 18 years polishing that stool into a perfect wood-worn impression of his ass. He tells everyone the bar is named after him. He says Carl is Old Norse for "Free Man," but to me there isn't anything free about being stuck on a barstool.

Mom willed me her interest in the family house but before her headstone was even up, Dad listed the house and didn't offer me a penny. By the time I got the job at Edward & Bliss, he had burned through the money and he called me.

~~~

My dad's gruff voice snaps me back to the diner.

You listening to me, Son? Why would you stop sending money?

I want to tell him he's lucky I ever sent a dime. I want to remind him he drank my inheritance. I want to get up and walk out. Instead, I just look over my menu at him and say,

I lost my job, Dad.

Dad covers one nostril, leans over and blows a string of snot onto the floor. He calls it a farmer's salute. He says,

It should be easy enough for a greedy stockbroker to find work in this drunken economy. You know damn well things are tough for me without your mother around. It ain't cheap for me keepin' up her flower service either, you know. You gotta honor your mother, Son.

I knew coming here was a mistake. In treatment, Mr. Shaw said I need to deal with my family issues to recover. But I only came here because I don't know where else to go. I need a base camp. Dad must read my mind.

You ain't staying for Thanksgiving tomorrow, he says. I won't be home—no siree. Pastor invited me to supper with them.

~~~

I remember Thanksgivings at our house, never a big deal the way they were for other kids. My mom would cook a royal feast but Dad made her serve it in the living room on TV trays and he would be halfway through his plate by the time Mom and I sat down to say grace— Dad the big Christian, Dad who carries his Bible around.

~~~

Dad, I don't care anything about Thanksgiving, I say. But I was actually hoping to maybe crash at your place for a while—just until I find a new job.

He clicks his tongue, shakes his head. He says,

I'd put ya up but ain't got no room cause I quit workin' to serve the Lord full-time and Pastor put me up in an apartment but it's a shoebox for Christ's sake. You'd think the damn church'd treat their elders better'n this—me followin' the good book'n all. I gotta walk around hunched over all the time.

He straightens up on his stool and measures his stature against mine. Then he slumps back down and pats his hand on his Bible. You're young yet, Son, he says. You'll figure something out—God always provides.

The punk next to Dad rolls his eyes. He leans over to his buck-toothed friend. Fucking Bible thumpers, he says.

Dad whips around. What'd you say, son?

Nothin', old man.

Dad smashes the punk in the face with his Bible, knocking him off his stool. Then he leans over and says,

Now that's what I call Bible thumping.

I jump up to get between them. My coffee spills, burning my hand. The punk picks himself off the floor. I stare him down while his buck-toothed friend drags him from the diner and threatens to return with friends, nail us to the wall, and beat the souls out of us.

Dad hops off his stool, blows another farmer's salute and then limps toward the bathroom. Calling back to me, he says,

I gotta go drain my snake. Order me some eggs, Son!

4 The Bridge

I roll onto the 580 and speed toward the orange glow burning in the western sky. A wave of determination lifts me over Altamont pass where tall wind turbines stand black on the horizon, their giant blades turning slow in the wind, and as Modesto fades into darkness in my rearview mirror, I release my dad and he slips away in a sea of memory and sinks beneath me like a shipwrecked skeleton resting on the dark and silent valley floor.

I hit the Bay Bridge. Drop a gear. Floor it. The Porsche pushes me back into the seat until she hits 110. The speed makes me feel immortal and I'm tempted to jerk the wheel right and fly, to plunge off the bridge and sail into the night, to cut free from the world and join the stars—one weightless wink that beats any drug.

The Yerba Buena Tunnel that splits the bridge saves me from a bad decision and as I speed beneath the orange lights on the ceiling 50 feet above, I feel fine—I feel clean—I feel alive. I'm being pulled along without consent, pushed by a thousand choices already made, and as the roof rips off the tunnel, I surrender to the night sky above.

And there she is, San Francisco!

A magic island coast. A tall chorus of black skyscrapers cuts a jagged edge against the burning sky—sirens caroling me to wreck myself against their wild concrete shores. The winking windows of a thousand janitors cleaning a million offices, the green glow of blurry harbor lights bleeding into the bay, the bright-white light atop the sparkling Transamerica Pyramid shining into the night like the star on a feral God's thousand-foot foldout Christmas tree.

Everything looks better from far away—earth from the moon, people from a postcard, San Francisco from the Bay Bridge.

There isn't one door in San Francisco that will open for me tonight and the addicts and thugs are already creeping from their holes to feed on the city like vampires, but I don't care—I know my way around.

ON THE DARK EDGE OF TOWN, in the shadow of the bridge, I park across from the La Hacienda Motel. Its blood-red VACANCY sign flickers against the black sky. A letter board reads ROOMS $49— WEEKLY RATE AVAILABLE.

I turn my pockets out and count my money—$37.

Reclining my seat, I settle in for the night. Beneath the stars, beneath the bridge, I huddle beneath my jacket. It's strange how just a thin piece of fabric can make a person feel safe—a tent on a cold mountain, a blanket in a dark room, a jacket in a beat-down Porsche.

The blood-red sign flicks across the convertible canvas top shadowing the strips of duct tape that patch the tear, the tear that's been there for 20 years.

~~~

I remember the morning after Dad hit me—Mom leaned over my bed and brushed the hair away from my swollen eye. I could always tell my mom loved me because she smiled when she looked at me. Not like other people. Other people smile and look at me but I know it's fake because sometimes I catch them right when they look away and the smile is gone before their heads turn. That morning, Mom smiled down at me from the edge of my bed. She said,

How do you feel about going away with me, Trevor? Away to San Diego? Fly south like those robins we love? I visited there once. When I was your age. I think about it all the time.

We had to lower the convertible top to fit our big green suitcase in the backseat. We were rushing—neither of us thought about how we would raise it again.

Mom looked pretty that day driving the Porsche—her hair in a scarf, her sunglasses on. She was smiling. I remember feeling the wind in my hair. I remember yelling over the wind to ask her jokingly if the sign that said PCH meant *Harold and the Purple Crayon*. She laughed and said the sign was for Pacific Coast Highway but to me, it still felt like a peaceful purple day that we were drawing with our own magic crayon.

I knew something was wrong even before I looked. When I did look, I knew whatever was wrong was bigger than the storm clouds gathering offshore. The smile drained off her face. Not quick, like those fake smiles leave people, but slow.

She pulled off the highway and stopped in front of a bridge. The sign read BIXBY BRIDGE 1932.

The black, yawning mouth of Bixby Canyon opens the high cliffs and from its throat, a creek trickles into the blue immensity of the Pacific. Bixby Bridge is narrow and tall and it stretches over the deep canyon, a concrete tightrope that even the nimblest of cars crawl across.

The gathering storm clouds reflecting the afternoon light painted a paradise on the south side of the bridge—red-clay cliffs hugging the rocky shoreline, distant hills of towering redwoods, and a gentle golden highway rolling away south toward San Diego.

Then the dark clouds swept in and hid the bridge, hid the canyon in a deep and sudden quiet that I dared not disturb with even a breath. Mom looked at me and she was crying, an apology in her eyes, and she reached out and touched the bruise on my cheek and a raindrop hit her hand and another drop hit the windshield and then a great rush of rain fell, pelting the pavement, pooling into rivers, running off the gutters of the bridge, and disappearing into the black.

Back at home, Mom covered the Porsche with a tarp and locked it away in the garage behind our house. She never drove it again.

RAIN STREAMS DOWN the windshield, beats on the canvas roof, and leaks from the tear in the convertible top waking me. I don't remember dozing off and it must be late because the flickering motel sign is dead.

I start the Porsche, drive around the block, and pull beneath a covered parking garage. Settling back in, I look up at the tear in the convertible roof, the tear where our green suitcase cut the canvas when we forced the top closed, the tear marking the day Mom tore the illusion of safety from me.

The monument sign in front of the building across the street reads—SAN FRANCISCO HEALTH & RACQUET CLUB. I wonder if a shower and a shave will make me feel like a man again.

5 The Fat Man

The dirt of the valley washes off me and swirls down the shower drain. The racquet club is high-class—soft towels, hot shaving-cream dispensers, glass jars of disposable razors. I used to belong to a club like this in Folsom. Every day after work I swam laps and sat in the sauna before heading home to open a bottle of wine—sometimes two bottles—but as long as I swam my 50 laps I told myself I was fine.

As I finish shaving, another shower turns off. The Fat Man, buck naked except for a gold wedding band and pink flip-flops, bellies up to the next sink. His gorged gut rests on the counter and his floppy bologna tits hang against his arms.

He smiles at me in the mirror. Morning, he says. You getting away from a house full of family too? I hate Thanksgiving except for the leftovers. You know you really should wear flip-flops in here. Never can tell the kinda shit people step in. I picked up a plantar wart that took three weeks and four bottles of Dr. Scholl's to kill.

Ignoring him, I wash my face in the sink. He says,

My company imports a line of these Hawaiian sandals I got on here. I'd be happy to get you a pair gratis if you tell me your size.

I dry my face and when I pull the towel away, the Fat Man is facing me, his uncircumcised erection poking out from his tangled mass of black pubic hair like a little sausage wearing a roll-neck sweater. He winks at me and says,

You wanna take a steam?

I throw my face towel on the counter and walk away to dress. I wonder if the Fat Man has kids at home to go along with his wife. His beady eyes in their puffy sockets remind me of a sleep doctor my mom brought me to when I was 10. She brought me to the sleep doctor because I couldn't stay awake in school and I couldn't stay awake in school because I was up reading by flashlight and I was up reading by flashlight because I was terrified waiting for Dad.

~~~

We never made it to San Diego—I discovered Tolkien and Lewis and then I escaped into books. Dad never mentioned selling the Porsche again, but he fished Mom's wedding ring out from beneath the refrigerator and sold it.

I remember the winter was cold that year and Mom took a graveyard shift at the cannery to keep the heat on. Every night that she worked, I read in bed with my flashlight listening for Dad to come home from the bar. When I heard his emergency brake ratchet up in the drive, I killed the flashlight, stuffed it under the covers and pretended to sleep.

If Dad came home too early, he wasn't drunk enough and he kicked around the house yelling so loud the neighbor's dog took to barking. If he came home right when the bar closed, he crept into my room and kissed me goodnight with alcohol-soaked breath. If he came home too late, he was drenched with booze and sloppy sad and he dragged me into his bed and made me tickle his arm.

He made me play farmer. Made me rake my fingers down his thick forearm plowing the field. Made me tickle my way up to his shoulder watering the crop. If I stopped tickling before he fell asleep, he stirred awake and made me start over again. I remember lying in the dark, listening to him snore, smelling his foul breath, watching the shadow of his rising chest against the blue dawn slipping beneath the blinds, tickling his arm up and down, again and again, not daring to stop until I heard Mom come home.

I don't know why, but I always raced down the hall and dove back into my own bed before Mom even turned her key in the door.

Twice Mom took me to see the sleep doctor that winter. She stopped bringing me when Dad found his power-tool batteries dead in the garage freezer where I'd been stashing them. Dad blew his top. Mom told him he had put the batteries in the freezer himself and because he was drunk all the time, he believed her. Then Mom bought me my own batteries, gave them to me with a wink—but she never even asked me why I was reading with a flashlight.

By the time I hit 11, I threw away those books because I learned the truth—wizards and talking lions are just the fantasies of a little boy because the real world is full of rat snakes and fat men.

~~~

I grab my duffel and head for the locker room door. Stopping at the coat rack, I pat the pockets of the only coat hanging there. I pull out a wallet, open it, and take the cash. I look at the driver's license picture of the Fat Man, flip to a picture of his family—a wife and two boys. You cruise you lose, dude. I throw his wallet in the trash.

In the lobby, I snatch a newspaper from the counter and slip past the young receptionist with a thankful wink. I've learned you can hustle your way into almost anywhere with a smile.

As I walk to my car, I count the cash—215 bucks.

I throw my duffel in the Porsche boot. Then I pull out the roll of gray duct tape I keep in the corner and peeling the old, worn tape off the tear in the leaky canvas top, I patch a square of fresh strips.

6 *Never Been Better*

The hostess at Denny's looks like she's been there longer than the building has and she doesn't look happy to be working on Thanksgiving. She tells me to sit wherever I want and then she just stands there at the door like a coat check where you leave your hope.

Slipping into a window booth, I spread out the job section of the newspaper and pore over the short list of available broker jobs. Words jump off the blurry page and stick in my mind like newsprint on Silly Putty—experience needed, references required, performance history mandatory.

How do I explain being fired? How will I rationalize six months of unemployment? What do I say about rehab?

An offbeat waitress bounces by chewing gum and holding a coffeepot. I turn my cup upright. She fills it with burnt smelling diner sludge. Smiling down at me, she says,

I'm Summer.

Hi, I'm Trevor. It's nice to have a little summer drop in on such a gloomy day.

Gee, thanks, she says. Today's special is a turkey and roast beef Thanksgiving dinner with all the trimmings.

Is it lean roast beef?

She blows a pink bubble the size of her face. When it pops, she says, Lean roast beef? Are you fucking kidding me? It's Thanksgiving and you're at Denny's.

Yeah, well so are you.

Hey, I'm getting double time and my family's 3,000 miles away.

My family's farther away than yours is, I say.

Summer nods toward my newspaper and says,

We're hiring in the kitchen if you're looking for work.

Thanks. But I'm a money manager.

Oh! I could really use your help.

Well I happen to be free tonight.

She considers the offer, blows another bubble. She says,

I get off at seven if you wanna pick me up.

I'M HAVING SECOND THOUGHTS as I wait in my car across the street. Summer is cute, but I never would have dated her before and even though I need a place to crash tonight, I don't want to be just another Fat Man.

In treatment, Mr. Shaw told us about holiday sobriety meetings that just keep going 24 hours around the clock for people who are struggling. He said meetings are a good place to get connected and I thought about finding one, but drinking coffee from Styrofoam cups and listening to people bitch about their families isn't my idea of success. Besides, my problem is I need a job.

Summer steps from the diner door and looks around. She let her dark hair down and it scoops from her neck up to her cheeks. A black coat with a fake fur collar drapes around her shoulders and she traded her work slacks for blue jeans but she's still wearing her black heel-less clogs. She could be Stephanie's less-attractive younger sister.

She looks my way. I flash my headlights. She dodges across the street, climbs in and shuts the door. She says,

Nice Car. You'd think people'd tip better on holidays—cheap

bastards. You're cute, you know.

Summer pulls down her seatbelt and I latch it for her. You sure your friends won't mind me joining you? I say. Because I'm happy to just drop you off.

No. You're totally coming. My friends'll love you.

THE NOC-NOC BAR, a trendy neighborhood joint, is dark inside with graffiti-covered walls and zebra-striped columns framing private nooks that fill with an eclectic city crowd.

Summer pulls me to a table and introduces me to her three friends, all in their 20s. Tiffany, a blonde with a red braid hanging in her face, is clinging to Brad, a skinny rocker type wearing too tight jeans. Tony is taller than Brad is, but just as thin and the sour look on his face and his hard handshake tell me he was planning to couple with Summer.

After the introductions, Brad stands. He says,

I'll go get us some more drinks.

I'll have another fuzzy navel, Tiffany says.

Guinness for me, Tony says.

Summer smiles at me. Ooh, let's see now, she says, I think I'd like a screaming orgasm tonight.

How about you, Trevor?

Ah, just a Coke please.

Rum or whiskey?

No, just plain Coke.

Summer kisses my cheek. Oh, you're so darn cute, she says. Don't worry about driving, Trevor—I just live three blocks from here and we'll move the party over there later.

Yeah. I'm fine. Just a Coke.

Tony laughs. You a Mormon or something?

Why would I be Mormon?

Because you don't drink, dude.

You ordered Guinness, are you Irish?

Tiffany rolls her eyes at Summer. She says,

He at least smokes out right?

Summer looks at me. No, I say, I don't smoke out.

She steps away from me and folds her arms. She says,

If you wanna hang with us tonight, Trevor, you're gonna at least drink some shots!

They all turn on me so fast I can't think of anything to say. I back away from the table and then turn for the door. I didn't really want to spend Thanksgiving with a bunch of kids anyway.

As I exit the bar, I notice a sloppy drunk leaning against the brick wall bogarting a cigarette in his pale lips. The blue light from the NOC-NOC BAR sign floods down over him as he rocks back and forth like a corpse in the waves. I ask him for a smoke. He fishes in his pocket. They're American Spirit, he slurs.

I pluck a cigarette from the crumpled pack and light it with the trembling tip of his. Inhaling a long drag of calming smoke, I breathe a white cloud into the blue night air. I think maybe Summer will follow me out and apologize. She doesn't.

The drunk's eyes droop. He falls over to the side. I grab his arm and straighten him back up, lean him against the wall again.

You all right? I say.

He smiles. His cigarette drops from his mouth. He says,

Never been better.

MY TIRED FEET FALL, striking echoes in the quiet night, on wet cobblestones glistening in the amber glow of iron streetlamps, as I trudge the steep and narrow hillside streets of lofty painted ladies—Victorian row houses snuggled together against the cold.

I look in the windows—

Young couples lounge beside fires sipping wine.

Smiling families sit at long tables for Thanksgiving dinner.

Mothers lift steaming lids from casserole dishes.

Fathers clink spoons against glasses calling for toasts.

A boy plays with his puppy.

His sister watches cartoons.

Row after row of interconnected townhouses with warmth burning inside the windows and I wouldn't be surprised to see people stand and walk into their neighbors' homes to share the good cheer, passing in front of one another's windows—no walls on the inside, no partitions between the people.

A gust of wind lifts my shirt and blows through my aching guts. I pull my jacket tight and walk down the hill toward my car.

7 My Best Plan

A police officer rapping his flashlight against my window wakes me. He points his flashlight at the sign in front of my car—GOLDEN GATE PARK, NO OVERNIGHT PARKING. The officer crosses his arms. I turn the key in the ignition—it turns over twice and gives out. The officer pulls out a ticket pad. I turn the key again—it hesitates then starts. As the officer walks back to his cruiser, I drive off.

I follow the coast to the San Francisco Zoo. It costs 15 bucks to get in unless you hop the fence and you can spend an entire day there and nobody looks at you strange. I hang out at the gorilla enclosure for hours. Silverbacks get a bad rap—they're good dads.

I spend Friday night parked down the street from the zoo. It's nice to hear the waves from the Pacific but it's too cold.

SATURDAY, I drive to Daly City and buy a dress shirt from Value Village. In the parking lot, I peel off the two pair of slacks that I put on under my jeans in the fitting room and then I pull the three ties from my crotch. I always get an anxious ache in my gut when I steal. My mom always said that ache is God talking to me. But I don't feel bad stealing from Value Village because they're a big for-profit business but don't pay anything for their donated merchandise. One of the brokers at Edward & Bliss told me all about it. He knew a guy who was rich off it.

SUNDAY morning, I cruise downtown and watch tourists in Ghirardelli Square. The other zoo is better. Monday I'll get a job. I'm good at what I do even though I don't like it.

~~~

College wore me out—a full-time job waiting tables and I was still underwater. My path was to law school and McGeorge accepted me but as graduation loomed, I couldn't imagine doing another hard three years. Then Edward & Bliss came to campus career day. The recruiter said their average new-hire bought a Range Rover his first year and a house his second year. It only took me one year to buy both. I set the record for new accounts and the head broker Mr. Charles took me to his Granite Bay Country Club for lunch. Charles is his first name but he makes everyone call him Mr. Charles.

Then the money started pouring in and the other brokers took me out and showed me what I had been missing—VIP entry into hot clubs, after-hours parties, attractive young women, and the best pickup line ever—cocaine!

Stephanie and I were on-again, off-again. She planned to go on for her master's in English and money was tight for her so when I bought my house in Folsom, I asked her to move in. I thought it would help settle me down, get me back on track. She said no and broke my heart. It took a lot of convincing, but three months after I moved in she agreed and gave up her room in the dorms. Having her live with me settled me down—for a while.

PARKING IN FRONT of a coin laundry, I carry my black plastic-garbage bag full of dirty clothes inside and heft it onto the counter. Why do Laundromats always have ugly orange Formica countertops—the same ugly orange Formica countertops?

An ancient quarter-candy machine collects dust in the corner. It's nearly empty of the Boston Baked Beans it offers up, which means it's full of quarters. A cable secures the machine to the wall but there's plenty of slack. I pick it up, spin it upside down and shake it. The metal housing separates and quarters spill out onto the floor. I scoop up the quarters.

As I buy a miniature box of Tide from the vending machine, I notice three girls standing outside a bar across the street smoking— they point and laugh at me. I'm tempted to go outside and ask them if I should be separating lights from darks, but the girls stub out their cigarettes and push back into the bar. I load all of my laundry into one washer and run it on cold.

I flop into a plastic scoop-chair with the employment section from the newspaper. I need a plan. There's a YMCA on Mission and it's far enough from the city that parking is free. I can sleep in the Porsche. Shower at the Y. Dress for interviews. Bus into downtown. I have enough cash to drop into a Kinko's tonight and print off résumés. I'll use my old address and Barbara's phone number— should be good enough to get me in the door somewhere. Maybe get an advance. Maybe even hustle a signing bonus.

It's not much of a plan but it's my best plan and it has to work. If it doesn't, I'm beyond screwed.

8 It Is What It Is

I wait outside the Y for the desk clerk to step away. He's been diligent at his post for almost an hour. I'm about to give up when a homeless guy lumbers past me dragging an orange five-gallon bucket on wheels. He plows right past the desk without stopping and the clerk doesn't blink—a cardboard cutout welcome to the Y. I follow him and his orange bucket into the locker room.

I strip and head for a shower. The showers look out on a row of sinks in front of a long mirror. I watch the homeless guy unpack. He spreads an assortment of grooming products on the counter. Then he plugs in clippers and shaves his head, his dark hair piling on the floor around him. He lathers his face and shaves with a straight razor. He plucks nose hairs—clips fingernails, toenails—files a foot corn with a pumice stone. He spits out his dentures, scrubs them with bleach, rinses them and then slurps them back into his mouth. Placing everything in the bucket, he undresses. Layer after layer peels away until he is half the size he was before and his clothes pile two feet high on the bucket. His face, neck, arms, and hands are all brown from the sun but his body is white as porcelain. He inspects every inch of his flesh, rubs a purple bruise on his thigh. Then he drags his bucket past my shower and only a pile of his dark hair remains.

I smell his stench. I hear his shower turn on. Transfixed, I've watched him transform. My fingers are prunes, my feet numb. I kill the water and head to the mirror for my own transformation.

I MAKE THE ROUNDS with my new résumé and door after door closes behind me. Most places won't even take the résumé, they just tell me straight away that they're not hiring and then wish me luck with plastic grins. Looks like everyone is beginning to downsize.

My last stop for the day is Citigroup. A cute coed receptionist greets me. She glances at my résumé. You went to Slack State, huh?

You must be an Aggie then, I say.

Ugh! Davis? No way. I'm a Berkeley girl. I'm just answering phones here while I study for my broker license.

I lean in and drop my voice to almost a whisper. Can I tell you something?

She looks around, confused but curious. She nods. I say,

You'll rake in a fortune. Do you know what a rare combination intelligence and beauty are? In this biz? And you've got both. Come on, Berkeley plus your smile? You won't have to bother dragging your résumé around like I am.

She blushes. You're just saying that, she says.

Hey, I wouldn't say it if it weren't true.

She searches my face to see if I'm lying. I smile.

We're not really hiring, she says, but I know Miss Winters has one slot open.

The engraved gold plaque on Miss Winters' office door says MANAGING BROKER. I knock and a commanding female voice calls from inside, Permission to enter.

The office is all business and so is Miss Winters. She wears a dark blue suit with wide lapels and gold buttons. She has hair pulled back and bound so tight that when I hand her my résumé, she has trouble getting her reading glasses on over her ears. She reviews my résumé with military posture.

After enough time for her to read it twice, she says,

So, you have your Series 7?

Yes. Series 3, 9, and 34 too.

Impressive. Do you have a book of business to bring over?

No. I've been out for a little while now.

Miss Winters looks at me over the rim of her reading glasses. The skin beneath her eyes is thin and blue veins show through her makeup. She reminds me of my third-grade teacher. She says,

Why have you been out?

Just some family problems you know.

She sets my résumé down, pats it with her palm. No, I don't know, she says. Why don't you tell me?

I'm ready to get back to work, I say.

Miss Winters strips off her glasses and pinches her brow. When she removes her fingers, the indentations stay. She says,

We're only hiring brokers with clients of their own. I'm afraid I can't do anything for you.

TUESDAY morning I call on Merrill Lynch. The old-timer slouching behind the desk says he's filling in for their receptionist who's been out for a week with mono, which he says she got from some other broker named Bing. I hand him my résumé. He scans it and says,

Sacramento kid, eh? Welcome to the big city. It must be your lucky day. A broker just bailed for Schwab. Couldn't cut it full fee. That means Weaver's got a desk to fill. Follow me.

He walks me down the hall to the branch manager's office, but he stops short at the door and hands me back my résumé. He says,

I'm supposed to be covering the phones so just go on in.

Well what's his name? I say.

Mr. Weaver, he says as he beats feet back the way we came.

I knock on the door. A high-pitched voice calls,

Come in, come in.

I push the door open and step in. The office is filled with bulls. Mean market-making bulls, bulls with bowed heads and big horns. Statues of bulls, paintings of bulls. Mounted on the far wall, with a white muzzle and black-tipped horns, is a real stuffed bull's head. Beneath the bull's head, swallowed by an enormous desk, sits a sheepish little fellow with watery eyes and a comb-over. He must be somebody's relative. I step to the desk. I say,

Mr. Weaver?

Yes, indeed. That's me.

I'm here to fill your open desk, I say handing him my résumé.

He turns my résumé over again and again in small, nervous hands until I wonder if he expects something to appear on the backside in invisible ink. Then he lets the résumé fall to his desk with a sigh. He says,

You have a bullish résumé here—bullish!

Thank you, sir. I'm very proud of it.

Yes, of course you are, he says. But I'm just afraid we're not hiring at the moment.

But the guy who brought me in here said you have a desk that needs filling.

Yes, well, you see—it's just that I'm new here and I came from another branch of the firm and so, you see, this is their way of breaking me in here is all.

Breaking you in?

Making me deliver bad news. I hate delivering bad news, of course, you see.

Just give me a shot, Mr. Weaver. You won't regret it.

I like your attitude, I do—it's bullish. However, you see we're just not hiring. No one is hiring.

Won't you just give me a chance, sir? Please.

He holds his hand to his mouth and simpers an apology. No, no, dear me I wish I could, he says. So, so sorry you see. You have my word though. And you can count on me. Things will change. The bulls will be back. We'll give you a jingle.

After I leave Mr. Weaver in his office polishing his bronze desktop bull paperweight with his silk handkerchief and mumbling about how bullish it was of me to try, I hit wall after wall of rejections until I can't take anymore.

The bus drops me on Mission Street in front of a discount bakery. I buy a box of day-old donuts for a buck and a half and carry them to my parked car.

WEDNESDAY and I got a belly full of leftover donuts and my best bright-blue tie on. I'm playing my only card left today—I'm going to see Jack Strawberry.

When I started landing accounts at Edward & Bliss, Mr. Charles invited me to lunch at the private Granite Bay Country Club. When I screwed up, he fired me. He fired me for making excessive trades to earn commissions, trades that Mr. Charles told me to make. I went over his head. I left message after message with his boss Jack Strawberry. I was waiting for Mr. Strawberry's call when I drank my wine collection and lost my house. Mr. Strawberry never called, but who wouldn't back their head broker when the guy he fired is gone and the clients are happy because somebody took the fall?

The San Francisco branch of Edward & Bliss is on the 12th floor of a tower overlooking Union Square. The lobby is drab and minimalist with two old elevators. Hordes of office workers squeeze in and out. I get off on five different floors to let passengers behind me exit. By the time the elevator hits 12, the mob has thinned and I can breathe again.

The doors open onto an opulent lobby with money-green carpet and wood-paneled walls. A fountain trickles, green plants spring from every corner. The receptionist is much older than I am and she looks very proper in a white blouse and blue pants. She smiles and says,

May I help you today, sir?

Yes, I'm here to see Mr. Strawberry.

You're in luck, she says. He's just back from Palm Springs. His office is right there on the left.

Will you tell him Trevor Roberts is here?

She waves her hand. Oh no, she says, Mr. Strawberry has an open-door policy—just go right on in, dear.

I can't believe how easy that was. All week I've been fighting gatekeepers with wit and charm and fake confidence and here is Martha Stewart ushering me in from the cold for hot tea and butter tarts. I should have come here on Monday.

Mr. Strawberry sits behind his desk reading a *Wall Street Journal*. I've heard his voice on our weekly market conference calls and he looks exactly like he sounds—slick and self-assured. His gray hair thick and well cut, his suit conservative and well made. I tap on the door. He folds the paper and smiles up at me. Can I help you?

I'm here about a job.

Well, he says, the way the market's heading, I was just looking in the *Journal* for a job myself. Shall we look together?

Smile lines surround Mr. Strawberry's bright-blue eyes. I'm just joshing, he says. Never did have any comedic timing. Have a seat. Please. How is it you come to see me about a job, young man?

I'm Trevor Roberts.

He shakes my hand. Oh, yes, he says. How rude of me, I didn't introduce myself. I'm Jack Strawberry.

I know. I used to work for Mr. Charles in Sacramento.

Mr. Strawberry releases my hand when I mention Mr. Charles. His smile lines disappear. He says,

Yes, how can I help you?

I called you several times.

I did get a message or two, yes. I'm sorry but I just can't attend to every concern. That's why we hire managers.

Like Mr. Charles?

Yes, like Mr. Charles.

He told me to make those trades, sir.

Come on, Trevor, you know you're responsible for following the rules. This isn't kindergarten here.

I know that, Mr. Strawberry. But you have to give me another shot. You just have to let me prove to you that I've changed.

I'm afraid I can't.

You mean you won't.

No, I can't.

You're the regional boss, why can't you?

Because we're a family company and the founders believe in allowing management a say in running it. Every manager has veto rights over rehires and Mr. Charles vetoed you.

Pardon me, sir, but this is bullshit!

It is what it is. Everything is what it is. If you learn that now and stop fighting you'll be 20 years ahead of Mr. Charles, son.

I really, really need a job, Mr. Strawberry. I'm out of places to interview and this firing is following me.

How old are you Trevor?

Thirty in March, sir.

Mr. Strawberry leans back in his chair and looks down his long nose at me. His left index finger taps the folded *Journal* lying on his desk. Then he leans forward and spins his rolodex. He says,

I'm an old-fashioned man, Trevor. See my rolodex? I know people. You're a good kid. Ha! I say kid but when I was 30, my kids were nine and six already. You should have kids you know. Makes this other stuff seem silly. Here it is.

He stops his rolodex, pulls out a card and says,

No promises, but I'll call Mr. Feldman for you. He's a bit rough around the edges but he runs a thriving wealth management business. Mostly just a feeder fund.

Feeder fund?

Yes, he says, Feldman has access to an anonymous master fund with hot returns. Big-money types line up begging to be fed into it. Feldman's always hungry for young brokers to handle the traffic.

9 Excuse Me, Sir

Mr. Feldman's firm is called Strategic Capital Inc. His young receptionist looks like a souped-up model you'd rent from a temp agency to work a booth at a car show. When I tell her my name, she looks at me like an unwanted chore that showed up too soon. She hurries me back to a large office filled with smoke and introduces me to Mr. Feldman.

He's a no-neck thug in a suit. The late morning light fights its way through smoke-covered windows and glistens on Mr. Feldman's baldhead. He's not wearing a tie, his top three shirt buttons open showing off his shaved, puffed-up pecs. His cheap cologne manages to penetrate the smell of his cigar smoke.

He sets his fat Cohiba down in a crystal ashtray and squeezes my hand until it hurts. I pass him my résumé. He reviews it for about 10 seconds before wadding it up in his steroid-pumped fist and throwing it at the trash can. He misses and my résumé bounces off the lip and rolls to the middle of the floor. It sits there crumpled into a ball and I want to tell him he owes me a buck-50 but I just sit there crumpled too.

Mr. Feldman smiles, his round face scrunches up like a pig in pain. Impressive résumé, son, he says. But résumés ain't worth the paper to wipe your ass. Old Strawberry said something on the phone about you taking six months off for personal reasons. What reasons were those?

Mr. Feldman picks up his Cohiba and crams it in his mouth, puffing to no avail. Damn things go out the second you set them down, he says. He clinks open a gold Dunhill lighter and puffs the cigar lit again. He blows a thick, gray cloud of smoke at me and when it clears, he says,

I asked you a question, son.

Beating around the bush isn't working, so I try outright lying. Wanted to give something back, I say. Did some deep soul searching. Joined a church. Went to Peru. Helped build a poor village school.

Sure you did, kid. Why doesn't Strawberry take you back over there at Edward & Bliss then? He likes do-gooders.

He wanted me back, I say, but he's more like a mentor than anything to me and he said your firm would be a better opportunity.

Feldman puffs his cigar, blows smoke out his nose. You're a good liar, kid, he says, but not a great one.

The phone on Mr. Feldman's desk chirps and the receptionist comes on its speaker—Sir, Paul is on line one.

Mr. Feldman holds his hand up, signaling me to be quiet. Then he jerks the phone off the cradle. Hey there, big guy. Whataya know?

He leans back in his chair, the phone against his ear, listening. He puffs on his cigar and blows a smoke ring. Well you know the market's down, he says. Folks are getting margin calls. They're scared. And your fund's as good as a gold. Good as a money market. It's the first place they turn for liquidity. That's all. Don't worry about us— I'm working on a new fund for you. Seeded it myself.

Then his features scrunch together again. He leans forward in his chair, lowers his voice. He says,

You wouldn't cut me off. You don't mean that. Whataya mean you're here? Here now? At my office? Okay, sure—give me a minute.

Mr. Feldman drops the phone back in its cradle. He looks dazed for a moment and then he sees me sitting across from him. He jumps to his feet, stubs out his cigar. He says,

Sorry, kid. You're not a fit for us here.

I was thinking he scheduled the call from his receptionist just to end the interview, but he looks like he just hung up the phone with a ghost. There's no use arguing so I stand and head to the door.

Take your résumé there with you, he says.

I can't believe he wants me to pick up his trash after he treated me so rude. I want to tell him to fuck off but I've lost any will to fight and instead I veer past the door and lean over to pick up my useless education and job history printed on dollar-50 paper where it lies crumpled in a ball on the floor.

I reach for my résumé.

Before I can grab it, a red boot steps on top of it. And not just any red boot, but a red Michael Anthony crocodile cowboy boot I saw in a *Robb Report* for 9,000 bucks.

I look up.

The owner of the boot is staring down at me. His pale features are chiseled and perfect but something about the way they arrange around his intense, dark eyes is more unsettling than attractive. His thick black hair is just messy enough to be stylish. A coffee-colored suede jacket hangs loose on his shoulders over a seafoam silk shirt with oyster-shell buttons. The shirt hangs untucked and he wears faded blue jeans. He's trying hard to look casual, but the custom boots give away his wealth.

I pull my hand away.

I stand up.

We lock eyes.

He's not quite as tall as I am, and not as broad, but he has a heavy presence. He's holding the office door open and fresh air blows in from the lobby carrying the scent of his Clive Christian cologne with it. He doesn't say anything, he just holds my stare.

After several seconds, I look away from his eyes and down at his red 45-hundred dollar boot parked on top of my crumpled dollar-50 résumé. I say,

Excuse me, sir.

Then I brush past him through the open door.

10 Second Chances

I sit on a metal bench and look up at the skyscrapers piercing the gray fog overhead, fog so thick I can't see the building tops. The streets are sober and silent. I've been turned down and stepped on everywhere. There's nowhere left to go. I reach in my pocket and count the last of my money—seven bucks and change, not even enough for a box of rat poison.

A gilded monument clock in front of my bench chimes noon, the fog lifts away revealing blue skies above and white puffs of clouds floating by, the gray streets fill with yellow, and then as if a lever has been pulled from the bottom of a grain silo, people spill out from the buildings.

Office women in skirts and silk blouses carry sack lunches to the park. Stuffed suits rush by on their way to expensive martini lunches. Young salesmen plead and persuade into cell phones. Pigeons flock around a woman tossing them crusts. A group of small children trots by following their young teacher and clinging to a bright orange rope.

In a trance, I watch the minute hand race around the hour and the people race around my bench and when the big clock chimes one, the people retrace their steps and then crowd back into the office towers, the fog rolls back off the bay and closes the sky again, and the yellow drains from streets.

I sit on my bench alone with the pigeons and a discarded sandwich wrapper blowing over my feet and along the pavement.

DRIVING ALONG THE RAGGED EDGE of the city, down a street lined with cheap car lots and corner markets with bars in the windows, I look down at my fuel gauge—empty. I pass a shabby building with a fenced lot of cars and an enormous letter board that reads WE LEND MONEY. I pull to the curb and park. The pawnshop sign says SECOND CHANCES.

~~~

When I was losing my house, I started selling things. I advertised my Land Rover but I owed too much and the bank did me the courtesy of picking it up. I sold my motorcycle and my hi-fi system. I sold the refrigerator. I sold everything that wasn't bolted down, everything except my mother's Porsche.

After my overdose, Barbara stopped by my house on our way to the airport and I stuffed a duffel with clothes. The only sentimental thing I took was my grandmother's wedding ring. My mom started wearing Grandma's ring when my dad sold hers. Near the end, it wouldn't stay on her finger any longer so Mom gave me the ring. I was planning to use it when I proposed to Stephanie.

~~~

I step inside Second Chances. It's small, cramped. Pawned goods hang from the wall, line shelves, and fill a glass display case. Behind the counter, an obese female pawnbroker reads celebrity diets in a *Star* magazine while eating from a loaf of Wonder Bread and an open jar of peanut butter. Light shines through the frosted windows highlighting blonde whiskers above her smacking lips and orange makeup sinks into her gaping pores. She smiles up at me with small yellow teeth. Well, well, she says, look at you—you tall drink of milk.

I lay my grandmother's ring on the counter.

The pawnbroker pinches the ring with flabby fingers and holds it in front of fleshy, fake-lashed eyes. She drops it back. Stone's too small, she says, not interested.

What are you talking about? Look—

I'll pay ya 50 for it, she says.

Fifty won't do nothing.

She points to a display case full of rings. I've got me too many broken heart rings, kiddo, she says. It's a sad world.

But I need some money.

She reaches across the counter and pinches my cheek. I've got me some friends over in the Castro, she says. They'll put those cute little dimples of yours to work if you need some money, honey.

I'm not a hustler.

Well unless you got something else to pledge, beat it!

She dips her knife into the jar of peanut butter and spreads it thick on a fresh piece of white bread. My eyes get wet again. My throat aches. It hurts when I swallow and say,

How much for a 1983 Porsche convertible?

IT'S DUSK WHEN I hop off the city bus. Across the street, the blood-red VACANCY sign blinks on. Here I'm standing right where I parked when I first got to the city, across from the La Hacienda Motel. It seems a lot longer than a week ago.

The attendant is old and bald and he looks like he'd have a South American accent if he spoke, but he only grunts and points to the list of rules as he hands me the rusted box-end wrench that acts as a chain to the room key.

I climb the stairs to the second floor. I pass a room sealed off with yellow crime-scene tape. I'm guessing some sorry dick had enough shit and swallowed his pistol. This is that kind of place. I wonder if he came here so his family wouldn't find the mess.

I turn the key in the lock of room 36 and swing the door open.

The air conditioner in the window throbs cold air into the dark room—it smells like a meat locker. I pull its plug—the AC sputters to a stop. I flip the light switch—a single lamp with a crooked shade turns on. I toss my duffel on the floor and walk to the window, part the curtains and look out at the blood-red sign flickering in the dark.

I pull the thick wad of cash from my pocket—six grand. That's what my mother's memory is worth. The Porsche must have a book value three times that much. The pawnbroker wrote it up as a loan but I know I'll never get my mother's white Porsche back.

~~~

My mom didn't say it, but I think she knew her cancer was back when she gave me her Porsche. I won a partial scholarship to Sac State but I didn't want to go. I didn't want to leave Mom alone with Dad. Sure, he quit hitting her when I got big enough to intervene, but Mom had been sick on and off for a long time and instead of Dad caring for her, she still catered to his drunken ass.

The morning after I told her I wasn't going to university, I woke up to Mom sitting at the foot of my bed humming the Judy Garland song "Smile." I asked her if everything was okay. She said she had a feeling it would be. Then she asked if I knew how much she loved those robins that dart around our yard each spring. She said as much as she loved them it was okay that they flew away each fall because they always came back to sing again. Then she kissed me on the forehead and handed me the keys to her Porsche.

And I came back again, the very next spring. But not to sing. I came back to watch her die and say my goodbye.

~~~

I walk to the bed, pull the sheets back and check the edges of the thin mattress for bedbugs. Then I flop on my back and stretch out. The hard mattress reminds me of my treatment center bed but it feels like heaven after a week sleeping in my car. The white popcorn ceiling is stained and I try to find patterns in it. I've been here three minutes and I'm bored.

I spread the cash on my chest, pull the pile of bills to my nose, and inhale the musty odor of American money. I read somewhere that over half the dollar bills in circulation have cocaine residue on them. I can't go back to the coke but maybe all that BS they fed me in treatment about a drug is a drug is a drug was just that—bullshit!

~~~

Mr. Shaw always rattled off pithy little sobriety sayings—cute sayings like "One Day at a Time" and "Easy Does It." He had a saying for everything. He talked about the steps too. I remember in one of our private sessions I told him that 12-step stuff was great for people who need it, people who can't stop drinking on their own. Mr. Shaw said I was comparing my insides to everyone else's outsides. Then he asked me if I thought I was unique. When I didn't answer because I didn't know, Mr. Shaw took a deep breath and when he let it out again he said, Do you think you're alcoholic, Trevor?

His question hit me like a bullet. Nobody had ever asked it and I didn't know how to answer it. I thought I was coming to rehab to learn how to drink normal, or maybe learn to abstain, but me an alcoholic? The way I saw it, three types of people filled the treatment center beds—

The young, but already repeat offenders trying to beat drug court who treat rehab like it's the new black—mostly a bunch of spoiled indigo children whose New Age parents fucked them up into thinking they were so special that they went out and bashed their self-righteous heads against the real world until there was nothing left of themselves and still, that nothing is all they think about.

Then there are the placaters who are just getting off the streets and spinning dry so they can go back out and run again—guys who have no real interest in getting sober—guys looking to cruise through their 28 days so they kiss ass and tell the counselors everything they want to hear and the counselors lap it up.

Then there are the real alcoholics. Alkies are usually older and hard-worn—their lives pissed-down barroom drains. Alkies come to rehab to stop the bleeding. They're losing things—losing jobs, losing wives, losing their health.

One old alky broke my heart when he told us in group that he went to the hospital with jaundice and came out with a diagnosis of late-stage pancreatic cancer, the symptoms of which he missed because he was drunk every day of his adult life. One of the indigo kids asked him why the fuck he was bothering with rehab if he was going to die soon anyway. A flood of tears burst from the alky's eyes. The group got quiet. One of the placaters punched the indigo in the shoulder. And when the old alky's weeping slowed enough for him to speak, he told us he came to rehab because he hoped to stay sober the short time he had left so his daughter might speak to him again so he could tell her goodbye.

Now, nobody ever told me I was special and I'm no indigo child, and sure, I've lost a job and a house and a girlfriend, but I'm young and I have my health and a hungry mind that learns from my mistakes so I'm no alky either, and I'm certain I'm no placater because I have no intention of ever going back to treatment and I don't give a shit what the counselors think about me, so when Mr. Shaw asked me if I thought I was alcoholic, I looked him square in the eye and said,

No, I don't.

Mr. Shaw's response was to stare at me across his desk tapping his pencil on a yellow legal pad. The tap-tap-tapping silence made me nervous so I jumped to fill it with an explanation. I've been here for three weeks now, I said. I haven't had a drop. I'm not craving. Booze or drugs. So my trouble was just a phase.

Mr. Shaw smiled and shook his head. You know, Trevor, he said, even if you squeeze all the rum out of a fruitcake, you're still left with a fruitcake.

And he might be right for most of those guys in rehab but not me. I am unique. My problems are unique. If anybody had to go through the shit I've been through, they'd drink too. I don't drink because I need to—I drink because I want to. It helps me forget. Forgetting is relief. And everybody needs a little relief.

~~~

The thud of something slamming against the floor above me shakes the cheap acoustic ceiling and a piece of popcorn falls free and tumbles down drifting toward the bed. In the time it takes it to land, I make my decision.

THREE BLOCKS from the motel, I find a place—no windows, a thick green door, red-neon sign that reads BAR.

Inside, the usual dive-bar suspects lean hopeless over drinks. A bucket sitting on the bar counter reads SMOKING FINE DONATION— 25 CENTS A CIGARETTE. The bucket is full of quarters and the bar is full of smoke.

A thin, veiny bartender tattooed everywhere except his eyelids blinks at me and says, What'll it be?

I take a deep breath and let it out. I say,

Double vodka straight.

The tattooed bartender tosses a coaster on the bar in front of me—a cutout from a porn magazine wrapped in clear tape. He sets a jam jar on top of the coaster and fills the jar with well vodka. The clear liquor magnifies the dismembered tits on the coaster.

The bartender says,

Rough day?

So this is how it happens—just like this. No fireworks, no thunder, no lightning. Nobody screaming, Don't do it! Just a jam jar full of cheap vodka served up on a pair of headless breasts with no questions asked. Mr. Shaw always said to think through the drink so I try, but all I can think about is how good it will feel to get that vodka in me. Mr. Shaw said to pray, but that makes me think of my dad and he and his God can go to hell. Mr. Shaw said to pick up the phone before I picked up a drink, but whom would I call?

I don't realize I'm clutching the bar until the bartender knocks his knuckles in front of me. He says,

Eight bucks, buddy!

Is there a phone in here?

The bartender points to a dark pay phone in the back of the bar. When he turns his head to another customer, I grab a fistful of quarters from the smoking bucket and head for the phone leaving my vodka untouched.

I dig the treatment center's card from my pocket, put the heavy black receiver to my ear and dial the toll-free number.

A faint female voice answers on the fifth ring—

Brave Ascent Recovery Center.

I need to speak with a counselor.

What's your name, sir?

Trevor Roberts.

And who are you with?

Who am I with? I only lived there for a month.

I'm just the night operator, sir.

Won't you just get me a counselor?

I said I'm just the operator, sir.

How about Mr. Shaw? Is Mr. Shaw there?

I can take a message.

What kind of bullshit is this? It's like calling the suicide hotline and being put on hold. I crumple the card and drop it in the corner.

Hello? Sir? Do you have a message?

I hang up. Pumping in quarters, I dial Stephanie's cell phone. It rings three times then goes to voicemail—

Hi! You've reached Stephanie. You know what—

I hang up and head back to my vodka.

The pay phone rings behind me. I rush to answer it, catch it off the cradle and put the receiver to my ear again—Stephanie!

Hello. Trevor? It's Barbara.

Oh. Hi, Barb. How'd you—

We saw the city number on Steph's cell screen and I knew it was you. Trevor! Are you okay? Where are you staying?

I'm fine, really. Everything is fine. It's just been tough you know—job hunting. Is Stephanie there?

Trevor, you have to be patient.

Okay, I get it, Barb. I need to prove I've changed.

Silence on the line. Barbara sighs. She says,

I've been praying for you.

I grip the receiver tighter and change the subject. Anyway, I say, it's nice to hear your voice. I'm glad you called back.

I got a call for you this afternoon from—let's see—hold on—here it is—Valombrosa Capital. They said they could see you about a job Friday. Friday at two. Oh, that's tomorrow.

Valombrosa Capital?

That's it, yes.

It doesn't sound familiar.

Do you need the address? It's on California.

I'll find it. Two o'clock?

Two o'clock.

Thanks, Barb.

Oh, booger me, I nearly forgot, she says. Jared called for you.

Shit!

What's wrong?

Nothing. Did Jared leave his number? Hold on a sec.

I can't reach the card that I dropped in the corner so I search my pockets and pull out the photo of the boy, the photo Evelyn left for me on the train. Using the pen attached to the phone book by a chain, I write Jared's number on the backside of the photo.

Thanks, Barb. Thanks really. You've been a lifesaver.

Before she'll hang up, Barbara makes me promise to call her after my interview tomorrow. Then she tells me to make sure I'm eating. I thank her again and set the phone back in its cradle.

I return to the bar and push the jar of vodka back to the bartender. I say,

You got coffee?

Does this look like Starbucks to you? he says holding out his tattooed hand. Eight bucks for the vodka.

11 *Are You Sober?*

The next afternoon I hop off the bus at the corner of Montgomery and Washington streets. I look up at the Transamerica Pyramid and wonder whose job it is to climb up there and hang the light every year—the light I saw from the Bay Bridge on my way into the city, the light that shines from Thanksgiving through the New Year.

I walk three long San Francisco blocks through honking traffic and people hurrying by bent over BlackBerries. Nobody looks where they're going. The people in the financial district remind me of windup toys plodding along in whatever direction their office-tower bosses point them.

On California Street, dead center of the block, I stop in front of a stone and glass skyscraper. Tall letters carved in the granite façade above the doors read VALOMBROSA BUILDING.

The revolving doors spit me out into the silence of a cavernous marble lobby. An armed guard sits like a sphinx behind a reception station in front of two separate banks of elevators. I cross the lobby and smile at the guard. I say,

Which floor is Valombrosa?

Name?

Valombrosa Capital.

Your name?

Oh, sorry, Trevor Roberts.

The guard programs the elevator from his station. The doors slide open. I step on. The doors close and the elevator takes me up to the 30th floor without me pushing anything.

When I step off, a sleek receptionist sits behind a zebrawood desk that matches her smooth dark skin and hard edges. She has her phone headset on upside down to avoid messing up her shampoo commercial hair. She looks me over cold and says,

You're Trevor Roberts?

Well it's not fair unless I know your name too.

She adds annoyance to her cold look. She says,

Mr. Valombrosa is very busy, but he read your résumé and he asked me to set up an interview. Mr. Valombrosa doesn't interview many people.

When you say Mr. Valombrosa, you don't mean the guy whose name is on the building, do you?

She cocks her head and removes her headset. She says,

Follow me.

She leads me down a long hallway hung with expensive art. I lag behind, wanting to get my bearings, look at the art, prepare myself—but she charges ahead like a runway model, working long, slender legs in a gray pencil skirt. At the end of the hall, she stops at copper double doors. She pushes them open, waves me in, and then shuts the doors behind me.

His back to me, his BlackBerry to his ear, Mr. Valombrosa leans on the edge of a teak desk looking over the city outside his windows. He wears a tailored gunmetal-gray suit with a faint chalk stripe. He runs his free hand through thick, unkempt black hair and his ruby cufflink catches the light. Then he speaks into the BlackBerry—

I don't care if you know which horse is gonna win what race next year, you still gotta do something with the money between now and then. Besides, I'm bored.

I can see myself standing in front of the copper doors in the reflection of the window he's looking at. I begin to wonder if he even knows I'm here. Then he says,

I gotta go—I got a new guy here.

When he ends the call, I pull my shoulders back, walk to his desk, and stick out my hand. It's an honor to meet you Mr.—

He turns around. I see his face, stop short, stumble forward and step on his red Michael Anthony crocodile boots.

I remember him from Mr. Feldman's office the other day. He's the guy I bumped into, the guy who was standing on my résumé. Smiling, he grabs my shoulders and helps me regain my footing. I step off his boot. He pats my shoulders and says,

Just ask if you wanna dance with me, kid.

I'm sorry, I'm so clumsy. I didn't—

Don't worry about it.

Did I scuff your boots?

They're cowboy boots, kid. They should be scuffed.

But they're Mark Anthonys.

Yeah, well I walk on 'em, why shouldn't you?

When I was learning sales at Edward & Bliss, they taught me how to maintain eye contact and establish control. I never knew what it felt like to be on the other side of that until now because Mr. Valombrosa just keeps smiling and looking into my eyes until shyness forces me to look down. I see my crumpled résumé unfolded and smoothed out on his desk beneath a reading lamp. He says,

Have a seat, slugger.

Yes, sir. I slide down into a chair.

He lowers himself into his chair. Then he leans back and smiles at me with white teeth. He says,

Do I remind you of your father?

What? I mean—no, sir.

Then don't call me sir.

Yes, Mr. Valombrosa.

Paul.

What?

My name is Paul.

Yes, sir—I mean, Paul.

He picks up my wrinkled résumé and looks it over. I study the office. On the wall, a painted portrait of a stern bald man resembling Mr. Valombrosa must be his father. A sitting area pointed at a wall-mounted flat-panel TV. A bar in the corner. The carpet is green, the faux ceiling painted to look like Italian plaster. An oil-rubbed bronze chandelier hangs over his desk.

Then I see her—

Sitting on his desk in a gold frame is a closeup photo of a woman in partial profile jumping a horse. Her face is so calm that I'd swear the photo was staged if the film hadn't frozen her long blonde hair streaming out behind her as they jump. Her skin is smooth cream poured over high cheekbones. Her nose is small and delicate with just a slight upturn at the tip above her red swollen lips. Long, thick lashes curl away from her eyes—eyes that are as deep and green as Hawaiian pools—eyes you could swim in. All her features cast a perfect spell of symmetrical shadows. She looks like she was carved by Michelangelo and painted by da Vinci.

You like horses, Trevor?

I look up. Mr. Valombrosa is watching me.

Yes, I say, they're very beautiful animals.

Your résumé says you were at Edward & Piss before.

Bliss—Edward & Bliss. Yes.

Well? Why did you leave there and what have you been doing for six months?

Uh, I had to . . . well, truth is . . . I had a problem.

What kind of problem?

I intended to lie, but for some reason—perhaps because Mr. Valombrosa is staring at me with piercing dark eyes, or maybe because I'm sick and tired of being sick and tired, but whatever the reason—I tell him the truth. I say,

A drinking and a drug problem.

Mr. Valombrosa stares at me without responding. Maybe I said too much. Maybe he meant my problem at work. I say,

I made some bad trades at Edward & Bliss.

I watch Mr. Valombrosa for a reaction. He gives up nothing. After several quiet beats, he says,

What kind of bad trades?

A promising startup was offering us big pops to sell their stock. I had discretion over a few of my client's long-term accounts and my boss, Mr. Charles, he told me I should buy and sell with them. Startup sank. The clients were upset. Mr. Charles blamed it all on me. They accused me of churning.

Paul leans forward in his chair. Were you?

Was I churning?

Yes, churning.

Yeah, I guess I was.

What did they do?

Fired me. My license is still good though, and Mr. Strawberry wanted me back—he said so—and he would have hired me two days ago, but Mr. Charles vetoed my rehire and . . .

Mr. Valombrosa looks disinterested in my explanation so I let it die. He smiles. He says,

Tell me about the booze and the blow.

My throat swells. My heart rate runs. My lips quiver. I say,

When they fired me, things got worse. I fell behind on bills—drank a lot—overdosed—went to the emergency room—girlfriend left me—lost my house—I just got out of drug and alcohol treatment and I need a job pretty bad, sir—I mean, Paul.

He looks away out the window. It's quiet. So quiet I can hear a clock ticking somewhere. I shouldn't have said it. I knew better than to tell the truth. I blew my only shot. I know the interview is over. Sparing him having to tell me I'm not a fit, I stand and say,

Thanks for seeing me, Mr. Valombrosa.

It takes forever to walk the long, empty distance to the doors and just when I reach for the handle, he says,

Are you sober?

I turn around. So far, I say.

What if I told you I was sober too?

You're sober?

My question hangs in the air.

His BlackBerry rings. He looks at the screen. I have to take this, he says. We'll call you if something opens up, Trevor. Then he turns his back to me again and answers his ringing BlackBerry. Hey there, gorgeous. Still mad at me?

I trudge the long hallway with my head down. I pass the hair model receptionist, she doesn't even look up. I step onto the waiting elevator. The doors close. The elevator descends. I slump against the wall and watch my life drop with the floors.

The elevator stops at the lobby level.

The doors don't open.

I push the door open button—nothing.

I push the lobby button—nothing.

The doors won't open.

The elevator begins to rise. It rises all the way to 30 again and then stops. The doors slide open and Mr. Valombrosa's receptionist stands in front of me. She says,

Mr. Valombrosa wants you here Monday at 8 A.M.

12 Soles for Sale

I spend Saturday at the main library on Larkin Street. The library building spreads out covering an entire block in white stone and inside, it's a maze of bridges connecting floors around a five-story atrium. You can walk the rows of books for hours before you see another soul.

I sit at the microfiche terminal and look up every news article I can find on Valombrosa Capital. I don't find much. VC is a private equity hedge fund known for great returns and they're selective about the investors they accept. Valombrosa even turns away investments from some big clients for no apparent reason. He's a mystery. Smart. Makes investors eager.

A story in the *Chronicle* that profiles Mr. Valombrosa as the King of Capital explores the background of his success. The article says Valombrosa grows up an orphan in New Orleans. He recycles scrap metal for a conversion van and RV builder then works his way up and buys in as a junior partner. A year later, the owner dies in a warehouse fire. The partnership agreement includes a life insurance policy. Valombrosa is cleared of any complicity in the arson. Over the next several years, he grows the company into a national player before selling out to a division of General Motors. Then he moves to San Francisco and starts a venture capital firm. After several hits and some big misses in the tech runup, he makes a small fortune on a bunch of bullish oil bets. In 1997, he founds Valombrosa Capital with a prominent Napa wine family as his first investor.

The reporter requested an interview but Mr. Valombrosa declined with a letter that said he prefers to stay out of the spotlight. The reporter did snag a quote from Mr. Feldman at Strategic Capital, the asshole that wadded up my résumé that day. Feldman said—

Valombrosa's not an activist investor but he sure can generate amazing returns. He doesn't have any hobbies but he's a hell of a guy.

The details in the story drop off citing the lack of transparency in hedge-fund models but it does say that industry experts estimate Valombrosa Capital to have as much as $16 billion in managed assets.

I look up an armful of books on hedge funds. When a library worker tiptoes by and whispers that they're closing, I gather up my books, head to the front, and use my old address in Folsom to get a library card. This is the first library card I've had since I was 10.

SUNDAY, I pick through the packed racks at Ross Dress for Less. I buy five dress shirts and one pair of slacks—shirts need to be laundered but slacks never get dirty.

Then I wave down a taxi, ride to the Upper Haight, and pop into a consignment store on Ashbury. I find a black three-button Brooks Brothers suit. The sleeves are an inch too short but unless I stretch my arms out, nobody will know. Between the shirts, the slacks, and the suit, I piece together a workweek outfit on the cheap. But the one thing you can't fake are good shoes.

After passing Buena Vista Park with its benches full of cruisers flagging a rainbow of bandanas from their back pockets like horny, fatted mandrills showing off swollen multicolored callosities, I turn onto Haight and walk through the quiet lane of Victorian storefronts where I find a boutique men's shoe store called Soles for Sale.

Inside it smells like leather and Kiwi shoe polish. The red-faced proprietor, wearing a clean white cobbler apron, looks up at me from a pair of shoes he's inspecting. His twinkling eyes and rosy cheeks make him look like Santa Claus after a shave. He sets the shoes on the counter with a clack. Good afternoon, he says.

I was wondering, do you buy souls too or just sell them.

He laughs. I don't buy them, he says, but I do repair them. I'm more cobbler than salesman, but nobody bothers to repair anything these days. They just throw everything away and buy new.

Well it's a catchy name, man.

Yeah, sign used to say SOLES REPAIRED but my wife came up with SOLES FOR SALE—said it would bring buyers in.

It brought me in.

That it did. What can I do for you?

I'm starting a new job tomorrow morning. I need a new pair of dress shoes.

The cobbler steps from behind the counter and looks at my feet. Size 12? he says.

Yep, and flat as flapjacks.

I know just what you need then.

He strips off his apron and ducks in the backroom. When he comes out again, he's carrying a shoebox. He lifts the lid. Nestled inside, protected in blue felt bags, is a shiny pair of size 12 Salvatore Ferragamo dress blacks. While the cobbler laces them, I strip off my old shoes.

He uses a silver shoehorn and slips the Ferragamos on my feet. They fit perfect. I stand and walk a circle around the shop. They feel great. I stop and look at my feet in a small angled mirror attached to the fitting bench. They look amazing. I say,

How much are they?

They're 640 and worth every penny.

Six-hundred and forty?

He clears his throat and says,

The shoes make the man and those Italian lace-up oxfords make you the tops.

Thought you said you were more cobbler than salesman.

He chuckles. A fella's gotta learn if he's gonna eat, he says.

Okay, I'll take them.

For another $20, I'll polish up your old shoes and glue on some zip soles—they'll be good as new.

No thanks, you can toss them. I'll wear the Ferragamos out.

See, he says, nobody repairs anything. He smiles and carries the box to the counter and punches the sale into his register. He grabs a pair of Superfeet insoles and tosses them in the box.

I'm throwin' the insoles in, to help with your flat feet, he says. No charge. Maybe I'll ask my witty wife to add a tagline to our sign—GIVE YOUR SOUL A LIFT.

BACK AT THE LA HACIENDA, I study my library books until 10. Turns out there are many different styles of hedge funds and they're easy to start. They popped up like mushrooms during the bull market in the 1990s. Most funds charge a set percentage fee. Then they take a big hunk of the gains they earn. Hedge funds dodge the heavy Wall Street regulations by only being open to sophisticated investors—high net-worth individuals, pension funds.

Fixed-income arbitrage, bonds, interest-rate swaps, insurance derivatives, mortgage-backed securities—it's all a blur and I'm so tired by the time I quit reading, I can't remember a word of the last five pages.

I pull down my best new shirt and hang it on the bathroom door to steam the wrinkles out. The motel shower is the size of a broom closet and I have to duck to get my head beneath the hot water but it feels good running through my hair and over my body. Between the clothes at Ross, the Brooks Brothers suit and the Ferragamos, I've spent almost a thousand of my cash already and tomorrow I need to pay the motel for the week. I turn the water off and the pipes rattle in the wall then settle down.

I wipe the steam off the mirror. It's cracked in the corners and the surface is so worn the black backing shows through in the middle. I smile at myself and practice my greeting for tomorrow— Good morning, Mr. Valombrosa. Good morning, Paul.

It's funny how sometimes the universe lines up to help you if you just hold on long enough. In treatment, Mr. Shaw said not to give up five minutes before the miracle happens. When I told him that I don't believe in miracles, he asked me if I believed in buses. Of course I do. Then he tells me to forget about miracles and to just not leave the stop five minutes before the bus shows up. I'm glad I waited for the bus.

I hang the steamed shirt in the closet next to my secondhand suit and my new Ferragamos with the bright blue Superfeet insoles. I'm excited to dress for work tomorrow.

I throw my stolen Value Village slacks in the motel trashcan. Then I remember the photo in the pocket, the photo of the boy that Evelyn gave me on the train, the photo with Jared's phone number written on the back. After that incident with Rooster, Mr. Shaw said it was good I was Jared's roommate. He said we all need somebody to look up to. He said Jared looked up to me. I wonder how Jared's doing now that he's out.

I sit on the bed with the photo. Evelyn was right, her grandson does look like me. I flip the photo over and look at Jared's number— 209 area code. Stockton. I remember Jared said his dad has a muffler shop in Stockton. I pick up the cheap-plastic motel phone—no dial tone. I'm too tired to go down to the office tonight. I'll call Jared tomorrow from my first day on the job—he'll get a kick out of that.

I flop back on the bed and click on the TV. The screen's not much bigger than a toaster but at least the little remote works. I can't believe this shit they peddle on nighttime TV—wipe yourself into a good tan, electrocute your stomach into fitness, smell your way into weight loss. Who buys this crap? I flip through until I find the financial channel where a newscaster with fake teeth and fake tits recaps last week's stock market news. She's smiling as if she just won a Pulitzer Prize while she delivers the depressing headlines.

On Friday, the markets closed down for the 13th straight trading day. But all eyes are on Monday's opening bell and what the weekend job report will do to investor confidence . . .

My eyes close.

. . . In other news—a young stockbroker—Trevor Roberts is guilty of selling futures when there isn't one—guilty of trading options when there aren't any—and the judges sentence him—to be exposed—on the floor of the New York Stock Exchange. Bells ring, papers fly, screens blink, and busy traders dart back and forth signaling one another and I stand naked in the center of the exchange dripping with the mucus of afterbirth and pulling at a long umbilical cord stretching out from the hole in my gut up to the press box where the newscaster holds it clutched in her nailed hands as she grins down at me—

This is hell. It's waiting for you.

13 Valombrosa and Me

When I wake, the TV is still on and a panel of experts prattling on about foreign markets has replaced the newscaster. I try to remember my dream but the horror slips away as soon as I click off the TV.

In the pitiful La Hacienda lobby, the old bald clerk now wears a dragon print hat as he sits behind the counter working on a greasy carburetor spread out on a motel towel.

I ring the bell on his counter but he doesn't look up. I say,

I want to pay for the week.

Keeping his head bent over the carburetor, he speaks from beneath the bill of his hat. He says,

Two-forty-five if yer payin' cash. Charge tax if yer usin' plastic.

I count the cash into his greasy hands. He folds the bills in half and tucks them in his shirt pocket. I say,

The phone in my room doesn't work.

He grunts and taps his finger on a faded sign taped to the counter—PHONE DEPOSIT REQUIRED.

MR. VALOMBROSA'S SECRETARY clacks across the marble floor as she charges toward the elevators in her black six-inch heels. She looks me over as if she's grading beef. You're early—that's good, she says. Then she turns to the guard and says, Trevor's with us now.

The guard nods.

She leads me onto the elevator, swipes her key-card and pushes floor 30. Are all these floors Paul's? I say.

Paul? she says. Boy, don't you move quickly. Just 28 to 31 are ours. The other bank of elevators services the lower floors—Mr. Valombrosa leases them out to different companies. Don't mind the guard—he'll warm up to you. I'll issue you a key-card that will get you access to our floors and to the garage so you can park your car.

Don't worry about the garage, I take the bus.

You don't have a car?

I didn't say that. I'm just reducing my carbon footprint.

The elevator stops at 28. Our research floor, she says. The doors open on dim rows of faces glowing in the blue of computer screens. A young researcher lurches onto the elevator. He half smiles at Valombrosa's secretary but loses his courage and looks down. He swipes his key-card and pushes 29. The elevator rises and the doors open on a beehive of activity where a less attractive receptionist fields phone calls to eager brokers buzzing around cubicles. Our trading floor, she says. The researcher steps off and the doors close. The elevator rises to 30. The doors open. What's on 31? I say.

Thirty-one is our hedge-fund floor, she says. You're not allowed up there! You'll be working here on the executive floor with Mr. Valombrosa and me.

You mean, Valombrosa and I.

No, she says, it's Valombrosa and me. It's been Valombrosa and me for—years. No one says with I.

She smirks as she leads me past her desk and down the long hallway. Today, I take my time, look at the art, and while I'm no connoisseur, I recognize Picasso's signature when I see it.

Down another hall, left of Mr. Valombrosa's copper doors, she stops at a small interior office. She throws open the door. The office is bare and white—desk, chair, computer, phone—the only color from a tall stack of green file folders.

Welcome home, she says as she waves me in.

What's this, no view?

Don't push things.

I drop into the chair and test it. It feels good to be back in the saddle. Leaning back with my hands cupped behind my head, I prop my Ferragamos up on the desk. I say,

You know you never did tell me your name.

Get your shoes off the desk.

You like them? They're Ferragamos.

She pats her hand on the stack of file folders. Mr. Valombrosa wants you to review these commodity-trading patterns, she says. I suggest you get started.

Where is Paul?

He's out of town all week and if you knew Mr. Valombrosa well enough to use his first name, you'd know that. Now get to work.

She turns for the door, looks back before closing it. My name is Britney, she says. Then she shuts the door and I'm alone in the quiet office. I drop my shoes off the desk and open a file folder. I spent my first year at Edward & Bliss analyzing commodities so at least this is familiar work.

I pick up the desk phone. Nine gets me an outside line. I dial Stephanie's cell number. Three rings and her voicemail answers—

Hi! You've reached Stephanie. You know what to do.

This time I leave a message—

Hi monkey—I mean Steph. I wanted to call and tell you I'm in the city. Give you my new work number—I'm over at Valombrosa Capital. I thought—well, I hoped that maybe we could grab a coffee or a bowl of chowder this weekend. Or we could even go skydiving, or smoke a joint or something—just kidding about the joint, of course. Maybe we'd go to church. I'd love to see you—

A female computer voice cuts me short, thanks me for my message, and then tells me I can send it with urgent delivery by pressing one, but doesn't give me an option to erase it. I hang up. I sounded like an idiot. I didn't even leave the number here and it's printed right on the base of the phone. I pluck the receiver off the cradle and dial her again. After three rings, she answers—

Hi, Trevor.

What? Oh. Hi, Steph. How are you?

I'm sorry I've been out of touch—

That's okay. I understand.

It's been hard, you know—

I know. You staying at your mom's?

Yeah, just until next quarter starts then I got a dorm. But you probably don't—

No, I'm fine. I mean everything's fine. I just left you a message.

What did it say?

You can listen to it later if you want.

Okay, then.

I'm glad you picked up, I say.

A long silence. It feels like I'm talking to her in an old movie on an antique phone over a cable stretched across the Atlantic Ocean with a 30-second delay. Then she says, Trevor?

Yes, Stephanie.

You wanna meet up this weekend?

14 *Ambitious Bird*

Brad Pitt and Angelina Jolie stand together looking at us with permanent smiles. Stephanie stands between them reflected in the museum window with posture as perfect as the wax figures, the top of her head level with my shoulder—in my month away, I forgot that I'm a foot taller than she is. I also forgot how turned on I get by her long dark hair, her exotic face, her full red lips.

She smiles up at me. Look, she says, it's your doppelganger.

Yeah sure, I say, I'll bet people stop Brad Pitt in the street all the time and tell him he looks like me.

I take Stephanie's hand and we walk on together down Jefferson Street. The air crisp, the sun warm, the smell of fried seafood wafting on a gentle breeze—a perfect San Francisco afternoon.

Giggling groups of tourists bump past us along the old warped wood piers of Fisherman's Wharf and as we pass a cluster of shrubs on the busy sidewalk, a street performer disguised as a bush springs out at us and roars! Stephanie screams and jumps back into my arms. Then she laughs and I laugh too. I lean down, our lips touch—she shakes her head and pulls away.

Several tourists, already wise to the trick and milling about to see the next victim, clap and laugh. I smile and throw five bucks into the bushman's basket as we pass.

Stopping at a chowder stand, we order two wharf specials from a concessionaire with a toothless smile and wispy strands of hair hanging from his shiny head. We watch as he ladles our steaming clam chowder into sourdough bread-bowls. I whisper to Stephanie that he looks like a 70-year-old newborn. She elbows me in the ribs.

We carry our chowders to the wharf's edge and listen to the sounds of San Francisco—gulls swarm overhead calling for crumbs, gentle waves lap at the pier, distant sea lions bark fighting for space on a large floating buoy.

So far today, it's been all small talk between us. We were always good at avoiding things, it's part of our problem. I tear off a piece of bread-bowl and toss it to a gull. Stephanie stirs her chowder but she doesn't eat. After a long silence, she says,

So?

So what?

So, how was it?

You mean how was treatment?

Yeah, treatment.

It wasn't bad.

Wasn't bad?

Some of the guys were all right, I guess. And the food was good.

The food was good?

It wasn't like this, I say holding up my chowder, but it was good.

I wasn't asking about food, she says. What did you do all day?

Group therapy mostly. Everybody trying to out-do one another with their stories of woe.

And what was your woe? she says.

Oh, I don't know.

You don't know?

Why are you drilling me? It was drug and alcohol treatment. What do you think we did all day, every day, for 28 days. It's just a bunch of guys trying to find their way back.

Did you find your way back?

I'm here aren't I?

Were there girls there too?

Is that what you're afraid of? That I met a girl.

I'm not afraid of any such thing, she says.

~~~

Then I remember something Jared asked me, a question the morning I left rehab, something he said his mother asked him before she left. What did he say? He said—what would you do if you weren't afraid?

~~~

Stephanie grabs my arm. Where are you? she says.

What would you do if you weren't afraid, Stephanie?

I don't understand you, Trevor.

You ever think about leaving?

Leaving where? Why?

Going somewhere new and starting over, I say.

Are you doing okay, Trevor?

You mean am I sober?

Yeah, I guess, she says. Are you sober?

I like seeing the concern in her eyes so I don't answer her right away. I toss another piece of bread to the circling gulls. Then I say,

I haven't touched a drop.

Has it been hard?

I held on.

Stephanie squints into the setting sun, her chowder untouched in her hand. Then, without looking at me, she says,

Do you think you're alcoholic, Trevor?

Do you think I am?

Stephanie pats my arm. Hey, tell me about your job, she says.

The job's great, I say. Mr. Valombrosa—he likes me to call him Paul—he runs a massive hedge-fund for rich people. Makes them big bucks too. And everyone loves him. The *Chronicle* even did an article, called him the King of Capital.

The gulls circle our heads begging. I toss my last hunk of bread in the air and a big gray swoops down and snatches it. Stephanie says,

Where'd you meet this Paul person?

Did I tell you he's a billionaire?

Ya, but what's he like? Is he nice?

Paul's sober too, I say.

He told you that?

In not so many words he did. We have a way of spotting each other, you know. Us sober guys. Like a secret club.

So you're sober now?

I told you, I haven't touched a drop.

Well, I just hope you know what you're getting yourself into this time, she says.

A fat gull swoops down, snatches Stephanie's bread-bowl in his beak and flaps away with it, landing on a nearby pylon. We watch with equal admiration and alarm as he struggles to swallow the entire sourdough lid, getting it caught in his throat and choking as sallow foam drips from the sides of his beak.

Stephanie looks right at me. She says,

Ambitious bird!

AT GHIRARDELLI, we order an enormous ice-cream sundae. The menu calls it The Earthquake and the server asks us three times if we're sure. I was sure until he brings it out on a dish that covers the entire table between us.

Stephanie has one bite and then decides she's not in the mood for ice cream. Watching me pack away the sundae, she says,

You eat like you used to drink.

Then she laughs at her own joke. I fling whipped cream at her. A young brother and sister sharing a smaller sundae watch us. The little girl dabs whipped cream on her nose—I dab whipped cream on my nose. The little boy eats a bite fast—I eat a bite fast. Stephanie joins in and lobs a cherry into my mouth. The kids giggle. Stephanie giggles. We all giggle.

It feels good until their parents catch on and admonish the kids with hushed anger and then drag them crying from the creamery.

WE TAKE OUR TIME strolling in the heavy twilight toward the Embarcadero BART Station. I love twilight. Everything looks clean and new and anything seems possible.

When we get to the tunnel entrance, I stop and soak up one last look. The narrow streets tumble down to the bay, a streetcar climbs a distant hill, the sky hangs blue over red brick buildings, and white clouds billow from steam-plant stacks.

Yellow sodium vapor lamps replace the blue sky as we descend into the underground station. I want to kiss Stephanie. I've wanted to kiss her all day. Instead, I walk to the edge of the platform and peer down onto the sunken tracks. Stephanie pulls me away from the ledge. She doesn't let go right away and I can tell she doesn't know what to say either.

Sure you gotta go, I say.

It's late, Trevor.

Well maybe we can get together next week sometime?

The train slides in from the tunnel. The doors hiss open. I reach into my pocket, pull out the blue Tiffany & Co. box and hand it to Stephanie. Her eyes light up with surprise and then she smiles.

What's this? she says.

Just a little something, I say. You can open it later.

Stephanie throws her arms around me. I kiss her head, breathe her in, smell her sweet vanilla shampoo, and commit the moment to memory. Then she breaks free and runs onto the train. She looks at me through the glass as the doors seal closed.

WALKING BROADWAY STREET above, I feel that ache in my gut again. Stephanie will ride BART back to the parking terminal in Tracy and then drive her Honda Civic home. By the time she gets there, Sacramento will be asleep. But San Francisco never sleeps and the writhing city streets stretch out their lights like hungry lovers tempting me with sweet oblivion.

~~~

I remember in treatment, Mr. Shaw told me that the alcohol and drugs never were my problem. He said the alcohol and drugs were my solution and that was my problem. And he was right.

~~~

Red-neon light shines on two bikini-clad strippers shivering on a smoke break outside their club. One calls to me. Hey, handsome, she says, lonely tonight? Three-dollar drinks. Five-dollar dances. I put my head down and keep walking. The stripper yells at my back,

Screw you then, faggot!

~~~

I remember Mr. Shaw saying, If you don't want to slip, you need to stay away from slippery places.

~~~

Farther along a dealer lurks in the dark shadows of a doorway slinging rock. His dead, milky eyes flash in the headlights of a passing car. Whatcha need tonight, slick? he says.

~~~

I remember Jared showing up to rehab, huddling in a corner twitching, picking at his skin, coming down, and I remember him telling me I was lucky I never got into crack or ice or junk.

~~~

Just keep walking, I tell myself. Today was great. Tomorrow will be better. Every day I'm sober things get better. Nothing is worth throwing my sobriety away. Think the drink through.

Another three blocks and I pass a homeless man lying crumpled in a doorway with a cardboard sign propped against his threadbare coat. The sign reads: THE DEVIL MADE ME DO IT.

I stop and look down at his wrecked body curled up with a bottle of booze in a brown-paper bag. His whiskered mouth hangs open with a spray of vomit in front of it and with each raspy exhale, his swollen tongue pushes his one remaining loose tooth out past his lip and then his inhale sucks it back into his mouth again. I pull out a 20-dollar bill and stuff it into his jacket pocket.

Walking on I focus on the rhythm of my steps. It's a long way to the motel but the bitter night air feels good pressing against my face and the sidewalk sliding beneath me calms my thoughts.

~~~

I remember Stephanie's face when I handed her the Tiffany & Co. box— the surprise, the smile. I hated to part with any more money but I figured Mom would approve. I remember Mom taking me to the city once, I remember looking through the Tiffany & Co. window, and I remember her saying the color of the boxes reminded her of a robin's egg. She loved robins. She said they brought spring.

~~~

Now I need to figure out how to buy the Porsche back from Second Chances. Last week Britney barely said boo to me as I passed her desk every morning and I'm tired of studying copper and oil prices—it's a waste of time, crap that Mr. Valombrosa could get off a thousand websites, stuff any of his researchers could throw together.

~~~

I remember stepping on Mr. Valombrosa's red boot, I remember my crumpled résumé unfolded on his desk, and I remember him saying, What if I told you I was sober too?

~~~

I'm beginning to worry that I'm a sobriety-charity case. Then again, nobody told me how much I'm being paid or when I'm being paid and I haven't even filled out any employment papers.

The sidewalk sparkles with tiny flecks of crystal reflecting the streetlights—the shopping district. I look up. A sharp black Armani suit in a storefront window catches my eye.

~~~

I remember when I hired on at Edward & Bliss—Mr. Charles told me to buy some business suits and I told him I didn't have any money and I remember he said, You gotta fake it till you make it, kid.

~~~

I gaze at the Armani suit and see myself reflected in the white mannequin's mouthless face. The store sign says they're open.

Tomorrow I'll talk to Valombrosa about getting paid.

15 Valombrosa II

When I step off the elevator, the phone rings unanswered at Britney's empty desk. Down the hall, Mr. Valombrosa's copper doors are closed and I wonder if he's here.

I go to my office and grab the commodity reports. I check my reflection in the mirror. My new Armani suit looks sharp. Confident. I knock on the copper doors. I hear Mr. Valombrosa say something from inside so I swing the doors open, walk in and say,

Sir, I finished those commodity reports—

Just give them to Britney, sport, he says.

Britney stands from beneath Paul's desk, tucks her blouse into her skirt, and walks to the door. She shoots me a lipstick-smeared smirk, plucks the reports from my hand and exits without a word.

If Mr. Valombrosa cares that I walked in on him and Britney, he doesn't show it. He just buckles his belt.

Sorry, I say. I didn't mean to barge in.

No need for sorry, kid, he says. We're all family here.

Then he turns his attention to paperwork on his desk. I stand there for almost a minute, half in and half out of the room. I'm not sure what to do with my hands. I put them in the pockets of my new suit. Too casual. I take them out again. Not sure of what to say, I say nothing. Paul looks up. He's surprised to see me still standing there. What's up, slick? he says.

Oh, well, I'm sorry to have to bring this up but I need—

Don't ever say you're sorry. Now what do you need, champ?

Well I wanted to talk about pay.

About pay?

Yes, we never—

There's no fee.

No fee?

For your internship.

Internship?

Apprenticeship if you prefer.

I can't believe what I'm hearing—he expects me to work for free? Not all this money I spent on clothing, not all this time bent over these bullshit commodity reports—no way. I step closer to his desk. I say,

I think we misunderstood each other, sir. I can't work for free. I came here asking for a job, not an apprenticeship.

Whoa, easy, slugger—I'm just having a little fun.

You are?

Yeah. You're gonna get paid.

Oh, thanks. I'm sorry—

Quit with the sorry.

Got it. What a relief. Thanks.

You're a college boy, right Trevor?

My BA's in political science, I say, but my real major was in campus social studies.

Social studies?

Yeah, you know—bars, cars, and campfires.

Ha! Now you're having a little fun with me, he says. See how it goes, prentice? Tell me what you know about teachers, Trevor?

I know their favorite months are July and August.

Paul laughs at my lame joke. Then he stares out his window. His brow is tight around the bridge of his nose and it looks like he's deciding something. He turns back to his desk. He picks up the gold picture frame with the blonde beauty jumping the horse. He looks at her photo. Then he sets the picture down and hits the intercom button on his phone. Britney answers before it even rings. Paul says,

Call the club. Tell them to dewinterize my yacht before lunch. And add Trevor to the reservation.

Paul ends the call and looks back to me. He says,

You're joining me for lunch today.

Okay, sure. Thank you, sir.

Sir is what a hooker calls me after I've fucked and paid her.

I'm sorry—

Stop with the sir, kid. Stop with the sorry.

I will. Thank you, Paul.

Better. We can talk about your pay after lunch. We leave at 11. Now I have a call to make if you don't mind.

As I turn to leave, Paul says,

And, Trevor—

I turn back.

He smiles. Nice Armani suit.

THE YACHT CLUB RESTAURANT overlooks Belvedere Cove and, farther out, across the cove, the city skyline rising from the shores of San Francisco Bay. The ride with Paul in the town car was quiet. He did tell me we were meeting Benny Wilson for lunch. He said Benny is the CEO of CalTEARS, the California Teachers, Educators and Administrators Retirement System. They have more dough than some small countries and Paul said that even though Benny controls billions, he's cheap as hell and for me not to be surprised if he brings his tip calculator to lunch.

And after our long and boring lunch, I know what Paul meant.

Benny Wilson sits across from me scanning the table for the bill. He's 50. Neat. Conservative. Chews every bite until it swallows itself. He's getting nervous as we finish and he must be expecting a sales pitch from Paul.

Benny wipes his mouth, leans back in his chair, and pulls out his wallet. Paul shakes his head. He smiles at me to say I told you so, and then he looks back to Benny and says,

Lunch is on me, Benny.

Benny opens his wallet. I insist on going Dutch, he says.

Your money's no good here, Paul says. They charge everything to my member account.

At least let me get the tip.

Benny pulls a crisp $20 bill from his wallet but before he can lay it down, Paul throws a wrinkled $100 bill on the table. Benny frowns at the $100 and stuffs his $20 back. Then Paul says,

Now, about our business—can CalTEARS start transferring assets over as soon as the first of the year?

We haven't made a final decision just yet, Mr. Valombrosa.

Your board's all for it, Benny. So is the State Controller.

Because of your pressure they are.

Maybe they just like our returns.

You charge big fees for those returns.

We're setting ourselves a hurdle rate against the T-bill for your investments. We don't perform; we don't get paid.

Benny sets his jaw, narrows his eyes. He says,

I'm concerned about risk.

What risk? Paul says. This is a relationship business, Benny. It's about trust. What more do you need? How many more lunches? Tell him about our hedging, Trevor.

I almost choke on my water. Then I take another long drink to buy time. Valombrosa Capital is a hedge fund with rich, steady returns—but even all my research didn't tell me how we invest to generate those returns. Benny must know that investment strategies are like secret recipes to hedge funds. I set my water glass down and smile at Benny. I say,

Yes. Well, you see, Benny—may I call you Benny? We have a failsafe method of diversifying the risk using a mix of derivatives and mortgage-backed securities. Of course, as you know, hedge funds aren't in the habit of discussing their exact positions and models. If everyone knew the mechanics of how we do it, then we wouldn't be the best. And the only reason you're here is because we're the best. Isn't that right?

Benny shakes his head. Derivatives aren't safe, he says.

The way we hedge, it's as safe as America!

Safe as America? Oh, you're cute. Paul, why is your man Friday here pitching me as if I'm a housewife investing in encyclopedias?

Before I can jump in to defend myself, Paul holds up his hand. He smiles at Benny and with kill-me-calm he says,

I'm assigning Trevor as your personal contact at Valombrosa.

Benny rubs his chin and looks me over. How long have you been with the firm, Trevor? he says.

I look at Paul, but he gives me no guidance so I look back to Benny and say,

Seems like forever.

Benny leans back and looks me up and down. Then he turns to Paul. I need more data, he says. I need to ensure our investments will be safeguarded.

We'll deliver some risk reports, Paul says.

Fine, Benny says, have Trevor here deliver them.

Benny throws his napkin on the table and stands, signaling that our lunch is over. Paul and I stand too. Benny shakes Paul's hand and when it's my turn, Benny squeezes my hand a few seconds too long and then he says,

It was wonderful to meet you, Trevor.

Then, insisting that the next lunch is on him, Benny thanks Paul and walks away. I know Paul is watching me, but I can't help letting out a sigh as soon as Benny is gone.

Paul laughs. Safe as America? he says. Good stuff, slick. I hope you don't get seasick because I have something to show you.

Paul leads me into the yacht club. We walk over travertine floors inlaid with nautical tiles and walk past walls lined with sailing trophies and meticulous models of members' ships. A wood fire roars in the gentlemen's lounge. Oiled wainscoting shows between tall cases of sailing books in the library. Even when I was high-rolling at Edward & Bliss, I never had business lunches anywhere like this.

When we get to the yacht club manager's office, Paul knocks on the open door. He says,

Drinking on the job, Francis?

G'day, Mr. Valombrosa.

Francis would look like he just stepped off a yacht if he weren't trying so hard to look like he did. His legs are crossed, his sockless feet stuffed into white felt loafers. White trousers, white shirt, a blue sweater wrapped over his shoulders. He's leaning back in his desk chair sniffing a crystal glass of brandy with his bulbous nose. Paul introduces me. Francis says,

Nice to meet you, mate. How was your lunch?

Before I can respond, Francis spins around in his chair and paws through a cabinet of hanging keys. He talks over his shoulder. We're very proud of our buffet here, he says. I always want a second plate, but I know if I do, I'll be uncomfortable. Now, which one is your key? They just brought them back. Here! I should remember yours. Shall I give them to the new man?

Francis hands me a set of keys. On the end of the chain is a small curved, black horn in a silver setting. Francis taps the horn. That horn charm reminds me of a dik-dik, he says.

A what?

Dik-dik!

Paul grabs the keys from my hand. It'd be a small dick, he says, and I don't see why you keep saying it twice, Francis.

Francis chortles. No, he says, not cock-and-balls, mate—dik-dik. He holds his index fingers against his temples to make horns. It's a little African antelope, he says. Makes a warning call when predators are near. Goes dik-dik, dik-dik!

When we're clear of the club and walking down the docks, I ask Paul about Francis. He says Francis is just Francis and that he's been here so long nobody knows who can fire him.

The marina is filled with sailboats and motor yachts tucked away in slips. The boats nearest the gate are smaller, but the farther out we walk the larger and taller they grow, each one bigger than the next.

At the very end of the dock, parked in a wide berth, floats the largest boat yet—an antique motor yacht with clean lines accented by polished teak and brass fittings gleaming in the sun. Painted on the back in elegant black script is VALOMBROSA II.

Paul hops aboard. Untie us, sport, he says.

I unbutton my suit jacket and struggle with the huge knots tethering the yacht to steel-dock cleats. Paul starts the engines and revs them like a teenager impressing a girl at a stoplight. He backs the yacht from its slip with no warning. I jump aboard. The yacht lurches forward, turns too soon and squeezes the giant rubber bumpers against the dock. I make my way toward the bumpers to pull them in, but I nearly fall in the water when the yacht turns sharp again, this time to avoid colliding with a small sailboat motoring into the protected marina.

We cruise into Belvedere Cove and turn out for San Francisco Bay. I climb into the pilothouse, loosen my tie, relax. It's beautiful. The sun bores a hole through the perfect blue-dome sky and the deep-blue bay is flecked with silver running like fish on its surface. The sailboats plying the waters in front of the San Francisco skyline look like toy ships in some looking-glass snowglobe world and the whole city seems a mere movie set to be folded up and shipped ahead of Paul when he travels. I say,

Wow! I've never seen the city like this before.

The wind tousles Paul's thick hair and he looks like a Kennedy when he flashes his white smile. He says,

I'm going to show you lots of things you've never seen before.

I walk over to Paul at the wheel. Why do you call your ship *Valombrosa II*? I say.

Because my old-man's boat was named Valombrosa, he says. Quit asking questions, kid. Go down and get us something to drink.

I leave Paul at the wheel and drop down into the plush interior. Passing polished wood and gold fixtures, I stop to take in a regal, painted portrait of Paul grinning beneath coiffed hair. He's even wearing an ascot and it looks so much like portraits I've seen in museums, I can't decide whether it was posed as a joke. The painting is the same style as the painting of the bald man in Paul's office, the painting that looks like his dad. Paul said his dad's yacht was named *Valombrosa*, but I remember reading in the *Chronicle* article that Paul grew up in New Orleans as an orphan.

The galley is bigger than the kitchen was in my house. Polished wood panels conceal high-tech appliances. Granite counters swirl with black and gold marbling.

I open the refrigerator. It's empty except for a martini shaker and two chilled glasses. The freezer has a bottle of Kauffman, the only vodka I've ever seen with a labeled vintage. I search the galley cabinets. They're empty too. I find a built-in climatized cellar full of expensive French wines, but nothing else.

I climb the stairs back to the pilothouse empty-handed. Where's our drinks? Paul says.

Don't you have any club sodas, or juice, or something? All that's down there is booze.

Paul shakes his head disappointed.

That's a great painting of you down there though, I say. It reminds me of the one in your office. Is that your dad? In the other painting? In your office?

You're perceptive, kid. I like that—but not too much.

Who's the other one? The photo on your desk? The woman on the horse?

Tara, he says.

Who's Tara?

Paul grins. You'll see, he says. Come over here.

Paul motions for me to take the wheel from him. He stands behind me, puts his hand over mine, and turns the yacht toward a long white Beneteau under sail. He places my other hand on the dual throttles and pushes them wide open. The engines scream to life. At first, not much happens but then we pick up speed and charge straight at the Beneteau.

What are you doing? I say.

Paul pushes the throttles harder. I turn the wheel away. Paul grips my hand, turns the wheel back. I pull away from the wheel. Paul pushes himself against me. As I struggle with Paul, the Beneteau crew screams and waves from the deck. At the last second, the Beneteau turns to avoid a collision—its captain flipping us the bird as the ships pass within feet of each other.

Paul releases me. He grabs my shoulders, rubs them hard. Then he pats me on the back and laughs.

I HAVE NO IDEA what that game of chicken was about and when I asked Paul, he just grinned and steered us back to the marina.

My adrenaline is still running high and I can hear my heartbeat over the motors as Paul pulls the yacht back into its slip. Relieved to be on semisolid ground, I jump onto the dock, bend over and secure the main line to the cleat with a figure-eight hitch.

When I look up, Paul tosses me the yacht keys. He says,

Make yourself at home, pal.

I look down at the black dik-dik charm in my hand. Home?

That's right, he says, home. I told Francis you'd be staying here awhile. He'll treat you like family.

But I—

Cut the shit, kid. I know that fleabag motel you're living in.

How could you know that?

You think I don't know the man I'm doing business with?

We're doing business?

Everything's business. Benny for example, he's not as straight as he lets on.

You mean he's on the take?

I mean you did real good today. He liked you. Payday is Friday. Britney will get you a company car tomorrow.

I have a car.

You have a car?

Well, I had a car—I put it up for a loan.

Who gave you the loan?

A place on Mission called Second Chances.

Paul shakes his head and smiles. I'd say living on a yacht is one hell of a second chance, he says.

I look at the yacht pulling against the rope at my feet. I'm sure it cost millions. I look back to Paul and say,

I really appreciate this, Paul.

I know you do, he says grinning. Then he walks away leaving me standing next to the *Valombrosa II*.

16 Dancing with Strangers

Two weeks ago when I was getting out of rehab, if someone had told me I'd be living on a yacht drinking Coca-Cola from a martini glass, I'd have told them they were smoking crack. There's no silverware in the galley, just a gold wine opener, and all the delivery guy brought is chopsticks so I've been fighting with this box of Kung Pao chicken for 20 minutes and I'm still hungry.

I didn't feel right sleeping in Paul's stateroom last night but even the guestrooms on the *Valombrosa II* are larger than my room at the La Hacienda. I'd already paid for a second week there and when I checked out today after work, the old man in the dragon hat just pointed to the fine print that said—NO REFUNDS. I didn't bother arguing with him.

Between the clothes, the Ferragamos, the Tiffany's necklace for Stephanie, and the Armani suit, I'm running thin on cash. Paul said payday is Friday. I'll just have to wait and see how much he pays me. I keep replaying that chicken run with the Beneteau yesterday. I guess Paul must have some beef with its captain because otherwise it makes no damn sense.

I hear voices outside and giving up on the Kung Pao, I step out on the deck to investigate. Laughter spills from a contemporary yacht across the marina. I see a couple of guys on its party deck and one of them sees me and waves. Hey there, neighbor! he says. Come on over and say hello.

Why not? I backtrack to the gates and get onto the other dock, but by the time I get there, I can't tell which yacht is which because they all look different from the back. I feel stupid. I'm about to turn back when the guy leans out from the door of a sleek yacht called the *SS Reel Talk*. Howdy neighbor, he says. I'm Scott.

I shake his hand. I'm Trevor.

He ushers me inside. What do you drink, Trevor?

Nothing.

You sure?

I nod. Why do people always ask me if I'm sure when I say no to a drink? Scott takes me out to the party deck and introduces me to Justin. Scott looks like a playboy, but Justin looks like a bird. There's a fat guy named Bill passed out in a hammock stressing beneath his weight. Scott tells me Bill started celebrating a little early. I ask what he's celebrating. Scott and Justin both laugh. Scott says he's probably just celebrating the fact that it's Tuesday.

I join them at the table where they're playing cards and sipping Scotch. Scott says,

You sure you don't want a drink?

Thanks, I say. But I'm sure.

I'll go get the hooker then, he says.

Just one? Justin asks.

Yes, but three people can do it.

I jump up and say, I'm not into that!

Not into fruit?

Fruit? What?

The hookah pipe, Scott says.

My face flushes with embarrassment. Oh, God, I say, I thought you said hooker.

They laugh at my mistake. No way, man, Scott says, hookah just fucks your head. Hookers are a whole other thing.

Scott goes inside to retrieve the hookah and Justin picks up the conversation. How long have you been a member? he says.

A member?

Of the club.

Oh, I'm just visiting.

Where from?

Well, from here. It's just that I'm watching my friend's boat.

How long you staying?

Not sure—awhile.

Scott returns carrying a tall chrome hookah pipe with a scoop at the top and three rubber hoses stretching like umbilical cords from its swollen middle. He sets it on the table, pulls out a torch lighter and fires it up. He says,

The torch is just a fast start. I take this with me everywhere.

You ever been pulled over with that in your car? Justin says.

It's just a hookah, Scott says, not a bong.

Scott hands me a hose. I say,

What's the difference between a hookah and a bong?

Well, it's . . . it's kind of like a bong, Scott says, but we only smoke dried fruit.

Scott and Justin puff the hookah. They blow out thin sprays of gray smoke that dissolve into the cool night air. I hold my hose but don't raise it to my lips.

Scott nods toward the *Valombrosa II*. How do you know that Valombrosa fellow? he says.

I work for him.

You work for him?

That's a nice ship, Justin says, what's this fella into?

Scott pulls the hose away from his mouth and says, Some kind of fancy fuck-people-over-hedge-fund guy, right Trevor?

We sure don't fuck anyone over, I say, and we do institutional investing too.

Same thing, Scott says. You money-business guys are always cooking up new ways to steal it from people like us who have it.

I don't know what happened but these guys are turning into dicks. I stand up and stick my hand out to Scott. I'm a little tired, I say. Think I'll go crash.

Scott just looks at my hand and sneers. Then Bill stirs awake in his hammock. I keep telling people that Valombrosa is a damn fraud, he says. Nobody listens.

I turn to Bill. Excuse me?

He props his huge head up on his hand, the hammock swings beneath his weight. I've read his prospectus, he says. Nobody can generate those returns.

The SEC Commissioner who owes him her job helps keep the heat away, Scott says.

I turn back to Scott. Well, you're such a big shot, I say, what do you do for work?

Work? he says laughing. Did you hear that, guys? The kid here wants to know what I do for work. Then they all laugh. I leave them on the deck and show myself out. It was a mistake to come. They're just jealous of Paul. Screw those guys.

I can hear them laughing all the way back to Paul's yacht.

THE NEXT MORNING, on my way up the dock, I look over at the *SS Reel Talk* moored in its berth and I rerun what those jerks said to me last night. It runs like a tape that won't turn off, and it plays until my scalp itches.

~~~

When I was at Edward & Bliss, before things soured, I went to the health club every day after work. Usually, I swam. Sometimes, I did cardio. It helped quiet my mind. In treatment, I was itching to get back to the gym but all Brave Ascent had was a flimsy ping-pong table propped up in the basement. Mr. Shaw said they didn't have a gym because sometimes people cross-addict into fitness. He said physical exercise is a plus as long as spiritual health comes first. But I suspect a gym would have taken away beds and beds mean dollars.

~~~

I pop into the office and ask Francis if the yacht club has a gym. He says they closed it down years ago to make space for wine storage but he makes a quick call and gets me a temporary membership at the Tiburon Tennis Club. Before I leave, I ask him about Scott and the *SS Reel Talk*. He laughs and dismisses my question with a flip of his hand. He says,

Don't bother yourself with those trust-fund fellas, mate.

PAUL'S NOT IN HIS OFFICE. Britney says he doesn't keep regular hours and I guess I wouldn't either if I were a billionaire.

On my lunch break, I walk to Union Square and buy shorts, a gym shirt, and a pair of sneakers from the Nike store.

After work, I drive past the yacht club a half-mile down to the tip of Tiburon and the Tennis Club. They have signs everywhere that say MEMBERS ONLY.

I check in at the front desk. The prissy manager puckers her small mouth and takes on the attitude of the rich clientele she serves. She says it's a member-owned club—she says there's a wait list—and she says she can't even get me in to see about getting on the wait list until next week. I tell her that Francis from the yacht club called this morning and took care of it. Three key strokes in her computer and her sour face stretches into a fake smile. She says,

Would you like a towel for your workout, Mr. Roberts?

Outside the club's windows, on this side of the caged, empty tennis courts, are two heated lap pools and a sunken spa. Men sit in the lounge drinking wine and watching the news from leather recliners. Private rooms have yoga and Pilates schedules on their doors and women hustle in and out of them working out their jaws chattering with one another.

The cardio room is empty except for a young lady on a treadmill. I climb on the machine next to her and when she smiles at me, I notice she has Down syndrome. She's watching VH1 on her machine-mounted flat-panel TV and she's dancing on the moving treadmill to Natasha Bedingfield's "Unwritten" video.

She grabs the handles of her treadmill and dances to the music while she jog-walks. She's happy and carefree and it's catching. I smile back at her and dance on my machine too. It feels good. She giggles and speeds up her machine dancing faster. I speed up my machine and swing along to the beat keeping pace with her.

She blushes.

We both laugh.

Then the door opens and a woman charges in gossiping into her cell phone about her pending divorce and how much money she's set to get. She sees us dancing and glares at me. As she approaches, I see she has the same hair as the young lady next to me but none of her smile. She stops her daughter's treadmill, tugs her off the machine by the arm, and without even removing the cell phone from her ear, she drags her daughter kicking from the gym.

It's as if these plastic people have nothing better to do than sit around, sip wine, gossip, and smoke hookahs while poking fun at working people. Their lives are empty shells, husks gilded in gold and diamonds and stuffed full of broken hopes. When I was a boy in Modesto dreaming of escape, I looked up to these people. Now that I've been here, fallen, and come back again, I see that their lives are nothing to dream for because they're all just trying to escape too.

I change in the locker room and head for the pool. Outside under the stars, it feels good to glide through the warm blue water. The smell of chlorine smoking off the pool as I stroke through the lane sends me back to the club I swam at in Folsom when I first started at Edward & Bliss.

~~~

I remember how nervous I was, how unsure. I remember the Men's Wearhouse salesman teaching me to tie a half-Windsor because the only necktie I ever wore was a clip-on for my mom's funeral.

I remember how included I felt accepting my first offer for after-work drinks from the guys, and having them accept my offer to buy a round when my turn came. I remember the thrill of learning all the different drinks—that whiskey isn't just whiskey—it's a family of Bourbon and Scotch, and Cognac is a brandy, and sweet vermouth plus whiskey and bitters make a Manhattan. I remember learning to mix a martini, decant a bottle of wine.

Then too, I recall the invitation to the after-party, the surge of anticipation I felt looking at a line of cocaine on a colleague's coffee table for the first time, the rush of euphoria and energy that swept me in infinity when the powder hit my nose, dripping its numbing epiphany down my throat—this is what I've been missing!

But cocaine is an unpredictable dance partner and I don't know when the music stopped, but that enlightenment faded and left only a smoldering discovery that the world is, and always has been, dim lit, and the future even darker.

I'll never know how cocaine made me a stranger to my own life. How it dragged me down without me noticing. How it turned my promising career into a nightmare of weary days broken only by trips to the office bathroom, trips I timed against the routine of my co-workers' bladders so I could snort blow without an angry line forming outside the door.

And I'll never know how my ethics disappeared leaving only the self-serving lie that says it's win-win the minute greedy Mr. Charles suggested a way to make easy rips by churning my clients' trust into commission checks cashed and spent on bottles and baggies and babes, how I forgot about Stephanie as our relationship lay dying with her in my lonely bed while I searched for sweet oblivion between the legs of lesser women.

~~~

This time will be different.

This time I'm armed with information.

This time I won't be caught in a circular track chasing the dreams of other men.

I've got a real shot with a real billionaire in a real business—a business that makes Edward & Bliss look like a corporate cage of hamsters spinning the plastic wheels of go-nowhere lives. I'm going to work hard. I'm going to do whatever Paul asks of me. I'm going to show him he made the right choice giving me a shot. Then I'll show Stephanie that I have changed and I'll ask her to marry me and I'll never take her for granted again.

It would've been easy to disappear but I'm not built that way and I came from nothing and made something of my life and it wasn't luck the first time and I know damn well I can lift myself up from the bottom again.

And this time, I'll do it right—with a fit, healthy body and a clear, sober mind.

17 Trust Me

Thirteen-hundred bucks for a Tiffany's diamond solitaire on a platinum lariat and Stephanie hasn't even called me.

It's Friday. Paul said today was payday but I haven't seen anything yet. I haven't even seen Paul since Monday when he gave me the yacht keys. All week it's been just Britney and me on the executive floor and analyzing these commodity reports is like eating paint. I've tried talking to Britney—even flirt with her a little although I know she's Paul's—but so far, my charm has failed to melt her ice-queen exterior.

I'm bored. I've been swimming at the tennis club and my body feels lean and fit, but I'm vibrating with energy and sex drive that I have nowhere to put. Maybe I should just stop waiting and call Stephanie. I pick up the phone. Britney knocks on my open office door. I set the phone back in the cradle and say,

Let me guess, Britney—you wanna ask me on a date tonight.

She almost smiles, but not quite. She says,

You're not my type.

Hey there, I say, I only have one feeling and you just hurt it.

Britney lays a large manila envelope on my desk. She says,

You're not free tonight anyway.

Is this my paycheck?

I don't know what it is, she says. Paul wants you to deliver it to his home after work. I wrote you directions on the outside.

I pick up the thick envelope—it's sealed shut and stamped across the seal in red ink it says CONFIDENTIAL. There's a lavender sticky note with handwritten directions to an address in Napa.

I drop the envelope on my desk. On Friday? I say. Really? All the way to Napa? How am I supposed to get there, Britney?

Britney smiles at me for the first time all week. She tosses the keys to my Porsche on top of the envelope. She says,

It's parked in the garage.

I LOVE THE EDGES of the day. I crack the car window letting the damp evening air trickle in. It smells like rain. I've been on the road almost an hour watching the sunset over grape vines rising and falling with the rolling hills and it feels like I drove right into a car commercial. Why have I not been to Napa before? Passing a roadside sign that says WELCOME TO NAPA VALLEY, I say it aloud. I like the way it rolls around my mouth. It sounds much better than "Welcome to Modesto"—*muy modesto*, meaning "very modest." There's nothing modest about Napa.

Atlas Peak Road snakes me past the wide green lawns of the whitewashed Silverado Country Club, then twists me up where it narrows and winds in switchbacks up a wooded mountain. The last light disappears as the trees close overhead and my headlights bore holes through the blackness in front of me.

I feel drunk on the night—invincible, immortal, infinite. This feeling is why I loved cocaine. But for the first time since treatment, for the first time since Edward & Bliss, for the first time since that first 40 of Old English maybe, I feel perfect peace without anything mind-bending in my body. Sober life is good.

Mine seems to be the only car on the road. Downshifting, I

accelerate and cross into the opposite lane banking a tight corner—the Porsche hugs the pavement. Another corner and the road dips into a deep gulch and my headlights shine on rows of miniature headstones. My mother's face appears in the night. The road cuts left. I floor it and her face fades with the pet cemetery in my rearview mirror. I'm done living in the past.

At the top of Atlas Peak, the road levels off and the Valombrosa mansion glows in the distance like Atlantis rising in a midnight sea. I don't even need to look for an address to know it's Paul's estate.

I pull up to black-iron gates with a golden V twisted into the center, a golden V for a golden name—Valombrosa. A call box rises from the ground like a periscope but before I can press anything, the gates swing open. I idle up the lantern-lit drive toward the massive Mediterranean mansion.

In front of the tall mansion, I round a giant marble fountain with a naked God wearing a headdress of grape vines tipping a jug of wine to the thirsty mouths turning up at him from three naked women lying at his feet. The fountain is dry. Combed gravel crunches beneath my tires. I park. I grab the confidential envelope, climb the wide stairs, lift the heavy iron knocker and tap it twice. Raindrops begin to fall on the gravel drive behind me.

Paul opens the door and plucks the envelope from my hand. Tara's sleeping, he says, meet me around back in the garden.

Then he closes the door. I stand there for a minute trying to remember what he just said about the garden.

I follow the path around the house. The side of the house is dark. My toe catches a paving stone and I trip and then catch myself, scraping my palms. I step behind the house. Pool lights reflect off fan palms and copper lanterns cast twisting glows through rosebushes and the shadows they make look like people in the gloom.

Paul emerges from a door wearing a red raincoat. He grabs my arm and pulls me along the garden path leading me out into the dark.

Thunderclaps. I hold my jacket over my head. The rain falls fast, drops so big they sound like frogs plopping in the pool behind us. Paul passes the pool house and leads me off the path. He clicks on a flashlight. The beam slices through the rain and penetrates the trees shinning on a crumbling replica of Michelangelo's *Madonna*. I wonder why it's abandoned out here. Maybe the garden used to go back this far before it went wild. The rain pounds down in buckets. I grab Paul's arm. Where are you taking me? I say.

He spins around with the flashlight beam pointed up at his dripping, hooded face like a kid playing monster in a tent. He says,

Trust me.

As we push farther in, the garden continues to give way to wilder plants until we come on the crumbling stone foundation of an old building. Paul shines the light on a wooden crate the size of a dog coffin. He pulls me to it. Then he sweeps dead leaves off the crate revealing a wine company crest. The crest has two skeleton keys crossing behind a banner that reads PÉTRUS 1989.

IN PAUL'S STUDY, I shrug off my wet jacket and toss it on a chair beside a cavernous gas fireplace. The orange glow of flames dances on the carved limestone mantel wrapping around the fireplace like a living sea of fantastic animal heads and twisted human faces. Bookcases on either side of the fireplace display just the right books in just the right places and a large antique dictionary sits on a pedestal with a brass lamp hanging over it. There's not a speck of dust to tell if any of the books are ever pulled out and read, but I doubt they ever are. A hog-hair sofa sits in a corner with dried pig hooves for feet. In the other corner, near the interior door, Paul stands at the bar examining a bottle of wine from the open crate.

I clear my throat. What was all that about? I say.

Paul grins, uncorks the bottle of wine. Tara had one of her little fits, he says. She ordered the maid to pour out all my alcohol but I saved the Pétrus—800 bucks a bottle and impossible to get.

I don't understand, I say.

I left a few bottles on the yacht. Come on, sport, don't tell me you haven't opened one yet.

You said you don't drink anymore.

Paul's grin widens and he says,

I don't drink any less either.

Grabbing a wineglass from the bar, he fills it and holds the glass out to me. I shake my head. I say,

I just spent two months drying out.

Relax, Trevor, he says. It's just one glass.

Thanks, but no thanks.

Paul stretches the glass closer to me. I insist, he says.

I shake my head. Paul's grin fades. His eyes get serious. You wanna play in my world, he says, you gotta pay!

I turn away from him and grab my jacket from the chair. Paul smashes the wineglass against the fireplace. Red wine drips down the white limestone mantel and hisses as it hits the flames. I spin around to face him. He says,

Where you gonna go—back to that shabby-ending motel? You go there and you're crawling back into a bottle eventually anyway. We both know that!

I try to steady my nerves, think before I respond. If treatment did anything, it made me self-aware. Drinking is bad news for me. Truth is I'm scared to drink. Scared to go back to that place it takes me. I don't want to beg, but I put on my best pleading voice and say,

Please, Paul—you know I just got out of treatment.

I know you did, he says. And I'll bet they brainwashed you with a bunch of God shit there. They did, didn't they? What did God ever do for you? I'll tell you what he did—nothing. But I did. I delivered you from that shit-hole motel and put you on my yacht. I gave you back your Porsche. Can't you see those people are just weak and that's why they need God.

Paul grabs the Pétrus and guzzles from the bottle. Wine drips down his chin like blood from a slit throat. Then he pulls the bottle away, licks his lips. He reaches for another wineglass and fills it. He thrusts the glass beneath my nose, holds the wine an inch from my lips. He winks and then he says,

It's not as if I'm asking you to marry me, Trevor.

My mind races a thousand miles an hour over my memories looking for something to believe in, something that will tell me Paul is wrong. But I can't find it. He's right. Nobody did shit for me until Paul gave me a job and a place to live.

Paul holds the wineglass steady to my lips. He doesn't blink and his eyes are so glassy-black I can see myself reflected in the firelight there. I look down. I can see the red wine glowing in the glass. I can smell it too. Sticking just the tip of my tongue into the glass, I taste the wine. Every decadent drop delivers craving straight to my brain.

I take the glass from Paul's hand, raise it to my lips and take a sip. I swirl the wine around in my mouth, feel the alcohol soaking into my cheeks, and then the road falls out beneath my racing thoughts and my mind goes quiet. I didn't even know I'd been fighting these last two months, resisting the relief, clawing at the ledge, until I feel myself stop and relax into the drop. Feels good to surrender. Feels good to be powerless. Feels good to be falling.

I raise the glass and drain it. Paul says,

Feels like the first time after so long without it, doesn't it?

As the wine warms away the cold ache in my gut, I say,

Feels like relief.

Paul hugs me with his free arm. He says,

They don't call it spirits for nothing, killer.

I sink into a chair beside the fire. Paul pours two more glasses of wine. Your problem was you were drinking cheap booze, he says.

I take a deep breath and relax for the first time in forever. I say,

Fill the glass this time, will ya?
Paul looks over at me proud. He says,
There's my boy!

18 Like What You See?

Nails hammer into my throbbing head. My eyes ache. My mouth is dry. My memory of last night develops with my vision like a brittle Polaroid in the bright morning light. The search in the woods for the wine. My surrender to that first drink. Getting lit by the fire with Paul. Glass after glass—how many bottles, three, maybe four? I'm lying in Paul's study on the hog-hair sofa. Someone draped an afghan over me.

I pull myself up. Too quick. My vision goes white. I rest my head on my knees and massage my temples but the hammering continues. Tossing the afghan aside, I stand. When my legs stop wobbling, I release the sofa arm and search the bar for something to drink. There's nothing. Any evidence of last night has been erased— even the fireplace mantel is clean. The hammering sounds again. It's not in my head—it's in the next room.

I walk into the hall and follow the sound. Stepping under a tall passageway arch, I peer into the great room. And there she is—

Tara.

The woman from the photograph on Paul's desk, the woman jumping the horse. She's standing in the center of the room. Long golden folds of hair cascade down her back, just grazing the top of her perfect ass. Her skintight black leggings tuck into her Ariat riding boots. She's facing away from me, addressing two Mexican workers on ladders. They're hanging a painting above the mammoth marble fireplace, an oil painting of a tall gray horse alone on a rocky hill at dusk—the type of haunting painting you can stare at for hours. But I can't take my eyes off Tara as she purrs directions to the workers—

I think a little lower, dears. More to the left. Ahhh, that's it. Right there. Yes. Yes! That's the spot.

Tara turns to face me. Her eyes are even greener than they are in the photo on Paul's desk. Her skin is pale but sun-kissed and her pouty lips part just enough to show the tips of her white front teeth. The blood rushes from my throbbing head and my dick gets hard. I forget about my hangover. She says,

Bonjour!

Ah . . . good morning.

Yes, it is. Who are you?

I'm Trevor.

What are you doing here, Trevor?

I'm—I'm—well, I came to deliver something.

You're a delivery boy, Trevor?

No. I work for Paul.

A smile flirts with the edges of her mouth. She raises her delicate hand, points her index finger in the air and motions for me to spin. She says,

Spin around for me, Trevor. Go ahead—turn around. Let me get a look at you.

I don't want to turn around but something in her voice makes it impossible for me to decline. I turn a slow circle, being careful to not stumble and look like a klutz. When I return to face her, a smile rises on her face and her green eyes glow. She says,

I see what Paul means. Do you like what you see, Trevor?

Sure, I mean what—do I like what?

Why the painting of course, she says.

Tara glides across the room toward the open kitchen. As she passes me, she brushes my hand with hers and electricity shoots up my arm. She pulls down two coffee mugs. I'm sure you could use some coffee, she says.

Where's Paul?

I didn't mean to mention Paul and as soon as it comes out, I wish I hadn't said it because Tara puts one of the coffee mugs back. She says,

He's in his office.

On Saturday?

His office here, silly. It's just down the spiral stairs at the end of the hall. Go find him and tell him he has my blessing.

Your blessing?

He'll know what I mean, she says.

DESCENDING THE STAIRS, I find Paul's office door ajar and lamp light leaking out from inside. I push the door open. Paul sits at his desk leaning over something. I tap on the open door and say his name but he doesn't answer. I step into the room and approach the desk. When I'm close enough to look over his shoulder, I see he's building a ship in a bottle.

Selecting a hand-forged tool from a dentist-style tray, he pushes it in easy, and then stands up the mast of the ship. I say,

I always wondered how they got those ships in there.

Paul doesn't look up. He says,

You should have knocked first, sport, I would have warned you—everything loses its magic once you realize it's just a trick.

As he drives a cork into the bottle with his palm, I look around the office and see 5, 10, 20—a fleet of ships in bottles lining the shelves and I wonder if Paul built them all. I say,

About all the wine last night—

Did you meet my wife? Paul says.

Yes, just now. Upstairs.

What did you think?

She seems great, I say, really great. Oh, and she said to tell you that you have her blessing. She said you'd know what she means.

Paul laughs. He sets the ship-in-a-bottle on a shelf with the others. Then he opens his desk drawer and tosses the confidential envelope onto his desk, the envelope I delivered from the office last night. He says,

Tell me what you think of these.

I pick up the envelope. It's already been unsealed. I open the flap and slide out several facedown 8x10 photos. I turn them over. They're color photos of Benny Wilson naked and balls deep in a young man on a motel bed. I remember Benny in his conservative suit, but here in the photos undressed, he's flabby and pale, but his face is twisted in ecstasy just the same as when he bit into his lobster cakes at lunch last week. I say,

Benny Wilson?

Paul grins. Yep, he says, locked up in a bottle.

So he's gay, I say, so what? So are lots of people—

Not married people, he says. And besides, that's his intern there he's got his little cock buried in.

Then it hits me. Yesterday after lunch when Paul said Benny wasn't as straight as he lets on, this is what he meant. And the only reason I can think to have these photos is to blackmail Benny.

You're blackmailing Benny? I say.

Paul smiles. No, he says. You're blackmailing Benny.

I'm blackmailing Benny?

When you deliver Benny those risk assessments he asked for, you're going to give him these for lagniappe.

For what?

A little bonus with his new account. He can jack off to them while he reads the reports.

I'm not a blackmailer, Paul!

Lighten up, kid. Benny's the one fucking around on his wife with his intern and using the CalTEARS expense account to do it. A man who does that deserves what he has coming. We're just getting him to do what his board wants him to do. It's not blackmail—it's encouragement. It's hedging. It's what we do.

Paul takes the photos from me and slides them back into the envelope. Then he puts his arm around me and says,

When we land this account, you'll be set up for life. You'll have so much shit you'll have to hire people to keep track of it all. Now come on, let me give you the nickel tour and show you a little of what I mean.

IN THE LIGHT OF DAY, I see what I missed driving up last night. The estate is a sweeping horse property. The mansion faces west across green lawns that separate it from a long stone and timber stable. I'm too caught up going over our conversation about the photos to hear much of what Paul is saying about the property. He's pointing things out with his free hand and carrying the envelope at his side as if it were nothing more than the morning paper.

We drop down past the stable to the white fence wrapping the riding arena. Tara is on the far side of the arena adjusting the saddle stirrups on a tall gray horse, the same horse from the painting hanging above the fireplace. Standing next to Tara is a giant of a man with a mop of straw-blond hair. When Tara climbs on the horse, he's still almost eye level with her in the saddle.

Tara looks back at Paul and me. She trots the horse to the end of the arena past a bar jump set in its center. Then she turns and gallops the horse toward the jump. Her blonde hair streams out behind her. They leap and the horse's rear leg catches the bar, knocking it to the dirt.

Inside the stables, a long hallway echoes with snorts of horses looking out from U-shaped openings in the bars of their paddocks. There's not a crack in the polished concrete floors. Gleaming brass fixtures fasten together the wood stalls. The whole place smells like horse sweat and money.

Tara enters from the other side with the blond giant behind her leading the horse. As we walk toward them, Paul says,

Why don't you just move up here, Heath? As much money as it's costing me to fly your sorry ass back and forth every week.

We might just take you up on that, Tara says.

Paul ignores Tara's reply. He says,

From now on, you're flying coach.

Tara lifts a warning eyebrow. Careful, Paul, she says.

Paul chuckles and turns to me. Trevor, meet Heath, he says, the only man on earth big enough to get under a 17-hand thoroughbred, pick it up, and adjust its back.

Heath's hand swallows mine. I say,

You're a horse chiropractor?

Heath smiles and nods. Tara says,

The best—and he's a masseur.

You two already met I understand, Paul says.

Tara tosses her hair. Yes, we bumped into each other. Trevor here was admiring my portrait. Weren't you, Trevor?

I don't know what to say and I just stand there like a dope. Tara smiles and tugs at Heath's shirt. She says,

I want you to check Ava—she's heavy with Conan's foal.

Heath closes the gray horse in its stall then follows Tara from the stables. As they disappear around the corner, Paul says,

You think she's fucking him?

I think you'd know, I say, that guy's a monster.

Yeah, I'll bet he's hung like a horse, Paul says, and then he laughs. Pointing to the gray horse, he says,

This stud here is Conan.

The horse in the painting?

Paul nods. Tara found him on a trip we took last year to the Isle of Man, he says. Poor bastard was put out to pasture and abandoned. Of course, Tara fell in love.

I reach in and scratch behind Conan's ear. Paul says,

Tara had to have him. And Tara always gets what she wants. I spent days tracking down the landowner. He had no idea what kind of horse he'd left out in the cold. Old Irish bastard sold him cheap—couple thousand bucks. Of course, it cost me 10 grand to fly him here. Now he lives like a king—fucking my mare, whose bloodline traces back to the Godolphin Arabian.

Does she race him? I say.

Tara wanted a stud, Trevor. Prick doesn't jump too well yet, but he sure can fuck!

PAUL LEADS ME from the stables in silence. I must have slept late because the sun has already fallen behind the trees and it casts a soft golden glow onto the estate. My head is still reeling over last night, this morning, the photos. I'm as overwhelmed as a kid at a carnival is. As we get up near my Porsche, Paul says,

Nice car. It's a little small to be sleeping in though.

It was my mom's.

Looks like it could use a new top.

It's an '83, the first year for a convertible.

Paul runs his free hand through his thick hair. He says,

There's nothing like feeling the wind in your hair.

Yeah. Mom swore she would put the top down one day and drive south! Drive so far south she'd never have to put it up again.

Well, that lard-ass loan shark sure took you for a ride with six grand at two times usury.

Thanks for getting it out of hock, Paul, I say. I'll pay you back every penny.

Pocket change, kid.

Paul holds out the envelope of photos. Several silent beats pass as I make up my mind. Then I lift my left hand and close my thumb and four fingers around the envelope and when Paul lets go, the envelope hangs limp from my hand.

Paul nods once and grins. Then he reaches into his coat pocket and hands me a BlackBerry and charger cable sealed in a clear plastic-freezer bag. He says,

Look, Tara and I will be in Paris until Christmas. You're on your own. Keep this phone turned on. Deliver the photos to Benny. Do not fuck this up, kid!

Then Paul reaches into his other pocket, pulls out a money envelope and slaps it against my chest. He says,

And this is to hold you over.

Tucking the photos under my arm, I take the money envelope from Paul. I open it and thumb through a thick stack of 100s—it must be $10,000. I say,

That's a lot of holdover!

Like I said, spare change, kiddo.

Then Paul sweeps his arm over the estate. You see all this? he says. We land this account and you'll be staked real good. Have your own mansion with your own showstopper in the stables.

I'll do everything I can, sir.

Paul's face cracks into a smile. He says,

There you go with *sir* again.

Then he turns and trots up his entry stairs. As I'm getting in my car, he turns back and calls from the door. Did she make it? he says.

Make it?

Your mom. Did she make it down south?

No—she died.

19 Worth Overdoing

The drive back is a blur. There are questions I need to answer, things I want to consider, but thoughts dart across my mind like bats chasing bugs. Every time I focus on one thought, another snatches it up and swallows it—900,000 thoughts chasing each other in the dark.

The distance between me driving north last night and me driving south tonight can't be measured in 24 hours—it can't be measured in time at all. I'm in another body, in another car, driving on another road, thinking another person's thoughts.

I can't focus because the envelope of photos sits next to me like a dead body. I reach over and toss the envelope in the backseat.

Trying to take my mind off the photos, I think about my mom. But Dad swallows Mom and then a wave of hate pours over me and swallows our house in Modesto until all I see is my dad's pale, dead face floating toward me, his bloated hands clutching a bottle.

I spot a strip mall, a check-advance place, a WESTERN UNION sign hanging in its window. I pull in and park, get out and stretch.

I count the money in the envelope that Paul handed me. Eleven grand in 100s. Ten-thousand makes sense, it's even, but what's with the extra thousand bucks? When I was working at Edward & Bliss, I used to wire Dad a 1,000 bucks every month. I can't shake his dead face and I feel guilty for wishing it. I try to imagine his face when I call the bar and tell him two grand is waiting for him at Western Union. Maybe I'll just have Hank tell him.

COUNTING 20 $100 BILLS, I push them beneath the glass. The wide-eyed money clerk asks for the second time if it's Carl with a K or a C. I tell him C as in cantankerous, but when he asks what cantankerous means, I just shrug.

As he finishes the money transfer in his terminal, he sips from a monster 72-ounce, plastic-keg coffee mug. I say,

That's an awfully big coffee mug.

Yeah, he says, doc told me I could only have one cup a day.

Well, anything worth doing is worth overdoing, that's what I always say.

He laughs. Ain't that the truth? he says. You wanna add any message to the transfer?

Yeah, just—Merry Christmas to you, Dad.

THE REST OF THE DRIVE, all I think about is Tara. When I get to the yacht club, I stop by the bar and order a whiskey and Coke. I'm the only customer. The bartender says his name is Charlie—good name for a bartender. He stands in front of me dusting bottles with a white bar towel.

The envelope of photos sits on the stool next to me. The freezer bag with the BlackBerry sits on top of the photos. The 9,000 bucks I have left is tucked away in my pocket.

I drain my drink. Charlie flips the towel over his shoulder and pours me another whiskey and Coke. He says,

You look a little forlorn, fella.

Yeah. Just bored I guess.

It's Saturday night, he says. A handsome young fella who looks like you do oughta be out on the town hunting ladies.

Not really interested.

Got a girlfriend?

No. Not really.

Fella, with your looks, you oughta be chasing the girls away.

Maybe that's the problem—I chase them away.

You the new guy?

New guy?

Staying on the *Valombrosa*?

Yeah, that's me.

Charlie pulls down a bottle and dusts it while he looks me over. Flipping the towel over his shoulder again, he reaches in his back pocket and flicks a card on the bar in front of me. He taps the card with his index finger and says,

You get lonely you just call that number there and tell them you're a friend of Charlie's.

CHARLIE MUST HAVE many friends at the yacht club because when I called, the service knew right where to send the girl. Forty-five minutes later and she's tapping on the yacht door.

I open the door. She has black hair, big dark eyes and high cheekbones. She's wearing heels and a skimpy emerald-green dress. A brown fur wraps around her neck falling open at her chest. She twists sideways so I can get a look. She's curvy—nice breasts, juicy ass. But she's not Tara. She's not Stephanie either.

She looks me over. Aren't you a nice surprise call for a change, she says. My name is Kari.

I take her offered hand but don't invite her in. I had just enough whiskey and Coke to call but not enough to go through with it.

Listen, I say, I'm sorry but I shouldn't have called.

She looks disappointed. She says,

You'll have to pay my cancellation fee.

I hand her $400, the price her service said she costs an hour.

She counts the money and stuffs it in her clutch.

She caresses my arm. You paid enough for an hour, she says. Sure you don't want a little company? You won't regret it. I promise.

Not tonight. Sorry.

IT'S SUNDAY NIGHT, I just masturbated in the shower and I couldn't finish.

I didn't leave the yacht today. I watched some TV, ordered Chinese again. This time I asked for a fork but I still didn't eat much.

The BlackBerry that Paul gave me worked well enough to call the escort service, but I can't bring myself to dial Stephanie. Actually, I've dialed her 10 times. I just can't bring myself to hit Send.

I called the bar and asked Hank to tell Dad about the money waiting at Western Union. I made Hank promise to remind Dad to bring Mom poinsettias on Christmas. Mom loved poinsettias.

I shut the envelope of photos away in a galley drawer. I try forgetting about them but I can't. I'm surprised they haven't sunk the yacht they're so heavy. Maybe this is how the wealthy do things. Even at my top at Edward & Bliss, I was nothing but a junior account rep compared to this kind of money—Paul's kind of money, CalTEARS' kind of money.

Tomorrow starts the last week before Christmas so I know I'll be going to see Benny Wilson soon. I wonder if I can go through with it. If I can, I wonder if it will work. If it works, I wonder what Paul meant when he said I'd be set up for life. I've been thinking about all kinds of things and I can't stop thinking—

Thinking about Stephanie.

Thinking about treatment.

Thinking about Benny Wilson.

Thinking about blackmail.

Thinking about Paul.

Thinking about Tara.

I don't want to drink today. And not because I can't, but just to prove to myself that I can stop whenever I want to. So I'm trying everything else to loosen up. So far nothing has worked. Not even masturbating in the shower.

20 Eureka!

I can't bear carrying the loose envelope of photos—feels like everyone is looking at me. Before work, I dodge into a men's store around the corner from the office. Eyeing a wall of briefcases, I spot one with a double lock.

The salesperson rolls his eyes at me when I ask if it's a good briefcase. He says it's Chiarugi. He says it's made with Italian Tuscan leather. He says that they prefer the term attaché. I tell him for 600 bucks I'll call it a lunchpail if I want. He gets even more pissed when I pay with cash because he has to run next door for change.

The Valombrosa security guard nods to me now on my way to the elevators but he still doesn't answer my good morning.

I wedge my new briefcase in the closing elevator doors and they slide back open. A shifty-eyed little man with round glasses stands in the back of the elevator, rising and falling doing nervous calf-raising exercises. Before I swipe my key-card, I notice the button for the 31st floor is lit. I'm curious so I pull back my hand.

After rising several floors, the little man says,

What floor are you?

Hi, I'm Trevor.

What floor, sir?

Excuse me?

Your floor.

I can't recall.

He reaches for the panel but he's too late—the elevator stops at floor 31 and the doors slide open. He steps off and turns to face me, blocking the entrance.

The doors close. I swipe my key-card and press 30. Britney is just hanging up her phone as I get off on the executive floor. I say,

Hey, who's the gnome with the bad hair, who works on 31?

That gnome's Mr. Chapel, our Chief Financial Officer. You're not allowed up there!

Then she hands me a thick, bound report. Here's the risk report for Mr. Wilson over at CalTEARS. Paul said you were expecting it. I phoned Mr. Wilson's office. He'll see you at four.

Four today?

Yes, four today.

I open my briefcase and add the risk report to the envelope of photos. Britney says,

Oh, some girl named Stephanie called here for you too.

AS I CROSS OVER the Tower Bridge into downtown, I see the CalTEARS headquarters rising in angles from the edge of the Sacramento River. I look at the elevator-door scuffmark already on my new Chiarugi attaché. That salesguy would really be pissed now.

The CalTEARS lobby is as sterile as the glass exterior and so is the receptionist. She tells me to wait. I sit on a contemporary sofa beneath a leaning wall of green, fretted glass that hangs over my head making me nervous. I put the briefcase on my lap. The clock above the receptionist desk reads five minutes after 4:00 P.M. so that's what I set the combination locks to—405.

An eager young man wearing a too-tight brown suit approaches me with a fast, feminine walk. He calls my name. I stand. I've seen him before—his pictures are locked in my briefcase. I feel powerful having them there. I shake his hand. He tells me his name is Doug and that he's Mr. Wilson's executive assistant and then he leads me into the building's less-showy interior, prattling on like a tour guide.

You might notice it looks a little sparse around here, he says. We're still moving in. We're quite proud of this building. It was built with 10 percent recycled material and cost $360 million.

Nice to know you're green, I say.

Yes, Mr. Wilson oversaw every penny. Came in on time and under budget. In fact, the very floors we're walking on are recycled rocks, marble, and glass. Did you know CalTEARS is the largest retirement fund in California? Seventh-largest public pension fund in the world?

Yeah, I know—with a $160 billion in managed assets.

Yes, well we provide benefits to nearly a million educators and their families. Here we are then.

Doug stops in front of oak double doors. Inlaid on the floor at my feet is the California Seal—Athena the Goddess of Wisdom and War stands in front of a river full of boats. As Doug opens the doors, he says,

Eureka is our State motto and means "I have found it."

The office is large, its walls lined with bookcases leading to floor-to-ceiling windows overlooking the Sacramento River. In the middle of the office, in front of a cherry-wood desk, Benny Wilson sits talking to an attractive older woman. The woman turns her head like an eagle.

Benny rises. Trevor, it's nice to see you again, he says. This is Mrs. Hamner, our very distinguished State Assemblywoman.

Mrs. Hamner holds out her white hand like a queen. I take it in mine. It feels cold and waxy. I make a slight bow. Pleasure, Madame.

Trevor's with Valombrosa Capital, Benny says. They've made some aggressive proposals to help us with our investment directives from the board.

Mrs. Hamner perks up. Oh! she says. Mr. Valombrosa is one of my biggest contributors. It's a special pleasure to meet you, Trevor. You look very sharp and very young. Well then. I hate to talk money unless it's campaign time, so I'll be leaving you boys to hash it out.

Setting her teacup down, she stands with iron posture, nods and then heads for the door. Benny follows her.

I hope you and Henry have a merry Christmas, he says.

Mrs. Hamner laughs. Oh, we're having the Speaker for dinner, she says, and I'm praying he chokes on a turkey bone and dies. Then it'll be a merry Christmas all right.

Benny holds the door for Mrs. Hamner. He keeps it open and waves Doug out behind her. Doug doesn't move. Benny says,

You too, Doug.

But I thought—

That'll be all for now, Doug.

Yes sir, Doug says and then exits.

Benny closes the door and turns to me. He says,

Have a seat, Trevor. Can I get you something to drink?

No thanks.

You sure?

I'm sure.

Did you have a long drive?

Not bad now that the fog's burned off.

Nasty stuff—that tule fog.

Benny walks to the sideboard. He opens a small, hidden freezer. Plucks ice cubes from a bucket. Drops them in a glass. Pours himself a Scotch. He carries it over and sinks into the chair next to me. I watch the light hit his whiskey and ice as he swirls the glass in his hand. He raises his glass, takes a sip, and lowers it again.

Benny sighs. This is quite a view isn't it, Trevor?

I nod, looking through the windows at the Sacramento River. Most of the year, the river's dirty water crawls through town, but the recent rain has it flowing fast and a tired boat struggles toward us making slow progress against the current. I notice there are no blinds on the windows. I say,

Can people look in from boats?

Who would want to look in?

I don't know, I say. Just wondered, that's all.

Strange thing to wonder, Benny says, but don't worry yourself—they're mirrors on the outside. We had to use special black mirrors that wouldn't reflect sun. Expensive but quite a nice touch overall.

I watch the boat dredging up river. I know I'll have to open my briefcase. My hands grip the chair. My armpits sweat.

Benny sips his Scotch, looks over. He says,

Paul's wanted this account for a very long time. I know what it means to Valombrosa to have our money. Even a little of our money is a lot of money.

Then Benny empties his Scotch glass. He crunches an ice cube between his teeth. He says,

And I'm sure it means big commissions for you.

I force a little laugh and smile.

Benny stands. Are you sure you won't have just one drink?

All right, I say, just one though.

With water or on the rocks?

You got any Coke?

Dear God no!

I'll take it straight then.

Benny shakes his head and walks to the sideboard. I watch him pull down the bottle of Scotch and another glass. I turn back to the window. The boat is much closer now. It's an old boat, its flat back stacked high with dock boards sinking the hull into the water, its engines struggling against the weight, its nose pointing into the air.

Benny reaches a Scotch over my shoulder. I grab the heavy crystal glass and hold it up to the light. The amber liquid is as thick and dark as maple syrup. I take a sip—it bites my tongue and then warms my throat and I feel Benny's hands rubbing my shoulders, kneading my knotted muscles, and it feels good but by the time the Scotch hits my gut, I realize what's happening.

I jump up. Set my glass on the table. Step away from Benny. His hands hang in the empty space above my chair. I grab my briefcase. Fumble with the combination. I say,

I have those risk reports here.

All business, huh?

All business.

You work for Paul, he says.

That's right, I do.

And why do you think Paul sent you?

Because you asked him to send me.

Well, why do you think he brought you to our little lunch?

Because I'm good with numbers.

Because you're good-looking. Wake up, kid!

I spin the locks, but can't remember the combination. I say,

Valombrosa can make a lot of money for CalTEARS.

I don't trust Valombrosa one bit, he says. And if Paul weren't pressuring me from every angle, including my own board, I wouldn't even consider it!

At 405—the locks snap open. I swing the case up to rest flat on my forearm and opening it, I reach inside and pull out the risk report. I hand the report to Benny. I say,

I think this report will help put your mind at ease.

Benny throws the report in the wastebasket. He says,

I've been at this a long damn time, kid—I don't trust reports. And I don't trust Valombrosa Capital, and I don't trust Paul. Now, unless you're going to give me a reason to trust you—leave!

I reach in and grip the envelope of photos. My gut twists up and drops like a roller coaster ride.

I remember feeling this way, 20 years ago when I was nine. I found a purse in the grocery-store parking lot and snuck it in our car. We were halfway home when Mom saw me with it. She looked through the purse for ID and found $1,500. She turned us around to return the purse. I knew we needed the money so I asked her why. She said you always know the right thing to do in your gut—it feels funny to do anything else—if you don't listen—you only hurt yourself.

~~~

I let go of the photos. I close the briefcase with shaking hands. I walk to the door, look back, and see Benny already behind his desk, fussing with paperwork as if I'm already gone.

I step out and close the door behind me. I lean my head against the door and look down at the seal in the floor—Eureka! Is there a Latin word for—"I have lost it?"

~~~

I remember Paul handing me the photos, I remember what he said too. He said don't fuck up, kid—he said Benny deserves what he gets—he said Benny's the cheat—he said we're only encouraging him—he said we're just hedging—he said I get this account and I'll be set for life—he said I'd have my own mansion with my own showstopper in the stable, and I know he meant I'd have my own Tara.

~~~

I walk back in the office. Benny smiles. I toss the envelope of photos on his desk. His look changes to concern. I say,

Tell me what you think of these.

Benny opens the envelope and slides the photos out. As he looks through them, a vein at his temple swells, snaking from his eye to his hairline where a bead of sweat gathers and drips down his cheek. His breathing becomes shallow. His face reddens. He says,

Where did you get these?

Does it matter?

I have a wife and two children.

126

You'd never know it by looking at those photos.

You should be ashamed of yourself!

I should be ashamed? Your on-staff fuck-buddy waits outside. Your wife waits at home. And you get me in here and you want to fuck me? What does Valombrosa want? Valombrosa just wants your business. Valombrosa wants to earn a better return for your precious teachers and their retirement.

Benny fiddles with his tie, loosening it. He says,

Listen, Trevor, I'm not very proud of myself for—well, for what you see here—but this is private business. It's got nothing to do with CalTEARS. With the duties of my office. You don't want to do this. Paul doesn't want to do this. You can't barge in here with this trying to take advantage of me.

Like the way you just tried to take advantage of me?

Benny drops the photos. He walks around the desk. His voice is loud and firm. He says,

We're responsible for the retirement of the people who teach our children. We're not some reckless hedge fund here.

You seem to have no problem—

Are you blackmailing me, son?

Giving you options.

Benny stomps to the door and opens it. He says,

I take the professional duties of this office very seriously—I am not for sale!

My heart is pounding out of my chest but I remain aloof, force a smile, and walk to the door. As I pass Benny, he grabs my arm. He clears his throat and in a low voice, he says,

I'll look over that risk report. You can tell Paul I'll get in touch after the holidays.

21 It's Just Wine

I sit alone at a window table for two in the Delta King restaurant. If it were still light outside, I could see the CalTEARS building downriver, but I want to forget Benny Wilson, so I read the boring history lesson on the table card for the third time.

The Delta King is a retired paddlewheel steamboat permanently moored in Old Sacramento. In the roaring 20s, it took 10 days to steam passengers through the Delta into San Francisco. During World War II, it transported troops across the Bay. In 1982, it sank and lay on the sand-bed seafloor for a year before it was resurrected in Sacramento as a floating hotel and restaurant. Some people claim it's haunted and I think it would be great to see the faces of the pretentious capital-city patrons if the engines fire up on their own and we take off upriver during dinner. My hand is still shaking when I sip my water.

I see the mustached host leading Stephanie to the table. I stand. She wears a simple yellow dress that looks stunning against her dark skin. The Tiffany's diamond solitaire hangs from her neck catching the light. I take her hand. I say,

You're beautiful!

Thanks, she says, you look handsome, Trevor.

You wore the necklace.

Stephanie clutches the necklace and blushes. I slide her chair in as she sits and then I take my seat across from her.

I wish I could have afforded a bigger stone, I say. You should don a diamond the size of a robin's egg.

I like the one you gave me, she says.

Yeah, but the way things are going with Paul, I'll be able to buy you a better one soon.

Our server sees that my companion has arrived and rushes over with menus. She's a young redhead with a quick smile and cute freckles. She says her name is Courtney. She asks us if we would like to start with a drink. Stephanie says she's fine with just water. I say the same. We decide we're both hungry enough to order right away and as we look over our menus, Courtney says,

The chef's special tonight is the king and queen, a petite filet paired with a four-ounce lobster tail—

I snap my menu closed. We'll have two of those, I say.

Stephanie peers around her menu at me and says,

I don't eat meat, Trevor.

Oh, yeah, right—sorry.

Courtney beams a smile at me as she takes my menu. How do you like your meat, sir?

Bloody.

Courtney blushes. She turns to Stephanie. And for you, Miss?

The diver scallops, please.

Courtney nods, collects our menus. The sommelier will be right out, she says and then she heads off toward the kitchen.

When I called Stephanie back this morning, she sounded happy to be talking to me. I told her I was coming to town and suggested dinner. She said yes right away. I've been thinking a lot about getting back to when things were good with Stephanie and me and now that money's rolling in again, I think it's time.

I reach in my pocket. I feel the cold metal of my grandmother's ring. I brought it just in case. But now that she's across from me, I'm having second thoughts. I've never compared Stephanie to another woman, but I look at her now and size her up to Tara—Stephanie's not as pretty as Tara is.

Stephanie sees me examining her. We share an awkward silence. Why were you in ugly Old Sacramento anyway? she says.

Oh, just a little meeting over at CalTEARS—the $160 billion pension fund, the largest one in California.

That sounds really important, she says. What were you meeting with them about?

It's a new account, I say. Paul has me working with the CEO.

Nice. Have you seen your dad?

I sent him some money. How's school?

Fine. We're on winter break now.

When will you graduate?

I'm going for my TESOL certificate now, so next year.

TESOL certificate?

Stands for: Teaching English to Speakers of Other Languages.

Still want to teach, eh?

The money's no good but I love it, she says.

Stephanie takes two quick nervous sips of her water and when she sets her glass down she touches the Tiffany's necklace. She closes her eyes, opens them again, and says,

Trevor, I've been thinking a lot since we hung out the other weekend—since two months ago really—

Me too, I say.

And I've been talking with my mom. She's your biggest fan—

I like your mom very much.

Well, if you're really serious about things, I think I'd like to give it a try—give us another try—our relationship, I mean—but only if you still feel the same—

Your 1989 Château Pétrus, sir, the sommelier interrupts her. The sommelier is tall, thin, a tuxedoed cartoon vampire, and he grins down on me with purple teeth and presents the bottle. You have fine taste, sir, he says. Shall we open it now and allow it an opportunity to breathe? He deftly sets two wide-mouthed Bordeaux wineglasses on the table. Then he uncorks the bottle and pours me a sample. I taste it, nodding my approval. He fills Stephanie's glass, and then mine. He sets the bottle on the table, spins the label to face us, smiles, and then retreats with a bow.

Stephanie gapes at my glass of wine. She says,

What is this, Trevor?

It's a very rare French Bordeaux.

You're drinking again?

It's just wine, Steph.

Just wine?

The other stuff was the problem. You know that.

I know the problem starts with just wine, Trevor.

Relax, Stephanie, pull in your horns already. I'm not gonna start drinking again—I just wanna be able to enjoy a glass of wine with you. Like the good times.

There was nothing good about those times.

Come on, we had lots of good times.

You didn't touch me for months, Trevor.

I was a little depressed is all.

You overdosed!

Come on, I thought we'd celebrate.

Celebrate what?

Let's celebrate getting engaged.

I pull my grandmother's ring from my pocket and hold it out to Stephanie. She stares at the ring in silence. Then she looks at me with wet, glistening eyes. She grips the table. She says,

They pumped your stomach. You almost died. If I hadn't found you, you would have died. Right there in your stupid hot tub, Trevor. Don't you get that? You're heavy, you know. Too heavy for me to lift. You weren't conscious. All I could do was hold your mouth above the water until the medics got there. Now you're drinking again. And you want me to marry you?

I stuff the ring back in my pocket. Okay, I say, don't marry me then. But let's just drink this wine—we can't very well waste an $800 bottle in good conscience.

Stephanie stands and throws her linen on the table. She says,

If you have any conscience at all to go along with all this damn money that you're throwing around on wine, maybe you can pay my mother back for your rehab!

Sit down.

You haven't changed.

Stephanie storms out. I gulp my wine and decide to go after her. People stare at me as I rush through the restaurant. Bursting outside, I catch Stephanie on the dock and grab her arm. I say,

Why didn't you meet the train!

Stephanie spins around. She's crying. She shakes her head and says, This is too much, Trevor—too much, too much, too much.

She pulls free and walks off.

I yell at her back. Are you fucking someone else?

Stephanie spins to face me. She clutches the Tiffany's diamond solitaire around her neck. She rips it off and holds it over the railing of the raised dock. The necklace dangles from her hand reflecting yellow light from the windows of the Delta King. She lets it drop. The necklace tumbles toward the black water below. I rush to the rail and look over. The necklace plops like a pebble and then the inky ripples close around it and I can see myself reflected in the black water, my silhouette outlined by the orange dock light behind me waving on the water's surface—a shapeless shadow of a man.

When I look up, Stephanie is gone.

22 Christmas Ship Parade

The yacht club parking lot is full tonight. As I lead Courtney, the Delta King server, down the docks toward the *Valombrosa II*, partiers drift past us on their way to idling yachts. The black water reflects one-hundred-thousand colored lights strung from the ships and the waiting crews untie lines and lay dock plates down so the owners can board.

A boy passes us wearing a red Santa hat. He looks too young to be drinking the open bottle of Champagne he's carrying and when I call after him and ask what all the commotion's about, he looks back and he's not a boy at all but a small woman and she holds up the Champagne bottle and says,

It's the annual caroling Christmas ship parade of course!

Courtney's eyes get wide as I help her aboard the yacht. Her jaw drops when I throw the master switch and turn on the lights. Wow, she says, this is yours? You live here? Are you rich? Are you?

No, I say, I'm broke.

Yeah, sure, she says.

I'm tempted to open another bottle of Pétrus but I find a bottle of Vya dry vermouth in a galley cupboard and decide to mix martinis instead. When I pull the Kauffman vodka from the freezer, Courtney takes it from my hand and says,

Holy shit, dude! We serve this vodka for 80 bucks a shot.

While I shake the martinis, Courtney inspects her sudden stroke of luck. She wanders around the galley touching every expensive surface. Stopping to study the portrait of Paul, she says,

Is this your dad?

I ignore her question and fill the martini glasses. Courtney says,

So what do you do that makes so much money?

I blackmail people.

You're an attorney?

I hand Courtney a martini. Money manager, I say.

How'd you get into that?

I fell into it like a fucking grave.

She sips her martini. I'm getting my associate at American River College, she says. But I plan to major in business.

Business is good, I say. My degree's in poli sci and it qualifies me for jack shit—except maybe waiting tables. Sorry, I didn't mean anything by that.

It's okay, she says. I don't like serving either, but we all do what we gotta do, right?

The lighted ships are moving now and I walk out on the deck with my martini. Courtney follows me. She wraps her arms around me from behind and unbuttons my shirt. She presses her breasts into my back and slides her hands in my pants pockets, rubbing my inner thighs and the edge of my hardening boxers. She says,

What were you and that pretty girl fighting about?

Nothing.

Oh, don't tell me nothing.

Courtney pulls my grandmother's ring from my pocket and holds it up to me. Is this her ring? she says.

No, I say, it's not, snatching the ring from her hand.

I can't believe Stephanie threw away the diamond necklace I bought for her, I can't believe she told me I haven't changed, I can't believe I asked her to marry me, and I'm glad she said no. I wind up and pitch my grandmother's ring into the water. It doesn't even make a sound as it disappears into the black.

We stand at the rail in silence and watch the parade of lighted yachts pass by on their way out into the cove.

As the last ship passes, Courtney says,

Hey, that guy's waving at us.

Scott waves from the back deck of the *SS Reel Talk*. Ahoy, mate! he says. What's the problem, no Christmas spirit? That Valombrosa Grinch couldn't afford any lights? Scott and Justin high-five and everyone on his party deck laughs.

I leave Courtney standing on the deck and run out to the dock. I untie the lines and unplug the shore power. I jump back on the yacht. Courtney follows me into the pilothouse. I start the engines and back the *Valombrosa II* from its slip.

In the distance, the floating light show pushes out into the cove. I push the throttles forward and steer toward the yachts. Horns blow up and down the line of lighted ships like the wave moving through a crowded football stadium and the sound of caroling echoes across the cove. Courtney runs to the window. She says,

It's just so beautiful. I've never been on a boat at night—never been on a boat this big ever. Way cool. You must feel so free living on a boat. But it's not really a boat, is it? It's a yacht! We're getting closer. Look at the lights. Hey, they're caroling. Let's carol too. *I saw three ships come sailing in / On Christmas Day, on Christmas Day*. This is so great! Hey, there's your friend, there's the guy who waved at us.

Come and take the wheel, I say.

Courtney skips to my side and grabs the wheel with both hands. Yay, I get to drive! she says.

I stand behind her and steer our course for the *SS Reel Talk*. Then I take one of Courtney's hands from the wheel and put it on the throttles, pushing them wide open. The dual engines whirl and scream. We pick up speed. Courtney says,

Shouldn't we slow down a little?

She pulls back on the throttles. I push them forward again and keep us speeding toward the *SS Reel Talk*.

As we advance, a small crowd gathers around Scott on the party deck. When one person shouts and points, they all become frantic like ants in a smoking nest. Scott waves and yells—

Hey, what the fuck are you doing!

The distance closes between our ships.

Courtney twists like a held fish. Let me go, let me go, she says, you're scaring me!

I grind my hard-on into her ass. She turns around and kisses me. I pull back on the throttles and the yacht sinks back to the water line. Courtney reaches down and hikes up her dress. I unbuckle my belt and drop my pants. As the *SS Reel Talk* slips away, I pull Courtney's panties aside and enter her from behind.

Thrusting into her, I imagine that she is Tara. She lays her head against the polished-wood control panel and parts her lips. A moan slips out. Air pushes from her lungs with each violent pump. She reaches back, clutches my ass, and pulls me deep inside her. My scream bursts across the cove as I climax and then collapse on the deck panting. Courtney lies bent over the wheel housing with her dress bunched around her waist and her naked ass in the air.

The echo of my scream dies and the caroling carries back to us across the water—

All the souls on earth shall sing / On Christmas Day, on Christmas Day And all the souls on earth shall sing / On Christmas Day in the morning.

PART
II

23 Merry Christmas

I think my eyes are open but all I can see is darkness. The BlackBerry vibrates on the mahogany bedside table in the stateroom. It's been vibrating for half an hour.

It's a week since the Christmas ship parade. Courtney from the Delta King is long gone but Kari from the escort service lies passed out on the bed next to me. After loading Courtney in a cab that night, I called for Kari and 30 minutes later, she was tapping on the door. She said she knew I would call back. I handed her another 400 bucks and invited her in. While I shook us martinis, she kicked off her shoes and slid onto the couch. Then she opened her purse, pulled out a baggie and cut me a line. I snorted the coke and my brain lit on fire. That was a week ago, she never left.

I guess the escort-service number isn't the only one that Charlie gives out often because the "Doc" knew right where to deliver the cocaine. The Doc is a slick Mexican kid and he's crossed paths with the Chinese food-delivery guy so many times this last week, they've learned to say hello in each other's native languages.

I haven't left the yacht except twice to pick up boxes of bottles from Charlie at the bar. I can only imagine what my tab is now. My pile of cash is running lean. I quit paying Kari three days ago but she called in sick to her service and stayed. She's a cool chick when she's high—she's a bitch when she's not.

The cocaine was getting expensive and I needed to come down. I asked Kari if she knew where we could get some GHB. She didn't. But she went to her car and came back with a purple pharmacist's refill bottle of promethazine-codeine cough syrup. She called it Texas tea. She said it would help me sleep. And it did.

It must be windy because the yacht rocks in its berth and a yellow blade of light cuts beneath the blackout window shade. The BlackBerry vibrates on the table again. Grabbing it, I hit the answer button, raise it to my ear in the dark and mumble hello. Paul says,

Merry Christmas!

Huh? Oh, yeah, right—Merry Christmas.

Tara and I want you to join us for Christmas dinner, he says.

Today?

No, next Christmas. Of course, today.

I don't wanna intrude.

You won't be.

Are you sure?

I wouldn't be asking if I weren't sure.

Then I hear Tara in the background. She says,

Tell him I said to come.

Did you hear that, sport?

Okay, I'll come by your place then.

We're not at home, he says. Come to La Spa Rouge du Soleil in Rutherford. It's not far from our place. If there's anyone at the club today, they can give you directions.

I'll find it, I say.

When you get here, ask for the Champagne Suite.

Champagne Suite. Got it. What can I bring?

Just bring yourself.

Then I hear Tara again. She says,

Tell him to come as soon as he can.

You hear that, sport? We'll be waiting.

Paul hangs up before I can say goodbye.

Kari rolls over and groans, her sleep interrupted. I grope my way out of bed and pull on my jeans. I smell like booze and bad BO. I need a shower.

The BlackBerry vibrates again. I snatch it up and answer. Hello. I hear talking in the background. Hello. I press the BlackBerry to my ear. I hear Tara say, I'm getting the diamond facial. Paul says, I want the six-hands massage and the caviar-hair treatment. Hello. Nothing.

Paul must have pocket-dialed me. I hang up. I jerk open the stateroom door and step into the main cabin. The burst of light sends me cowering blind against the wall. I squeeze my eyes and wait for the headache to pass.

When I open my eyes again, I'm stunned to see a mile of blue water in every direction—the *Valombrosa II* is floating adrift in the middle of San Francisco Bay.

I feel better after a shower. I feel almost good after some cold chicken chow mien. And by the time I have a couple swigs of Jack and a line of coke, I have wings.

Kari isn't happy but when we get the yacht back to the marina, I give her a fistful of cash and the last of my cocaine and then send her away. She'll be less happy when she figures out it's Christmas Day.

THE YACHT CLUB sits on Belvedere Cove just off Highway 101. Driving south, 101 follows the coast until it turns into the PCH and runs into Bixby Bridge. From there I think it goes clear to Dana Point where you can see the beaches of San Diego. Driving north, 101 leads me through a soft rain toward Napa.

The shallows between the hills hold a thick fog like soup bowls and the rows of grape vines rise from the fog and roll over the hills to meet distant groves of naked winter trees. There's a kind of strange allure in the grape vines of Napa Valley. Even when they're winter bare, the thick, gnarled vines wrapping around their wires look like long lost Eden waiting to spring forth with juice-joy temptation. I wonder if Napa would be as charming if they planted rows of corn.

Spotting the sign for Rutherford Hill Road through the quiet rhythm of my dull wipers, I turn east to follow the vines upward.

After climbing, dipping down, and then climbing again, the road turns sharp to the left and leads me up a massive tree-dotted hill. Halfway up, I rise above the fog and rain and then the road widens into a private drive lined with silver birch trees. I pass a monument sign that reads LA SPA ROUGE DU SOLEIL, NAPA VALLEY.

Coming to a stone guardhouse, I stop at the white gate and lower my jerky-power window. A young guard in a pressed blue uniform leans out and looks over my Porsche. My dull wipers squeak back and forth on the windshield. The guard frowns at me with suspicion. Where you headed, he says.

The Champagne Suite to see the Valombrosas.

He turns his back to consult his computer. Without turning around again, he raises the gate arm and says,

You're good.

The vine-covered lodge is nestled into the bluff and a steep relief gives it the appearance of cantilevering out over the valley. To the left, down a gentle slope, stone paths lead through an olive grove to other stucco buildings terraced into the hillside. I pull beneath the carriage porch, toss my keys to the eager valet, and ask him where I can find the Champagne Suite. He points me toward a stone path and tells me to follow the signs at my feet. I hand him a 20. As I head for the path, the valet calls to me. He says,

Hey, Mister, you staying overnight?

I look back. No, I say. Just through dinner.

The path leads me down through lawns speckled with garden sculptures, winding me around twisting Napa Valley oaks. Olive trees dot the lower hills that roll down to the valley. Copper signs at my feet mark each tributary path. One reads HILLSIDE VIEW SUITE, another reads COGNAC SUITE—MERLOT SUITE, ZINFANDEL SUITE, BORDEAUX SUITE—and then the CHAMPAGNE SUITE.

The Champagne Suite break-off path ends at a white-adobe bungalow tucked into the hill. A wooden sign hangs from a rope on the gate—THE VALOMBROSAS.

I unlatch the gate, swing it open and step onto the stone terrace. The valley sweeps out beneath me. The French doors leading into the bungalow are open and white-lace curtains sway in the breeze.

I turn to the doors and knock against the wood frame. There's no answer. I knock again. Hello. Still no answer. I lean my head in past the curtains and take in the room. Whitewashed walls run up to dark-timbered ceilings and shag rugs cover the tile floor. Overstuffed pastel furniture surrounds an enormous stone fireplace and in the corner, a tiny tabletop Christmas tree hung with silver ornaments sparkles in the gas firelight.

Strong hands grab my shoulders from behind.

We almost gave up on you, Paul says.

You spooked me.

Paul laughs. You're like a horse that way, he says.

I follow him into the bungalow. He walks to the bedroom and when he parts the curtains, I see a tall California king bed piled high with white pillows. After a minute, Paul emerges from the bedroom wearing a white terrycloth spa robe. He hands me another robe and a small pair of black Yimps shorts. He says,

Put these on.

PAUL DISROBES and steps down into the steaming spa water. I guess Paul is smaller than I am because his shorts are tight. I toss my robe on a chair and get in the water quick. We sit across from each other, our arms along the spa edge. I'm reminded of a couple birds I see drying their wings every morning in the marina.

The pool area sits between the Champagne Suite and the main lodge on its own private terrace overlooking the valley. A few paces away from the spa, Tara swims laps through mist rising from the heated pool. The rain has stopped but fog lowers from wispy clouds and licks at the wet hills below us.

Paul smiles. Now this is living, he says.

Yeah, it sure is, I say. Do you come here a lot?

Whenever the mood strikes us.

Paul runs his hands through his thick damp hair. Then he says,

I look like a fucking bank executive on a mental health retreat, here. Look at you! You look like my tanned tennis coach. You been on vacation or something?

Yeah, to Sacramento. Hey, about Benny—

No business today, stud, he says. You're here as our guest.

There's a splash from the pool and Tara pulls her lean topless body from the water. She strolls toward us with complete comfort. Her ivory white skin is broken only by dark nipples on firm teardrop breasts just big enough to fill a wineglass.

I stare at Tara as she steps down into the spa. Paul stares at me. Tara glides over to Paul and French kisses him. Then she looks over her shoulder at me and says,

I'm glad you came, Trevor.

Yeah, I'm glad I came too—this place is gorgeous.

A young masseuse stalks toward us carrying a clipboard. She's a cute Eurasian and her waist is no bigger than one of my legs. She must be 90 pounds soaking wet. She asks if I'm Trevor with a tone that apologizes. Before I can answer, Paul says,

Take good care of my man here. Have fun, sport. Meet us at the lodge at eight. I'll leave the room open so you can dress for dinner.

I climb out from the spa, trying to act cool even though my shorts are so tight my hard-on is obvious. I shrug on my robe, avert my eyes from Tara's breasts, and follow the masseuse.

HER NAME IS ZIN, like the wine. She lights a lavender oil diffuser and starts a mixed CD spinning in a player on a shelf next to a lion's head fountain. She holds a white sheet up to the massage table making a curtain and asks me to strip off my shorts. I wonder what Paul meant when he told her to take care of his man.

I lie naked on the massage table. Zin drapes the sheet over me. My hard-on makes a tent in the fabric. She giggles and says,

Maybe we should start with you facedown.

I smile up at her and say,

Maybe you could release the tension in my front first.

She raises her eyebrows, turns her head away, and lifts the sheet waiting for me to flip over. I'm glad she doesn't see me blush. I guess Paul didn't mean take care of that.

I look at the floor through the face hole in the massage table while Zin works on my back muscles. The brushed-stone tiles have streaks running through them and if I half close my eyes, they remind me of the silver veins of the delta snaking through the valley as I flew over heading to rehab. In some ways, it seems like 10 years ago—not two months. In other ways, it seems like I'm still on the plane.

As Zin moves down my back to work my legs, Delerium's song "Silence" with Sarah McLachlan comes up.

~~~

I remember when this album released, the same year my mom died. I bought the CD the day before the call came. I played it driving home, I played it driving back, I played this CD so many times that year the aftermarket player in my Porsche broke with this album stuck inside.

~~~

The music flies me higher. I imagine Zin has me strapped down boiling in a pot and is stripping the meat from my bones. This is the feeling I'm looking for—somewhere just this side of alive. Dead, but not quite. Zin massages my feet, the lyrics massage my mind and I sink into the silence and fall asleep.

IT'S LONG SINCE DARK returning to the Champagne Suite. The room is empty, the lights dim, the fire burning. My pants lie folded on the bed with a new collared shirt next to them. On top of the shirt is a note that reads MERRY CHRISTMAS!

Under the shirt, sunk into the white comforter like an egg in a nest, rests a platinum diamond bezel Rolex Day-Date Masterpiece.

I pick up the Rolex and turn it over in my hand. I've seen this Rolex in a *Wine Spectator* magazine ad and they didn't even list the price. I fasten it around my wrist—a perfect fit. I hold my arm out and test its weight. It's heavy, but not so heavy that you can't forget you're wearing it.

How can I accept it? It's too much. I'm not sure what one costs, but when they don't list the price in those magazine ads it means you can't afford it if you have to ask. I'll bet it cost more than the down payment I lost with my house. Can you say no to a gift like this?

I look at myself in the mirror—naked except for a terrycloth robe and a platinum diamond bezel Rolex. I feel like a million bucks.

THIS NIGHT FEELS like a slow-motion version of a foreign film. At the restaurant, a white-jacketed Maître d' delivers me to Paul and Tara's table.

Candlelight reflects from a decanted bottle of wine. Paul wears a suit jacket but no tie. Tara wears a white chiffon dress with a neckline that plunges to her navel, a blood-red ruby and yellow diamond necklace draped around her neck. After filling Tara's wineglass, Paul looks up at me. He says,

You found the shirt.

And the Rolex—Wow! Thanks.

I hold out my wrist and let the Rolex glitter in the candlelight. Paul frowns and clicks his tongue. He says,

Ooh, that's my Rolex. I must have left it by mistake.

Blushing like an idiot, I hang my head and unclasp the Rolex.

Even Tara laughs at me. Paul fills my wineglass. He says,

I'm fuckin' with ya, kid. Merry Christmas.

Really? You mean it's mine?

It's yours, sport, he says. Tara picked it out.

Tara laughs again. She says,

It looks good on you, Trevor. You're very handsome.

Thanks, Tara, you look beautiful. Paul, are you sure about the Rolex? It's too much—I don't know what to say.

You already said it, pal—thanks.

I pick up my wineglass and take a taste. Paul smiles. Tara runs her slender index finger across the rim of her glass. It's quiet. I can hear forks on plates, wine pouring, a blowtorch for someone's tableside crème brûlée. A fragile-looking veteran waiter approaches with two other waiters behind him. They set a delicate plate of rare-seared tenderloin filet in front of each of us. Paul leans back, pats his belly, and says,

Wagyū beef! Flown in fresh from Japan just for us.

The senior waiter presents an ornate ebony case to Paul. The waiter raises the lid and inside the case, nestled in red velvet, are three tortoiseshell-handle folding steak knives. Paul plucks one from the box, snaps open the long slender blade and hands it to Tara. Then he does the same for me. The knife is heavy, the blade razor-sharp. There's a golden V inlaid on the tortoiseshell handle. I say,

You bring your own steak knives?

Paul snaps his knife open. He says,

I never cut my meat with another man's knife.

The waiter closes the case, bows to Paul. Anything else at the moment, sir?

Yes, Paul says. Bring another bottle of my '95 Château Margaux for the table and two Glenfiddich 40s neat for us men.

A little water on the side with the scotch, sir?

No. And don't pour us drams either. Fill them up.

IT'S PAST MIDNIGHT when the tired captain comes over and suggests, after many compliments, that we might enjoy the services of the spa better tomorrow if we call it an evening—just a suggestion, of course. Paul orders him to bring out a bottle of Louis XIII and four cognac glasses. Then Paul makes him join us for a drink.

I've never met anyone with enough money or power to make a captain, waiter, and bartender stay three hours past closing on Christmas night. I can only imagine the tips Paul leaves.

As the three of us stumble along the lantern-lit path toward the bungalow, Tara says the garden statues look like they want to dance with us. I grab the arm of a bronze boy holding a daisy and do a grapevine one-step but he doesn't want to dance. I run to catch up with Paul and Tara. I say,

Paul, what about that guy trying to cut our drinks off tonight? Who gets cut off in a place like this anyway? We do. That's who!

That's right, buddy, he says, we do. I can buy this place tonight and fire them all and they know it.

Tara just whistles.

We enter the suite. I stretch out on the couch beside the fire and look at my Rolex. The diamonds glow in the soft light of the flames. Paul and Tara sit in a loveseat across from me. They light a joint. I haven't smelled marijuana since college.

Paul nods in my direction. Tara brings the joint over and sits on the edge of the couch beside my head. She's light—the cushions don't sink at all. She holds the joint to my lips. I take in a long pull of hot, acrid smoke, holding it in as long as I can until I cough it out.

Tara leans down and kisses me. I push into her kiss. Her tongue searches my mouth. She tastes sweet. She grabs my hand and cups it on her perfect breast. Paul says,

You can do anything you want, except fuck her!

I pull my mouth away from Tara and look up. Paul is smiling down at me with a camera in his hand. He says,

If you fuck her I'll castrate you, you got that? But you can do anything else. And whatever you do, look like you're enjoying it.

I wriggle out from beneath Tara and jump to my feet. I say,

It's late. I really should go now.

Tara takes my hand, holds up the Rolex, smiles. You got your Christmas present, she says, now it's time for me to unwrap mine.

Then she pulls me into the bedroom. She unbuttons my shirt and peels it off my shoulders. Then she slips off her dress, steps out of it and slides onto the bed naked.

24 A Forgotten Prayer

un pours through the open windows and warms the soft white bed linens as I drift in and out of weightless sleep. I'm floating on a cloud. Memories pass beneath me like a silent movie I saw in another life. I smell wood smoke from a distant fire and it reminds me of summer camp when I was 10.

~~~

I don't remember where the camp was, but I remember it took Mom two hours to drive there. I pretended to be sick because I didn't want to go, but Mom laid me down in the back of our old station wagon with a blanket and pillow. It felt good to close my eyes and listen to the hum of highway rolling by beneath the floorboard. I remember hoping we would never stop. Knowing my mother was driving made me feel safe—nothing could touch us, we were invincible.

I was terrified when she dropped me off. In one hand, I held an envelope with $20 for the candy commissary, in the other I held two weeks' worth of clothes stuffed in a duffel.

They put me in a cabin with five older boys. The next morning everyone went to the lake. I stayed in the cabin pretending to still be sick. A camp counselor came to see me. I wish I knew his name but everyone just called him Red because he had red hair. The other kids said he was a volleyball coach or something, but I thought maybe he was in the movies because he always said, That's the ticket.

Red sat on the edge of my bed. He didn't ask me what was wrong. Instead, he told me about his first time at camp. He said he was scared of the other kids because he wet the bed. He said he was scared of a woman counselor because he thought she was pretty. And he said he was scared of the horses just because. I'd never heard a man admit he was afraid of anything before. When I told him I couldn't swim, he laughed. It wasn't a mean laugh—it was a no big-deal laugh. He said he'd teach me to swim and he did. By the second week, I was jumping off the cliff into the lake. I got a ribbon for most-improved swimmer and Red pinned it on my shirt, smiled and said, That's the ticket.

The last night there, we built a bonfire by the lake. I was sad to be going home. Everyone was. The headman stood in front of the fire with his walking staff and talked to us about Jesus. Then he asked whoever was willing to make a decision to give his life over to God to come up and say a prayer. Red was looking back and smiling at me. I felt like he wanted me to go and I couldn't let him down. I was the first to stand and walk to the edge of the bonfire.

The headman got down on his knee. He took my trembling hand in his soft, wrinkled palm. He asked me to repeat a prayer after him and I did. But I was so focused on getting the words right, I forgot the prayer as soon as it passed my lips. But something happened. For the first time, fear completely left me. The world was full of magic and beauty and the bonfire smoke carried mystery on the air. I floated back to my seat and when I passed by Red, he smiled wider than ever.

Mom picked me up the next morning. I sat in the front seat of the station wagon and talked her ear off the whole way home. She nodded and smiled, but she didn't say much. When we got home, she sat me down at the kitchen table and explained what a mastectomy is and why she was missing a breast.

I lay in bed that night and tried to remember the bonfire prayer but it was lost with the smoke. I tried to find the fearless feeling but it was gone too. I wouldn't feel it again until college when that 40 of Old English hit my guts.

~~~

I open my eyes. Parked next to the bed is a bamboo tray stacked with bowls of fruit, baskets of breads, and a silver pot of coffee. Behind the coffeepot is a bottle of Roederer Cristal Rose in a copper bucket of ice. I reach for the Champagne. The Rolex surprises me on my wrist. The baguette diamond bezel is blinding beautiful in the morning light. I pull the Champagne from the bucket, ice water drips from the bottle onto a page of thick spa stationery. There on the tray, written by a flowing female hand in back-slanting light-footed cursive that dances across the paper, is a note—

Thanks for a great night! Stay as long as you'd like, but be at our place tomorrow night—We're having us a little party!

25 *Sorry, Ma'am—I'm Empty*

The Valombrosa gates are wide open like hungry black jaws. The drive is lined with candles glowing in little red-paper bags. The front of the mansion looks like a Beverly Hills showroom packed with every expensive make of vehicle. Two young women, who must be parking valets, stand on the steps wearing red vests and black button hats. I've been parked at the entrance with my lights off for 10 minutes.

I couldn't sleep last night so I called the Doc. The coke he brought blew my mind and I forgot about the Champagne Suite. But I'm thinking about it now. I felt rebellious and an exciting kind of guilty when I first woke up in that room. I remember Tara kissing me. I remember her lying naked on the bed. I remember spreading her long legs and tasting her. And the memories should be sweet, but my conscience keeps going off in the background like Paul's flashbulbs lighting everything up for what it was—me being used. I feel stupid. I feel dirty. I feel embarrassed. I wasn't going to come tonight but I dressed and then drove here on autopilot.

I'm leaving. I start the Porsche and reverse back into the street. I look at the Rolex on my wrist—can't leave. I remember Paul's camera—leaving. I think about the yacht—can't leave. I shift into first and drive up to the house.

The fountain is no longer dry. The wine God's jug pours red-dyed water into the naked women's upturned mouths. I park behind a black Bentley. When I climb out of my car, the tallest female valet bounces over. She says,

Hey, the service entrance is around back.

I was invited, I say.

She holds her hand out for my keys but I tuck them in my pocket and walk past her up the stairs.

Inside the foyer, candelabras cast a romantic glow on the polished wood and marble surfaces. Through the arch leading to the great room, I see guests in eveningwear mingling around a string band. The men wear white tuxedos, the women are clad in black, and together they look like a chessboard as servers dance between them refilling wine and delivering hors d'oeuvres. I'm not sure where I belong so I stay in the foyer.

Tara glides by with Mrs. Hamner, the State Assemblywoman. She spots me and stops. Tara's black dress clings to her body. She touches my cheek. She says,

Oh, Trevor—they'd open the studbook for you. I'm so glad you're here. I'd like you to meet—

Yes, we've met, Mrs. Hamner says grabbing my hand and petting it. In Benny Wilson's office, do you remember, Trevor?

How could I forget, Mrs. Hamner? Did you get your Christmas wish? I didn't read anything in the paper about the speaker choking on a turkey bone.

Mrs. Hamner squeezes my hand. You better be careful with this one, Tara, she says, he doesn't forget a thing.

Tara laughs. Trevor, Paul's in his study with the guys telling lies. Would you be a dear and tell him I'm making the announcement?

Then she whisks Mrs. Hamner away.

Paul's study is filled with more men wearing white tuxedos. They stand in clusters chatting with practiced boredom. Paul wears a white jacket with tails. He's opening a bottle and talking over his shoulder to the men nearest him. He says,

This is the best cognac made. It's aged in oak barrels under lock and key for 20 years. I first tasted it in Paris. Bought a controlling stake in the company so I'd never run out.

Paul turns around with two glasses of cognac. He sees me and smiles. He steps toward me, hands me a glass. He says,

Gentlemen, say hello to my new man—Trevor!

One of the guests, a fat man with a thick gray beard, looks me over and then he says,

He must have come straight from the office in that suit.

The room falls silent. A dozen pairs of eyes stare at me. Paul looks at me with a sly smile. I want to tell the beard it's an Armani suit, but I smile and take a sip of my brandy. After a heavy silence, one of the other guests says,

Where are those cigars, Paul?

And then another chimes in and says,

Did you buy a Dominican tobacco plantation too?

The men laugh. They forget about me and turn back to chatting. I feel better. Just as Paul opens the lid to his humidor, Tara pokes her head into the study. She says,

Those stinky cigars will have to wait, Paul—it's time to tally.

Paul closes the humidor. He leads the men into the great room where the guests gather around Tara. She stands in front of the string band holding a sheet of paper. When everyone is circled up, the string bass player plucks a few deep chords and calls for everyone to be quiet. Then Tara whistles. She says,

Okay, wild people, settle down—Bacchus will be back!

The murmuring turns to whispers and then the whispers turn to silence. I stand at the back of the crowd and watch. Tara says,

Years ago, I realized how hard it is to buy Christmas presents for my friends. What do you get people who already have too much of everything? Then the answer came to me. You get them that good feeling that comes from helping the less fortunate. You get them a little bit of their innocence back.

Someone in the crowd laughs. Someone else says, Good luck with that. Then everyone laughs. The bass player plucks a chord. Tara smiles. She says,

Well, we can try anyway. Now, for those of you who are new friends, here's how this works—every Christmas we send our favorite people an invite to this party—our black and white party. The invite has a space for you to write your favorite charitable cause. We collect the invites at the door and tally them up. Then we make a donation in your name to the charity of your choice. This year, we raised the donation to $25,000 per couple and $10,000 for singles—more for couples because we all know that a good couple is more than the sum of two people.

Someone says, Especially in divorce court!

Everyone laughs again, including Tara. Then she says,

Now for the tally—36 couples and seven singles showed up this year and Paul and I will make the donations in your names next week for a total of . . . wait for it . . . drumroll please . . .

The bassist slaps a percussive rhythm on his strings. Tara holds up the paper and waves it. She says,

A grand total of $975,000!

All the guests applaud. Tara bows deep, and then she swings back up, throws her arms in the air, and says,

Merry Christmas everyone! Your gift is a clean conscience for one night. Now let's use it up by getting good and drunk!

Tara whispers something to the bass player and he nods. Then she walks to me, takes my hand, and pulls me into the center of the room. The band plays "Unforgettable." Tara takes my hands, wraps my arms around her waist, and then she drapes her arms over my shoulders and leans into me. We slow dance. A few other couples join in but most drift to the sidelines and watch, their eyes raking over us, their mouths whispering, their wineglasses tipping to servers for more wine.

Tara feels like hot sex. She slithers in my arms. My hips slide against hers. I bury my nose in her hair, inhale her fresh scent. I need to taste her, need to be inside of her, need to mold my flesh together with hers. I whisper in her ear. I say,

I need to see you.

Tara brushes her hand against my hard-on. She says,

Hungry tonight?

The music stops. I notice Paul standing next to us. He presses a thick envelope of cash into my hand. Then Tara passes me off to a tall brunette wanting to dance. The brunette smiles. Tara winks and wraps her arms around Paul. I tuck the envelope in my suit pocket. I guess I'm my own charity.

I CAN HEAR the party winding down in the house behind me. I'm sitting on a concrete bench at the edge of the blue glowing pool. When I swiped the Champagne bottle from a passing server, I came out here to cool off. Now I'm cold, my tie loose, my hair hanging in my face, and I feel sick.

The patio door opens and Tara steps from the house carrying an empty Champagne flute. She floats over and sits next to me on the bench. She holds out her flute and says,

Fill me up, Mister?

I tip the bottle and pour the last drops of Champagne into her glass. Sorry, Ma'am—I'm empty.

Tara dangles the empty flute between her knees. She says,

You were the star of the party tonight. What did you think of old Mr. Kleinfeld's daughter, the leggy brunette you danced with three times? She was absolutely begging for a formal introduction.

I pat the thick envelope of cash in my pocket and say,

Did you tell her how much I cost?

Nobody's forcing anything, Trevor. We're all adults.

I'm getting another drink. I stand up, steady my legs.

Tara grabs my hand. She says,

I think maybe you've had one too many already.

I look at the empty Champagne bottle in my other hand and laugh. Who are we kidding? I say. One is too many.

The tallest female valet jogs over. She says,

There you are, geez, I've been looking everywhere for you. Your car's blocking a Bentley—I need your keys.

I look from the valet to Tara. I say,

I was just leaving anyway.

The valet follows me out. The impatient Bentley owner stands tapping his foot while his attractive young escort applies lipstick. I recognize him as the bearded guy who insulted my suit in Paul's study. I thrust the empty Champagne bottle at him. Confused, he takes it. No wonder you're impatient, I say, you must be paying your date by the hour.

A shocked hole opens in his gray beard but no sound comes out. The tallest valet tries to contain her giggle behind me.

I jump in my car and start it. I push the shifter up and to the left for reverse but I must have missed and hit first because when I pop the clutch, the Porsche jumps forward and smashes into the Bentley.

As I back out, I can hear the beard yelling. He says,

Did you see that? That punk just hit my Bentley!

Looking back one last time, I swear I see the valets smiling.

26 Measure of the Man

I'm not sure if it's still night, morning, or two days later but somebody is pounding on the door.

Pulling the shade aside, I peek out the stateroom porthole and blink into the daylight to see who it is. Reflected in the windows of the yacht in the next berth, I see a dark-skinned man wearing a double-breasted suit standing at the *Valombrosa II* door. He checks his thin reflection in the glass, straightens his tie, and knocks.

He's raising his fist to knock again when I swing the door open. Hello there, he says. Mr. Lussier at your service. We're here to get the measure of the man. The guy talks weird so I close the door. He knocks again harder. Persistent. I throw open the door. He's holding a black business card in my face. I snatch the card away and read the silver lettering—LUSSIER & SONS BESPOKE TAILORS, SINCE 1975.

Three and a half minutes later, I'm standing in my boxer shorts while Mr. Lussier measures me. He makes notations with a tooth-dented pencil he holds in his mouth. The Armani suit I slept in is piled on the floor and I can see the $10,000 envelope from Paul and Tara sticking out from its inside breast pocket.

Mr. Lussier looks up at me. He says,

Did we know our left leg is a half-inch longer than our right?

No, I didn't—I just hope it's not hollow.

Perhaps a chiropractor could straighten us out.

He turns to his bag and hands me tuxedo pants. I pull them on. What's all this for anyway? I say.

He grins at me and clucks his cheek. He says,

Mr. Valombrosa rushes his bespoke tailor, risking my reputation with a lousy made-to-measure tuxedo, and we don't even know what it's for? Well, all I know is we are to have it by New Year's Eve.

Then he holds out his hand and says,

Can we take off the Rolex?

I unclasp the Rolex and lay it in Mr. Lussier's outstretched palm. He inspects it before slipping it into his pocket. He hands me a shirt. I pull it on. As I button it, he says,

We're going to be the fanciest drake at the ball!

I wish I felt like it.

Ha! he says. If tailors could fix that, the world would be much better dressed, and there would be no psychiatrists.

I cluck my cheek, imitating him. I say,

Perhaps a psychiatrist could straighten *us* out!

Mr. Lussier smiles and slips a jacket on me. He marks the cuffs with chalk. Then he turns me toward the mirror and fusses with the lapel. He says,

When one is living the dream—waking at noon on a yacht, telling time on an $80,000 chronometer!—one could do worse, much worse. When one is young, one has to live. Plenty of time for dying later. This old tailor has made many suits for men who were dead but years yet from their grave. Trust us.

I don't trust anyone, I say.

Mr. Lussier hands me back the Rolex. He says,

We should trust people to be exactly what they have proven themselves to be, no more and no less.

Then he kneels to adjust the hem on the tuxedo pants. I clasp the watch around my wrist. Amazing, $80,000, he says. I look down at my suit on the floor, the envelope of cash sticking out from the pocket. Flaunting the Rolex in the mirror, I smile at myself and say,

I guess I am living the dream.

Mr. Lussier pokes my ankle with a straight pin.

27 Money's No Problem

It's funny how different the salesclerks treat me once they see the Rolex on my wrist. It's even funnier to watch their eyes light up when I pull out a wad of 100s and pay with cash.

At Nordstrom, I buy a new sport coat and designer dark-blue jeans. The girl behind the register says the jeans were designed for an NBA star. That reminds me of Mr. Charles. He uses the Edward & Bliss office fund to buy season tickets to the Sacramento Kings. Great seats too, three rows up from courtside. The tickets are meant for clients but Mr. Charles goes to every game himself. Sometimes he brings a top producer with him. He brought me once. The whole game, all he did was prattle about how expensive the seats were as if he'd paid for them. Mr. Charles would shit if he saw me now, if he knew how well I'm doing.

As the clerk rings my purchase, I ask her if she can recommend a sexy dress. She blushes and says,

For what type of occasion?

An evening of revenge, I say.

She giggles and says she knows just what I need. Then she takes me upstairs to the women's designer collections.

AFTER LEAVING Westfield Center with my shopping bags, I stop by a Walgreens on Market. I buy a prepaid Visa card and have the clerk load $2,000 on it. She has to call a manager over from the photo center to handle the cash and the manager probably earns 10 bucks an hour but he treats me like a drug dealer.

I walk back to the Valombrosa building where I parked. All the Valombrosa floors are dark except for the 31st floor. No one is working between Christmas and New Year's except that little CFO, Mr. Chapel. I'll bet he doesn't even celebrate his own birthday, let alone Christmas.

I ride the elevator up to my office. On my computer, I log on to StubHub. I use the prepaid Visa and buy a pair of courtside tickets for tomorrow's Kings game. Sacramento vs. Oakland, I know Mr. Charles will be at that game. I get seats on the floor, three rows in front of him. A $900 ticket is a lot, but it'll be worth it to see the look on his face. Maybe I'll wear my Rolex on my right wrist so he can see it when I walk three rows back to shake his hand.

SATURDAY WHEN I dial Kari, she's pissed at me for kicking her off the yacht Christmas Day. She says she's working, she says she doesn't want to see me, she says I'll have to call the escort service. I tell her I have courtside Kings tickets and a towncar and she says she can be ready in an hour.

I have the towncar take me to Kari's place on Potrero Hill. She answers the door, I hold up the Nordstrom dress bag. She hooks a hand on her hip. What? she says. I'm not dressed pretty enough?

I unzip the bag and show her the Cavalli dress. She gasps and then she kisses me. Stripping right there in her tiny apartment living room without even asking me to close the door, she slips into the new dress. The silk fabric hugs her heart-shaped ass and scoops her tits up like balloons holding water, her nipples poking against the fabric. She's not as pretty as Tara is but she's so different I don't mind. I grab her in my arms and pull her against me. I say,

You look good enough to eat.

She bites her lower lip, pouting. I say,

What's wrong?

She kicks up her foot and says,

Now my shoes don't match.

Well, just grab some other shoes.

She runs her hands down to my crotch, cups my balls. She says,

But I don't have any shoes that match.

I swell against my new jeans. I say,

We've got enough time for a detour I guess.

I HAVE STAGE FRIGHT and can't pee. The Ukraine Train is pissing in the stall next to my urinal. He's six-foot-ten, his head sticks up over stall wall, and he's singing the folksong "Where Have All the Flowers Gone?". I didn't know that courtside seats share a bathroom with the players. I flush the toilet, wash my hands, and step out of the bathroom. An old usher waddles up with his yellow arena shirt tucked tight into tan Dockers. He says,

Two minutes until tipoff, sir. We need to hurry along now.

The Edward & Bliss seats are still empty. In front of the empty seats, Kari sits beside the court with her legs crossed, the steel-gray Cavalli dress riding up her thighs, her new strappy silver Gucci platforms glimmering like jewels at the end of her smooth, dark legs shimmering in the stadium lights. Her breasts hang full and ripe and her dark hair waves down over her shoulder. The players from the visiting bench are checking her out. It feels good to be back on top.

All 17,000 fans in Arco Arena seem to watch as I walk to my seat. I hope the game is televised tonight and Stephanie sees me on TV sitting next to Kari. I take my seat. Kari kisses me. She says,

Why do you keep looking back at those empty seats?

Ah, just an old friend.

What's her name?

His name, honey. Just a guy I used to work with.

You would think that for almost a grand per ticket the seats would be leather recliners with built-in back massagers, but they're just padded metal-folding chairs lined up on the sideline. Even so, courtside is the only way to see basketball. Tipoff is right in front of us. We're so close, I could stick out my leg and trip a passing player.

The courtside crowd is too cool to cheer with the rest of the fans when the home team makes a basket, and the guy slinging beer offers our section red wine in plastic cups. I buy us two each, so we won't have to wait for him to come around again.

We skip the halftime show and head to the courtside club bar. We order lemon drops and chase them with Coronas. Every guy in the bar eye-fucks Kari. Whenever she catches them, she flicks her tongue at them, then leans in and kisses me. Then she checks to see if they're still watching.

It's well into the fourth quarter when we amble from the bar back to the game. I plop down in my seat and pull Kari onto my lap. She leans against me, her tits pressing into my chest, and we make out as the players run back and forth.

I can feel the usher standing over me even before I see him. He leans down to my ear and says,

She's a beautiful companion, sir. Can't blame you being eager. Nevertheless, season-ticket holders don't cotton to public displays.

I reach in my pocket, pull out a $100 bill, and hold it out to him. Run and get us two glasses of red will you? I say. Keep the change.

The usher stiffens. He says,

I think perhaps you've both had enough already, sir.

Kari climbs off my lap. She plunks down next to me in her seat. I look up at the usher. I say,

Screw you, man.

Do I need to call security, sir?

You need to call whoever sold you those Dockers and tell him they went out of style 10 years ago.

The usher smirks. I guess you can't buy manners, he says.

I stuff the $100 bill into his shirt pocket and say,

Why don't you see if you can buy a personality?

Then I take Kari by the hand and lead her across the court right in the middle of a home-team offensive drive. I hear the referee's whistle stopping the play as we blow out the back of the stadium.

ON THE ROAD BACK to San Francisco, the driver checks the game score on the radio. The Kings beat the Golden State Warriors 119 to 96. I ask him if the game was on TV. He says,

I don't think so.

Between $1,800 for two tickets, $500 for the towncar, almost $1,000 for Kari's dress, and another $600 for her Gucci platforms, I'm out $3,900 and Mr. Charles didn't even show.

Kari kicks off her new shoes. She leans into the car door and puts her bare feet in my lap. She rubs me with her toes. She says,

I feel like partying.

I scroll through the seven numbers programmed alphabetically into my BlackBerry—Barbara, Chinese Palace, Escort Service, Kari, Paul, Stephanie, The Doc. I dial the Doc. He answers. I say,

Hey, it's Trevor. Can you meet us with an ounce of candy?

The line is quiet for several seconds. Then he says,

An ounce is a felony, man. You sure?

I'm sure.

Runs 12 bills.

Kari's feet work in my lap, she flicks her tongue at me. I say,

Money's no problem.

28 The Plain of Oblivion!

I open the yacht door wearing my boxers. Paul wears a tuxedo, a Louis Vuitton garment bag draped over his arm. He hands me the bag. Get dressed, sport, he says.

I slide the zipper open—my tuxedo is inside.

Aren't you gonna invite me in? Paul says.

You don't have to ask, I say, it's your yacht.

Paul pushes past me and looks around the yacht. It feels strange to see him here in my space. He picks up an empty bottle of Jack and stands it upright on the coffee table. He chuckles. He says,

This is how I lived before I got married.

Then Paul walks over and peeks in the stateroom. He sees Kari passed out naked on the bed. He laughs and says,

I used to knock the ladies down like bowling pins too. Not bad, sport, not bad. But aren't you gonna get dressed.

Do you mind if I shower real quick? I say.

We got time, go ahead.

I grab my Ferragamos, fresh socks, clean boxers, and dive into the bathroom. I hang the tuxedo on the door. Turn on the shower. Brush my teeth. Wash my face. Run a razor across my cheeks. Jump in the shower. Lather up with soap and rinse off. Kill the water. Towel dry my hair. Step out of the shower.

I hear moaning coming from the stateroom. I cup my ear to the door—Kari. I crack the door and look out. Kari facedown on the bed, naked. Paul mounted on her from behind, gripping her hair, pants around his ankles, his pale, hairy ass pumping up and down.

I don't know whether to burst out and stop him or hide in the bathroom until he's done. I close the door. It's not like she's my girlfriend. And she is an escort. But I bought her. She's mine.

I focus on getting dressed. I pull the tuxedo pants on. Slide the shirt on. Button it. Tuck it in. Tie the bow tie. Crooked. Tie it again. Still crooked. I give up and lace my Ferragamos. Pull the vest over my head. Slip the jacket on. Look in the mirror.

Senior prom was the last time I wore a tuxedo and it was rented. The one Mr. Lussier made for me makes me feel like a film star.

I put my ear to the door again. It's quiet. I step out in my tuxedo. Paul zips his pants and walks over to me. He grabs my neck, pulls me to him, and reties my bow tie. I say,

How long did you take?

How long did I take for what, sport?

How long did you take with Kari?

Is that her name? he says. Just three minutes.

Well she's $400 an hour so you owe me 20 bucks.

Paul laughs. He squeezes my neck and says,

Bill me okay, sport.

Paul finishes adjusting my tie. He holds me at arm's length and inspects me. I Look down at Paul's high-polish tuxedo shoes. I say,

Are my Ferragamos okay?

Paul smiles. Kid, he says, you could wear purple Crocs and still win the prize tonight. Then he nods to Kari on the bed. Get rid of the whore. We gotta go.

Kari throws a shoe at Paul. He ducks and it hits the stateroom wall. Paul laughs. Kari jumps out of bed and pulls her dress on. She stomps around the stateroom plucking her things off the floor and mumbling something about dirtbags. Then she stands in front of me with her left breast falling out from steel-gray dress and her silver Gucci platforms cradled in her arms. She says,

How am I getting home?

I look at Paul. He grins and shakes his head. He says,

Give her a hundred.

I hand Kari a $100 bill. Guess you'll have to catch a cab, I say.

Her jaw drops. She slaps my face. You rotten bastard! she says. Then she storms off the yacht, slamming the door. Paul laughs. We both watch out the window as she pads up the dock shivering in the Cavalli dress and carrying her new Gucci shoes.

IN THE LIMO, Paul lights a joint and hands it to me. Just to prime the pumps a little, he says. I take a hit and blow the smoke out my cracked window. Now tell me about Benny Boy, Paul says.

Benny Wilson?

Yeah, Benny Wilson. How'd it go?

He threw me out.

So you gave him the photos.

You told me to give him the photos.

Paul laughs and slaps his knee. He says,

He threw you out, eh? God, I'd pay to see the look on his face. Did that vein at his temple swell? I bet it did. Just like when he's fucking that boy of his. Did he say anything else?

Said he'd get in touch with you after the holidays.

Paul reaches over and pinches the joint from my hand. He sucks it a quarter-inch down, holds in the smoke and then blows out a cloud. We lock down CalTEARS, he says, and the money will pour in faster than you can spend it, boy. You're gonna be rich.

Then he hands me back the joint.

I don't say anything about Benny making a pass at me.

I ASK PAUL WHY the other couples are staring at us. He says they'll look anywhere as long as it's not at each other. Tara laughs and says it's the marijuana.

Tara met us at the restaurant. She walked in and her sequined dress caught the light from a thousand bulbs in the great crystal chandelier. I heard a wake of clinking silver dropped on china behind her as she floated through the room toward us and, like a fish caught in a net, I couldn't look away.

The Fleur de Lys restaurant has no private booths and the tables sit in the middle of one big space with the grand chandelier hanging overhead. Pink brocaded walls suck the sound from the room and everyone sits on straight-backed chairs and talks in hushed voices.

A squadron of uniformed servers emerges from a hidden door. They swirl around the room delivering miniature crystal dishes of lemon sorbet. I pick up my tiny silver spoon and look at Paul. What's this, I say, dessert already?

One of the servers leans over from the next table and whispers,

A palate cleanser before your next course, sir.

Paul laughs and when he doesn't stop, I laugh too. Then Tara joins us. Now we're all laughing in the quiet restaurant and people are not only staring, they're pointing, they're whispering. Paul stands up and throws his linen on the table. Fuck this place! he says. Let's go.

We spill from the restaurant laughing and duck into the waiting limousine. Tara slides next to me on the seat. Paul sits across from us. He instructs the driver to take us to south of Market, Ninth and Mission. The driver looks concerned and asks if he's sure. Paul just rolls the privacy window up.

Tara opens her clutch and pulls out a crystal-cocaine bullet. We each snort a bump. Paul pours us whiskeys. He offers me a little yellow pill. I shake my head. Paul smiles and says it's a palate cleanser before my next course. I laugh and swallow the pill. I say,

What the fuck is a palate cleanser anyway?

Tara climbs onto my lap, straddling me. She says,

I'll show you.

Then she kisses me.

THE LIMO GLIDES to a stop in front of a huge, windowless warehouse on a dark street. A beefy bouncer wearing a beanie blocks the door. His hot breath makes ghosts as he talks down to a short companion. The short guy clutches a clipboard and hops from foot to foot. The cold air bites my skin as I step from the limo.

At the door, the bouncer asks for the watchword. Medusa's Mother, Paul says and the bouncer opens the door. As I pass, he puts his meaty hand on my chest. He says,

Sorry, pal—no solo dicks. Couples or extra ladies only.

Paul turns back and says,

He's with me.

Not anymore.

Paul points his finger in the bouncer's face. He says,

I'm Paul Valombrosa and this is my fucking party!

The bouncer looks down at his short companion who doesn't even consult his clipboard—he just swallows and nods fast.

Removing his hand from me, the bouncer straightens my collar. Yes, then—sorry, sir, he says. Then he touches a microphone sticking out beneath his beanie and says,

Two Adams and one Eve coming up.

We walk down a blood-red carpet toward the mouth of a freight elevator. A dwarf wearing a pirate's hat waves us aboard. He says,

Aye, for your behoof, step in!

The dwarf stretches onto his tiptoes, grabs the cage door and slides it closed. Then he looks at me with a knowing grin and starts the elevator moving up with a jerk. There's no light in the elevator and once we leave the first floor it's pitch black. Bass music throbs in the dark distance above and as we rise, black lights leak in and Paul's shirt glows white-blue. As we approach the final floor, red light spills through the elevator cage and Tara's sequin dress sparkles like the scales of a bloody koi.

Sliding the cage open, the dwarf removes his hat and says,

Who is for the Plain of Oblivion!

I step into a shadowy cavern the size of an indoor soccer field. Abbreviated walls cut a maze of semiprivate rooms along the edges of the warehouse and a dim kaleidoscope of light casts shadows of writhing bodies against the ceiling. A naked server, coated in red body paint with huge hanging breasts and rings in her nipples, steps in front of me with a tray of blue Curaçao shots. She says,

How 'bout a drink, handsome? Maybe something for your other hand there too.

She takes my hand and places it over her nipple. I look over to see if Tara is watching but Tara's not there. My right hand on her breast, I grab a shot with my left and gulp it down. She grabs my wrist, scoops her breast in my hand, and pushes it up to her mouth. She slurps up her own nipple and sucks it. Then clamping the nipple ring between her teeth, she pulls my hand away and her heavy breast falls, pulls against the ring stretching her nipple a thumb's length, and when she releases the ring from her teeth, her breast bounces and swings. I grab another shot and watch her sashay away with her tray.

Glass in hand, I push farther into the room.

I pass a group of bored-looking models lounging on a couch taking turns on a bong. A thin, vampire-pale Euro chick offers the pipe to me but I keep walking. Two young men built like Olympic swimmers and wearing only Speedos make out against a pillar. As I pass, one of them reaches out and grabs my ass.

I walk farther into the shadows, farther into the maze.

Primal beats pound in rhythm with the blood pumping through my veins. My feet go numb, my hands part the crowd, and as I swim through the lustful brine, a cacophony of images crashes into my consciousness and capsizes my mind.

A pasty fat man wearing a bird-beak mask has his hands tied behind a chair while an Asian transvestite gives him head.

A black woman with nipples the size of griddlecakes lies naked on a chaise longue and a leathery-skinned old man snorts thick white lines of cocaine from her firm pregnant belly.

A blindfolded man lies naked on a table and a couple take turns sucking him off while a shy woman who looks like his Midwest housewife snaps pictures.

A woman suspended from a ceiling swing, her legs in stirrups, leans her mane of red hair back and opens her mouth in ecstasy as another woman pushes a glow-in-the-dark King Kong vibrator into her. Men circle her head masturbating into her mouth.

More painted women come by with trays of even stranger drinks and a man in drag offers me candy-colored pills from a crystal dish and trance music pumps through the room from hidden speakers and the sweet smells of marijuana and sex fill my lungs and then I pass through a hall of staggered mirrors and fracture into a dozen selves—

I hold a lit joint I've never seen before.

I'm dancing with sharp-footed long-necked flamingos.

Soft swollen sounds tangle like kelp around my ankles.

I sink deep into a foreign world.

A stranger pulls her tongue from my mouth.

Her breath smells like oranges and cigarette smoke.

A sweaty strongman shakes me awake.

He says it's almost time.

An invisible demon voice counts—

Six—five—four—three—two—one!

Tara's mouth clamps onto mine.

Her tongue tastes like sweet milk in my mouth.

One hundred thousand voices cheer.

Tara pulls her lips away. She says,

Happy New Year!

She takes my hand and pulls me through the crowd until a giant naked African guarding a private door stops us. The African is aglow with white-blue tribal tattoos jumping off his dark skin and his height registers me at eye level with his huge endowment and through the head of this anomaly pierces a thick silver bullring with gold hanging cowbells. He takes himself in both hands, shakes the clanking bells at me and says,

It's so they can hear me coming.

He's with me, little man, Tara says, tugging me around him.

Once past, Tara grips the door handle, pushes it open, and pulls me into the private room. A stiff man-in-waiting greets us with a golden tray of Viagra and poppers. Tara plucks a Viagra from the tray and holds it above my mouth. I open. Take the pill. Swallow it dry.

The man-in-waiting steps aside and I see two gorgeous female models lying naked in the center of a vast, round floor-bed—one brunette and one blonde, beads draped around their necks, metal bracelets clamped on their wrists, their long, sleek bodies a tangle of hair and legs floating on a rust-colored sea of soft furs.

Paul sits like a wraith in the shadows. Next to him, a video camera points at the bed from a tripod. The camera's red record light glows like an unblinking alien eye.

Tara removes my tuxedo jacket, pushes me back onto the bed. She unlaces my Ferragamos and pulls them off my feet. The models wiggle free of each other. They slide toward me. Tara points her finger at me. She says,

You can do anything you want, except fuck them!

The brunette model pounces on my mouth and kisses me. I pull away and sit up. Tara stands before me with an aureole of golden hair surrounding her sequined curves. I want her, not the other women. I pull Tara down and kiss her. Another mouth joins ours. Tara slips her tongue into the brunette's mouth. Then the blonde joins. The three women hover over me kissing—tongues darting from one pair of red, swollen lips to the next.

Tara slides down to my waist. In the shadows, I catch a glimpse of Paul's hand jerking up and down. I try to stand but can't.

I want another blue Curaçao.

The man-in-waiting presents a bottle of Champagne.

No, I want the blue stuff.

Paul nods from his dark corner.

The man-in-waiting disappears.

The models crawl over my face.

They lick their way down my belly.

Tara unbuckles my belt.

I hear someone say,

La galette des Rois.

29 Wake Up, Shooter

A blasting horn blows me awake. I'm lying in a big brass bed. Blades of sunlight cut through wooden shutters illuminating dust particles floating in the dark room. A dresser stands against a wall. The wall is papered green. A light knock. The door opens. A plump Mexican woman holds clothes folded in her arms. Her lips move. Her voice fades in.

. . . I send *esmoquin* for cleaning. Here are pantaloons and shirt from Señor Paul.

She lays the clothes on the foot of the bed. Then she returns to the door and comes back carrying something else that she sets next to the bed before leaving the room and closing the door.

I roll over, swing my feet off the bed and sit up on its edge.

On the floor in front of me, the glistening red scales of Paul's Mark Anthony cowboy boots, catch the light slipping in through the shutters. They look like bloody, gutted crocodiles—a shimmering nightmare pair of Dorothy's ruby slippers.

~~~

I remember stepping on these boots. I remember feeling embarrassed. I remember apologizing if I scuffed them. I remember Paul smiling at me and saying, They're cowboy boots, kid, they should be scuffed and besides, I walk on 'em, why shouldn't you?

The horn blasts again. Paul yells from somewhere below—

Wake up, shooter! Wake up!

I part the shutters. A titanic luxury-tour bus idles in the drive. The horn blows again. Paul appears in its open door, looks up at the window. He says,

Wake up, shooter! You're holdin' up the show!

What day is it? How did I get here? I remember last night, Paul shouldering me onto the bed. Hands tucking me in. Voices arguing. Give his cock a rest. I own him. You're jealous. You're drunk.

I grab the pile of clothes. Stepping into Gucci jeans, I pull them on and button them. They fit. I slip a Brioni polo shirt over my head. It's tight in my shoulders but the fabric stretches. My Ferragamos have disappeared along with my tuxedo. I guess I'm supposed to wear Paul's boots. No socks, so I stretch out my naked feet and pull Paul's boots on left foot first. My foot catches in the vamp. I yank the tabs and force it through. When I get both boots on, I stand up. I'm taller. I feel different. Like I could walk over people in the street and stand on top of buildings.

Paul is still looking up toward the bedroom window when I step out onto the drive wearing his clothes. He sees me and says,

Racy boots, chief!

Tara walks from the house behind me. She smacks my ass with her riding crop as she passes. They look better on you! she says.

Paul's smile disappears. He says,

Get on, Trevor—you're holding us up.

Tara grabs my hand. He's riding with me, she says.

We have business to discuss, babe.

Tara ignores Paul. She pulls me toward a long, silver horse carrier attached to a white dual-wheel crew cab truck idling beside the stables. She climbs in the backseat. I slide in next to her. A young Mexican sits in the driver's seat. He smiles at us with a missing front tooth. All set, Miss Tara? he says.

All set, Carlos.

Carlos puts the truck in gear and eases us down the drive. We pass through the gates and turn down the mountain. I watch the bus follow us in the side mirror of the truck. Paul stands next to his driver in the window. We pick up speed and the distance grows between us until Paul is just a shadow against the windshield with the dark mountain rising behind him as we descend.

Tara relaxes back in her seat. She blows a hair away from her face. She watches me. It looks like she's deciding something. She twists her diamond wedding ring off her finger and holds it out to me. Confused, I hold out my hand. She drops the ring in my palm. Then she pulls out a pair of leather riding gloves and stretches them on. She says,

How's your head this morning?

It could only feel worse if you backed over it with this truck.

Tara leans up to Carlos. *Botella de whisky*, she says.

Carlos opens the center console and hands Tara a tarnished silver flask. She opens it and sniffs the contents. Then she plucks her ring from my hand and passes me the flask. She says,

Here, drink this—it'll help.

It must be homemade hooch because it tastes like a mix of gasoline and nail-polish remover, but it does the job and dissolves my headache before it hits my stomach. Tara winks. She says,

Carlos's secret family recipe.

Where we going? I say.

I have a little show today.

Horse show?

First event of the season, she says. This time last year we had a rare snowstorm but the fixture went ahead and we placed second. Today we're going to win. Aren't we, Carlos?

I think yes, Miss Tara.

I look through the back window of the truck, but there's no

window into the carrier. I say,

Is Conan back there?

No, she says, Conan's not jumping well. He's not ready. I'm riding Tabitha, my mare. Besides, Conan's going to be a daddy any day now. Ava's about to drop his foal.

I take another swig of whiskey. Tara says,

Do you wanna have a baby, Trevor?

I nearly spit the whiskey out. I swallow, catch my breath. I say,

Well . . . I mean, I never really gave it much thought . . .but, you know what, yes, I think I do want kids.

Was your family into horses, Trevor?

Nope. We sure weren't.

Well, what are they into, Trevor?

Guilt mostly. Why do you keep saying my name?

I like your name, she says. I gave guilt up for Lent when I was 12. Are you Catholic, Trevor?

My mom was. She liked the music—you know, the Gregorian chants they do. Anyway, she didn't take it too serious because she sent me away to a Protestant summer camp.

Tara looks out the window for a moment. Then she looks back to me. She says,

You said *was*.

Yeah, she got cancer.

And your dad?

He's not around.

I don't want Tara to see my eyes get wet so I turn away and watch the scenery roll past out my window.

The rest of the drive is hushed. Carlos points out several farms and orchards where he says he has relatives working, but during the long stretches in between, he just drives and grins at the road with his missing front tooth.

NORTHWEST OF NAPA, just on the other side of Hood Mountain, Santa Rosa spreads out in a plain east from Highway 101 to the Valley of the Moon. The highway glides past and when the mountain fades to a distant hill, Carlos pulls us off the road and we pass beneath a wooden arch into Fox Hollow Showgrounds.

As we circle the grounds to Tara's tent, we pass horse trailers and RVs spreading in a wide circle around the showground center. It reminds me of the way carnivals would set up behind tilt-up fences when they came to town.

At the tent, Tara gets busy setting up her tack with Carlos. Inside the canvas tent, it smells like fresh-cut grass and when Tara sets her saddle on its stand, the smell of oiled leather reminds me of my Porsche. The bus pulls up and eases to a stop. The door opens and Paul hops off. Tara opens the horse trailer and a hot wave of manure hits me in the face. I cough and fan the air with a sour expression. Tara laughs. Then she turns to Paul and says,

If you really have business to discuss with Trevor, why don't you go discuss it now in the stands?

LIKE A BULL'S-EYE in the center of the showground, tall white fences enclose the riding arena. Inside the arena, colorful bar jumps set at different heights make a course. On the far side of the arena sits a panel of judges above a golden table-banner that reads NOR CAL WINTER CLASSIC. Behind the judges, bleachers rise to a tall tent top that shades spectators from the sun.

Paul and I climb the bleachers and take a seat. We watch riders perform. One after another, they zigzag jumping the course. Some jerky and unsure, some powerful and energetic, some tired and going through the motions—but all with an attitude of disdain directed up at those of us watching from the comfort of the bleachers. Paul leans over and taps me on the arm. He says,

Don't marry a girl who's into horses, kid.

Why do you say that?

They cost a fortune, he says, and then when you're done with them, you can't get rid of them. They just hang around and get old. You can't even milk the fuckers. Paul slaps my knee. But you won't have to worry about that for a long time. Ain't that right, buddy?

I force a smile. Paul looks back to the arena. He says,

How was the ride over with Tara?

It's pretty country, I say.

Paul nods, smiling. Yes, sir, he says, pretty country indeed.

We sit silent watching competitors jump the course. My mind keeps drifting back to that cavernous warehouse of flesh that Paul and Tara pulled me into last night.

~~~

I remember I was lost. I remember bouncing from hand to mouth. I remember the New Year's countdown. I remember Tara kissed me, dragged me back to that final room, offered me up to those naked nymphos. I remember sinking into the bed in a tangle of arms and legs and hungry mouths. I remember Paul's shadow watched from the corner. I remember the unblinking red eye of his video camera.

~~~

The camera makes me think of what the video would look like to me now, sober and in the light of day, and I wonder what Paul does with the tapes and then I remember Benny Wilson's face when I handed him the pictures. I look over at Paul. I say,

Hey, Paul. Something Benny said has been eating at me.

Oh, yeah, what did Benny Boy say?

He said you sent me because . . . I'm young and attractive.

Paul smiles but keeps his eyes on the arena. Is that so? he says.

I'm asking you.

Asking me what, sport?

He also asked me at that lunch how we get those big returns. I made up an answer but I really don't know.

You did fine, he says.

How do we though?

How do we what, sport?

Invest for those returns?

Paul turns to me, his eyes hard, searching. He says,

What's your problem, kid? I'm not paying you enough? You want a jock-mount fee every time you ride my mare too?

What are you talking about, Paul?

Hey, there's my little coquettish mare!

Tara trots into the arena on Tabitha, an ink-black mare. Tara's seat is proud and sure, she's in complete control of the animal she's straddling. All the other riders wear green or dark-brown hunt coats but Tara wears a black shadbelly coat with tails in the back and a white ratcatcher shirt with a tie and pin. Her hair tucked up under her helmet makes her look like a perfect gentleman, except I know what's underneath the outfit.

Tara smiles right at me. Then with a slight lift of her eyebrow, she starts her mare moving. She leads Tabitha through the course with the confidence of someone playing easy with the younger kids. I watch in a trance as she jumps three perfect passes in two minutes. She is grace in the saddle.

When she finishes, the spectators in the bleachers let out a collective breath. Then when one person cheers her, they all join in. Tara halts Tabitha in the center of the arena. She bows, strips off her helmet, and then she throws her head back and her long blonde hair spills out behind her. Then she trots from the arena toward the tents.

Several other riders complete the course but none captures the admiration of the crowd the way Tara did. I want to go congratulate her but Paul says to stay put and let her be until the ceremony.

THE LAST COMPETITOR finishes and bows as dusk is draping itself over the showground. The horse and rider just clear the arena on their way to the tents when crews rush in like ball girls at a tennis match and dismantle the jumps. I wonder why the hurry but when I turn to ask Paul, he's gone.

As crews exit with the jumps, another crew wheels a collapsible stage into the center of the arena. They set up the stage, unrolling a deep-red carpet to cover it. A five-piece band appears humping instruments up to the stage and they prop themselves up to play in a corner. A red-faced announcer, sweating in a poorly fit tuxedo, drags a microphone stand to the stage while an electric boy untangles the cords behind him.

The murmuring crowd drifts from the bleachers down to the arena where they surround the stage. Several young men dressed in horse-head costumes trot through the crowd with saddlebags full of Champagne bottles filling plastic flutes for any takers. Someone throws a switch somewhere and faerie lights strung overhead from the tent above the bleachers blink once and then stay on.

The whole thing unfolds so fast nothing seems real and I feel like I'm watching roles cast for a play. One minute I'm sitting next to Paul on crowded bleachers as the sun sets on a rider and horse jumping the course. The next minute dusk drops down like a curtain and stage lights pop on. Now, I'm sitting alone on empty bleachers looking down on a celebrating crowd surrounding an announcer on a red-carpeted stage backed up by a band.

I don't feel part of the show.

I stay put and watch from the dark.

A young boy canters onstage carrying a trophy in both arms. When the boy wrestles the trophy upright, it's as tall as he is. The trophy is a golden horse leaping from the top of a platinum cup. Without looking, the announcer reaches down to pat the boy on the head and pats the trophy instead. Then he clicks the microphone on, taps it twice, and yells something to the electrical boy. He taps it again. Then taking in a deep and serious breath, which he holds in for effect, he lets it out in a stream of fanfaronade—

And now, Ladies and Gentlemen, hating hyperbole and platitudes myself as much as I know you all do, and knowing how anxious we are to hear the band and enjoy the night—especially after so many stunning performances today that escape description with mere words—I will give to you, without further ceremony, fuss, or ado, the winner of our prestigious Winter Cup, with an unheard of score of 42, our very own hunt seat queen, the lovely Miss Tara Loudon Bourdage!

Tara strides onstage and leans into the microphone. Oh, three names! she says. Thank you.

She takes the trophy from the boy and kisses him on the cheek. The boy blushes and kicks at the stage carpet. Tara lifts the trophy. The crowd chants—speech, speech, speech! Someone whistles.

Tara leans up to the microphone like a cat caressing its owner's leg and her voice purrs,

All right then. Well, I really have to thank my mare, Tabitha. She was even a bit sharper—in a good way—than she was last year. But there were so many good riders and good horses here today—I thought to be honest that I would be doing well to finish in the top three. But I guess I was a bit sharper myself too!

Everyone applauds. Tara bows. She exits the stage with her trophy and then the crowd swallows her.

I watch from the bleachers as the band warms up and the audience drains Champagne glasses. I scan the crowd for Tara but I can't find her. I walk down to the stage. Paul's boots pinch my feet and the joints of my big toes ache. A Champagne boy trots by. I take two glasses, one for me and one for Tara. Balancing the Champagne, I pinball through the partyers looking for her. I can't find her. At the edge of the arena, on my way to the tents, I drink both Champagnes and toss the plastic flutes away.

Propane lanterns hang from poles hissing light into the night and as I pass from tent to tent my shadow rises against canvas sides, lurking over me before slipping down into the darkness again as I pass the breezeways.

Nearing Tara's tent, I see a horse silhouetted against a canvas wall and as I get closer, I recognize Tara's truck and Carlos's voice as he coos and then cusses corralling Tabitha into the trailer.

I see Tara's shadow too and Paul's shadow perched over her and then I hear them arguing so I slow down my pace in order to listen. Paul says,

Well, they shouldn't have used your maiden name!

I hear the clink of metal as Tara tosses something into the tack box. Cut it out, Paul, she says. They used my family name because that's what's on my membership card.

Why haven't you changed your card?

I like my name.

You got a new name when you married me.

Tara's shadow straightens, hands on her hips. Maybe, she says, but Bourdage just sounds so much more elegant, don't you think?

I step into the light. Paul startles. Jesus, kid, you spooked me.

I laugh, trying to lighten the mood. Yeah, I say, you're like a horse that way.

Paul doesn't think it's funny. I hope you got a kick out of the show, he says, nodding toward the shadows. Then he sighs and claws a hand through his hair. He turns back to Tara. Let's load up in the bus and go celebrate, he says.

You go ahead, Tara says.

Go ahead? We're celebrating you.

Tara pulls her gloves on. I'm staying here to help Carlos, she says. Then she turns away from Paul and struggles to lift her tack box. I step over and take the heavy box from Tara. I say,

I don't mind staying to help.

Paul glares at Tara. He says,

I brought the bus so we could celebrate tonight.

I said you go on ahead, Paul.

Fine, he says. Come with me, Trevor.

Paul marches to the bus. Tara turns to me. She says,

You're welcome to stay here with me, Trevor.

Then she smiles at me, waiting to see what I'll do. The rope handles of the tack box cut into my hands. Paul yells from the door of the bus. He says,

Trevor, get your ass on the bus!

I hold the box out for Tara but she keeps her gloved hands at her sides. When Paul calls me again, I set the tack box on the ground at her feet and walk backward to the bus, my eyes locked with Tara's eyes. She watches me board.

Then Paul slams the door closed.

30 Intervention Tour

Paul's driver tells me his name is Tony. Tony looks like a Brooklyn bus driver. He's wearing an old-school duckbill cap and he's sitting in the pilot chair with the big steering wheel rubbing against his fat waist. Paul went back into a private room without a word and I've been sitting up here with Tony watching the big bus eat up the road.

Every soft surface inside the bus is a shade of tan. The latte-colored carpet is so thick it makes me want to strip off Paul's boots that mangled my feet raw. A cream-colored couch faces a matching leather recliner. Thick, beige fabric upholsters the walls. The hard surfaces are earth tones too. The wet bar is polished amber with bronze accents. A strip of rust-colored lights runs down the floor like an airplane aisle.

Just off the passenger side of the aisle, about 10 feet into the cavernous bus cabin, a gold-plated Keiser stationary spin cycle stands upright bolted to the floor. A stationary bike is a strange thing to see on a bus, but this bike would be a strange thing to see anywhere. Its shiny rear disc gleams like a golden deli-slicer blade. Its handlebar grips are curved Sable Antelope horns pointing off the bike front.

After several silent miles, Paul emerges from the back room wearing shorts and a black T-shirt. He grabs two Heinekens from the wet-bar refrigerator and tosses one to me. He says,

Good news, killer, we did it!

Did what?

I just hung up the phone with Benny.

We got CalTEARS?

We're all meeting tomorrow in my office at one.

Who's all meeting?

You, me, Benny, and their Chief Investment Officer.

He's bringing his CIO?

Paul grabs my shoulder. It's just a little formality, kid, he says. We got it!

Congratulations, Paul.

You did it, killer. You put the biggest ship in the bottle yet.

I really didn't do anything, I say.

Paul puts his hand on my head and musses my hair. He says,

Sure ya did, kid. If you hadn't made your photo delivery and persuaded Benny, we'd never have closed him. Now that we have, I'm gonna make you rich. How about a million dollars for your first commission? Not a bad way to pop your cherry.

One million dollars?

Not enough? he says.

No—I mean, yes. It's enough.

Paul drains his beer. He climbs onto the golden stationary bike and pedals. You like my shirt, stud? he says

Paul leans back, pulls his T-shirt straight. I read the tall yellow bloodshot letters screenprinted across his chest—MONKEY BRIDGE: SEE YOU AT MY INTERVENTION TOUR.

Isn't Monkey Bridge a hardcore rock band? I say.

Yep, he says, this is their tour bus. Found the shirt in the back—I kinda like it.

Tour bus?

Came with a record label I bought.

Didn't their drummer just overdose and die? It was in the news.
Paul grins. He says,

That's why I like the shirt so much.

I sip my beer. Paul said a million dollars for my commission.
What would I do with a million dollars? Buy a new house, a house
with a pool. I look at Paul peddling on the bike.

How much money is CalTEARS moving over? I say.

Tomorrow I tell them the minimum we'll take is one billion!

One billion?

One billion. And that's just a taste, he says. We'll slurp up the
entire pension fund by the time we're done.

Paul stands up on the pedals and with a shit-eating grin, he
bursts into a sprint that shakes the stationary bike straining the bolts
where they sink through the carpet into the floor. Sweat beads that
had been forming at his hairline drip down his brow and drop to the
floor dappling the latte carpet a darker shade of brown. Paul says,

A billion's the new million! Thing about greed, kiddo—it's a
disease. And the board's got it good. Greed doesn't leave any room
for prudence. Greed's all-consuming. If you want people to believe
you—tell them something unbelievable.

Paul sits down on the bike seat and pedals slower. He says,

Hand me another Heineken.

I open the fridge, grab a Heineken, crack the cap and hand him
the bottle. Paul guzzles half the beer down. Then he shakes his head
showering me with sweat. He runs his fingers through his sweat-
dripping hair. He says,

You think I'm losing my hair, sport? Did you know there are 40
million bald dicks in the United States alone and the sorry fuckers
spend a billion dollars a year on hair-growth treatments? Now you,
you won't have to worry. You got a good head of hair, sport. But tell
me the truth. Do you think I'm losing mine?

Before I can answer Paul's question, which I don't want to

answer, Tony calls back from the front seat and asks if he's dropping both of us at the house. Paul tells Tony we're not going to Napa, he tells him to keep driving to San Francisco, and he tells him we're celebrating tonight. Tony shakes his head. He says,

I can't, sir. I got my kid's play tonight.

Paul looks at me confused. Then he looks back to Tony. Fuck the play, he says.

I already mentioned it this morning, sir.

Too bad, Tony. We're going into the city.

I promised my wife I'd make the play, sir.

Paul gets pissed, raises his voice. He says,

A man shouldn't let his wife carry his balls around in her clutch! Now drive this bus into the city or you'll regret it.

Paul sets his Heineken bottle in a cup holder, grips the black sable horns, and pedals the bike fast and furious humping up and down as he pumps the pedals going nowhere. The golden disc-blade spins like a tree saw ready to split the bus down its middle. Tony sulks and drives in silence with his lips pinched together as the bus cruises slow and steady down the dark road.

Thinking about the meeting with Benny Wilson tomorrow makes me nervous. Blackmailing Benny is illegal and I took a risk when I opened my briefcase and walked back into his office with those photos. But we're just forcing him to do what his board wants him to do anyway. Somebody gets to manage their money for a fee, why not us? And Paul said I get a million dollars.

I'm still coming off the drugs from last night. Everything hurts. I think that yellow pill Paul gave me in the limo was a mother's little helper, and barbiturates mixed with cocaine mixed with Viagra mixed with blue Curaçao fly a guy pretty high and now I'm making reentry.

What a wild night that was. I've heard of swingers clubs or sex clubs but never anything like last night. It's all a jigsaw puzzle of images and it makes my stomach sick to try to piece them together.

The Heineken is softening the landing a little, so I grab another one from the fridge.

I can see that Tony is growing agitated. He keeps mumbling to himself and shaking his huge head. As we approach the Napa exit, he takes a deep breath, sits up straight, puffs out his chest and says,

I'm getting off here in Napa, sir.

Paul's head snaps up, his eyes drilling the back of Tony's head. Are you fucking senile or just stupid? he says. I told you three times already—we're going into the city.

I told you about my kid's play this morning, sir. I won't miss it. I'm pulling off in Napa and taking you home.

Mounted above the windshield is a wide-angle cabin mirror and I watch as Tony furrows his brow and looks at the upcoming NAPA exit sign. He pushes the turn signal on. There's a long silence filled with the clicking tickta, tickta, tickta of the blinker switch.

Paul picks his Heineken bottle up by its neck and raises it in the air like a bid paddle at an auction. The bottle magnifies the ceiling light and casts a green-glowing circle on the carpet at my feet. I watch an amber droplet of beer gather at the upturned bottle lip and fall to the floor where it joins the wet stain of Paul's sweat.

Then in a flash, before I can ask what he's doing, Paul rears up on the bike and tomahawks the bottle at the back of Tony's head. The bottle hits its mark with the hard, hollow crack of a boulder thrown onto a frozen pond.

Tony lurches forward clutching at his head.

The bus swerves on two wheels.

Crosses into the other lane.

Headlights, honking.

I rush to the front.

Leap for the wheel.

Grab it just in time.

Turn us back into our lane.

Tony comes to. He grabs the wheel from me, pulls the bus to the side of the highway and slams the shifter into park. He scoops up the Heineken bottle and winds up to throw it at Paul. I snatch the bottle from Tony's hand. Paul just smiles from the golden seat of his Keiser stationary bike. Tony stares at me with bulging eyes and for a second I'm sure he'll hit me. Then he snatches his hat from the floor and storms off the bus and out into the night. I drop the Heineken bottle and race after him.

I grab Tony's arm. He spins around and says,

That son-of-a . . . he could've killed us. He's crazy!

Paul leans out the door of the bus with steam rising from his sweaty back. He's laughing. Come on, Tony, he says. Suck it up, guy. Get your fat ass back here and drive.

Tony turns and walks away from the bus along the shoulder of the highway. Paul calls after him. Fine, he says, I'll give you a raise.

Tony keeps walking. Paul says,

I'll give you $20,000 more a year.

Tony stops, turns to face us. He takes off his duckbill cap and looks at it in his hands. Paul says,

And a $5,000 bonus.

Tony looks up. He mumbles something to the stars before tugging his cap on his head and walking back to the bus. As Tony climbs the step past Paul, he says,

I want holidays off too.

Paul pats him on the ass and says,

Don't push me, big boy. Now take us into the city—we're celebrating tonight.

PAUL MAKES TONY drive us to a place called Centerfolds. He sends Tony inside with a thick stack of cash he pulls from the floor safe. We wait on the bus. Paul changes back into his street clothes, but I can still smell the decay of his sweat. He opens a bottle of Patrón. I'm feeling sick so I tell him I don't like tequila. He pours me a shot anyway. While I nurse it, Paul slugs back two shots.

Tony knocks on the door. Paul sets his shot glass down and grabs an ice pack from the freezer. He opens the door and ushers a stripper onboard. She has a wall of sprayed hair and she's huddling beneath a puffy silver jacket. Paul pulls a second stripper onboard. She's spray-tanned the same shade of orange as the first stripper and they could almost be twins except this one's puffy jacket is red. Paul tosses Tony the ice pack for his head and tells him to wait outside. Tony begins to complain that it's cold but Paul slams the door.

Paul whispers to the strippers. I hear one stripper say,

That'll cost more.

Paul hands her another stack of bills. The strippers split the dough quick with fake-nailed fingers used to counting cash and then they tuck it away in their jackets before stripping them off. The first stripper sizes me up. She says,

We'd have charged less if you'd have sent this guy in.

The second stripper pushes past her. It's too late now, she says. Pour us some shots, handsome.

As I pour their tequilas, I look them over. They have too many rings on too many fingers. Their low-cut jeans have plastic jewels bedazzled into the pocket fabric. One wears a tight pink tank and the other just a mesh half-shirt showing off her nipples. I can tell they come from poor families because braces are expensive and they both have crooked teeth. Tara has perfect teeth. I wonder what Paul's doing with these cheap rental chicks when he has Tara waiting for him at home. Most guys would think these strippers are hot but if they didn't have hair extensions and bellybutton rings, and if they didn't have fake tits and fake lashes, they'd both be average girls that hate their fathers.

The tequila I'm pouring misses the shot glass and spills onto the counter as the bus jerks forward. The girls giggle. I look up and see

Paul sitting behind the big wheel and driving the bus away. Then I look out the window and see Tony running after us with his hat in his hand. Paul laughs. He says,

The intervention tour is officially under way!

THE STRIPPERS GRAB ME from either side. The strength in their hands shocks me and I feel like a felon being hauled to the hoosegow by the heat. They pull me toward the back bedroom. Paul turns around at the wheel. He says,

No, do it here.

He points to the couch.

The strippers look at each other. It's extra if you wanna watch, one says. Paul throws another banded stack of cash at them. They peel off their shirts and four melon-size, rock-hard saline boobs bounce out. I can see the ridges where the implants stop and the normal tissue begins and when one turns sideways, I see purple stretch marks on the profile of her breast.

They push me back onto the leather sofa. One wrestles with the buttons on my shirt. She strips it off. The other unzips my pants. She pulls them to my knees. Then she tries to jerk off Paul's boots but the boots won't budge. Pants at my knees, I sit there with my legs locked together like a dipshit taking a dump.

I can't get hard. Paul watches in the cabin mirror while both strippers work on me for five minutes before he pulls the bus over and offers me a Viagra. I shake my head and pull my pants up. I say,

I feel sick.

The strippers reach for their shirts. Paul snatches the shirts away. No, you don't, he says. I paid you two sluts good money to put out, now fuck each other!

The strippers sigh. They grab each other and make out. I dive into the bathroom and lock the door. I pretend to puke making sure I'm loud enough that Paul can hear. Then I run the sink to blot out the sound of tongue sucking and fake moans coming from the cabin. I rinse my face with cold water. I look in the mirror. I pass my wet hands through my hair and see a flash of Paul in my reflection.

I open the mirrored medicine-cabinet door to see if there's anything inside, anything to blot out the pain. There's just a bottle of expired antibiotics and a foot-fungus cream. I leave the cabinet door open on its hinges so I won't have to look at my face again. I had no idea what I was getting into two days ago when I pulled that tuxedo on and climbed into the limousine with Paul. The bus is suffocating me. Paul is suffocating me.

I turn the water off. I can hear Paul barking at the strippers through the door. He says,

Get into it you dirty whores! Lick that pussy. And I don't wanna hear any fake orgasms either. You're gonna earn your pay. I'll tell you what I'm gonna do, I'm gonna drive this bus to the Tired Trucker Tavern and make you two fuck every trucker there!

One of the strippers snaps back. She says,

Hey, it's not our fault your buddy's not into pussy.

The other stripper says,

Yeah, maybe if you suck him off he'll get hard.

I fall out of the bathroom looking as pale and puked-out as possible. I say,

Paul, I'm sick. I need to get back. If I don't get back right now, there's no way I'll make the meeting with Benny Wilson tomorrow.

31 The Virgin Athena!

As I step off the bus, Paul looks disappointed. He grabs me, holds out a Viagra in the palm of his hand. He says,

Sure you don't wanna power through, pal?

I shake my head. Well, be at the office by one then, he says. And don't be late. Then Paul pops the Viagra in his mouth and grins. I close the door and watch the bus swerve out of sight. My feet are killing me and I cannot wait to strip off these boots.

I catch Charlie just as he's closing up the bar. He hands me a bottle of Jack and says he'll put it on my tab. He asks if I had a good New Year's. I say,

It's been one hell of a ride.

He nods as if he knows. Then he hands me a whiskey glass to go with the bottle. He says,

Only drunks drink from the bottle.

It's a clear and quiet night. The stars hang low over the dark and blurry silhouettes of ships and the only sound is from a distant stream of water splashing into the still marina from an automatic bilge pump. It must be low tide because the air smells of salt water.

My mind races through the events of the last month and the images come at me so fast I can't focus. They all pile up and smash into my head. As soon as I'm inside the yacht, I strip the boots from my blistered feet and toss them in a corner. I grab the bottle of Jack and the glass and head outside to study the stars and sort through the wreckage of my thoughts.

I step onto the deck and there, leaning against the railing, is Tara. The water stretches out like a cape behind her and the stars swirl around her head. I try to hide my surprise. I say,

You make a perfect figurehead for a ship. The Virgin Athena!

A seductive smile rises on her lips. She says,

And are you my Perseus then?

I join Tara at the railing. I open the bottle of Jack and pour three fingers into the glass. I hand it to her. She smiles. I look up at the stars. I say,

Perseus, huh? I think I see my constellation.

Tara sips of her whiskey. She says,

Do you get lonely staying out here?

I'm used to it.

Living on a boat?

No, lonely.

How was celebrating with Paul? she says.

Celebrating? Ah . . . well, we just . . .

Tara grins as I stutter over what to say. Don't worry yourself, she says, I didn't come to make war.

Relieved, I take a swig from the bottle of Jack. Tara says,

I remember when Paul got this boat. Won it in some macho bet over a CEO being fired by his board. We used to throw great parties out here on the water in the summers.

I look over the railing at VALOMBROSA II painted on the yacht.

Did you ever see his father's yacht, I say, the *Valombrosa*?

Tara chuckles. She says,

He told you that did he? Paul's father has been buried on the floor of the Bering Sea for 35 years—with his rusty-old fishing boat.

Fishing boat?

Paul's father was a fisherman, she says. He died in Alaska when Paul was just a boy.

But the painting in Paul's office?

Paul commissioned it with an old photo. Prinked the old-sea dog up pretty good too, didn't he?

Fisherman? Really. Paul earned all this on his own?

Earned what? she says. I bought the house long before Paul came along. All he did is mark his territory by adding his initial to the gate. Then he used my money to remodel.

But he owns Valombrosa Capital. He even owns the building.

He leases that building from my family's real-estate trust, she says. Of course, he put his name on that too. Valombrosa Capital never gets off the ground without my family.

Then it clicks—her name. The announcer tonight introduced her as Bourdage. I know that name. I say,

Your maiden name, Bourdage—the famous wine label? Paul's first big investor.

Tara smiles. She steps back, places one foot in front of the other and curtsies. She says,

Oil money dahlin'. The wine's an attempt to wash all that dirty black off our hands. Mother even married a poor French boy just for his name.

Oil money?

Tara nods. She says,

Paul was nothing when I met him. He made his first real money off a tip he hustled from my grandfather.

How'd you two meet?

I met Paul at a fundraiser for pensioned thoroughbreds. An Evening under Californian Stars it was called. The idea is to save retired thoroughbreds from slaughter. I'm sure Paul was there to pick the pockets of the old-moneyed crowd.

Tara drains her whiskey. She tips her glass at me and I refill it with Jack from the bottle. She says,

I was young and rich and naïve when I met Paul. I was so bored. He was exciting. We danced that night and Paul invited himself to dinner the following week. But once I was away from him, his charm wore off. It was strange, but I knew then there was something mean in him. Something dark. An intuition maybe. I didn't want to see him again. That Thursday I instructed my staff not to open the gates for anyone. I remember it was the worst rainstorm we'd ever had and the power was flickering so I lit the house with candles and settled in with a book. A pounding on the door startled me. I grabbed a fire poker and went to the door. I opened it and there was Paul, soaking wet wearing that damn smile. He climbed over the gate.

Tara looks into the yacht where the portrait of Paul looks out at us. For the first time, I see lines of worry on her brow. She says,

He just never left. Now I wish I had never opened that door. Paul changes people, you know. He really does. I was much more innocent when I met Paul.

What do you mean innocent?

I mean *innocent* like you, she says. I wasn't into all this crazy sex stuff until Paul came along. He's changing you already too.

Tara takes another sip of her whiskey and then she looks at her glass, turning it in her delicate hand. She says,

You know, I was about to leave Paul when he brought you home. I was fed up with the games. The drinking. The drugs. I told Paul either he gets sober or he leaves. And I said it knowing he could never get sober. I even poured out his precious wine collection. But then Paul brought you home as a peace offering. And when I saw you, I couldn't say no.

I never thought of it before, but now it hits me—I'm not the first guy Paul's brought to bed with Tara. I say,

How many other men were there before me, Tara?

It doesn't matter, Trevor, because you're the last.

I swig from the whiskey bottle and rewind Tara's confession. It's as if she's given me the combination but minus one number and my mind won't quite unlock and let something I've been thinking out. Tara touches my hand. She says,

What was your mother like, Trevor?

My mother? Lit up every room she walked into.

Do you miss her?

Every day.

And your dad?

A terrible taste fills my mouth. The whiskey bottle is heavy in my hand. I pitch the bottle off the yacht deck. It hits with a splash, bobs once, and then settles in the still water. I swore I'd never drink like him, I say.

Was it bad when he drank?

A cloud hung over the house when he was home. My mom worked graveyard sometimes and I'd lie in bed at night and cringe when I heard his emergency brake ratchet up in the drive. We made a run for it once, my mom and I fled. Her dad left her that Porsche I drive now but as soon as Dad had blown the rest of the inheritance, he insisted she sell it. That's when he hit me. Next morning she packed us a suitcase and pointed that Porsche for San Diego.

Tara reaches over and caresses my hair. She says,

What did you do in San Diego?

We never made it South of Bixby Bridge.

I'm sorry, Trevor.

I fight back the tears. I say,

She locked the Porsche in the garage and never drove it again. She gave it to me when I left home for university. I guess she didn't want him to get it when the cancer came back to get her. Should have been Dad who got the cancer.

Tara takes a deep breath and holds it. Then she lets the breath out slow and at the bottom of it, she throws the whiskey glass in the water next to the bottle. I smile at her. I say,

I never told anyone all that before.

I'm glad you told me, Trevor.

Then she smiles. She rises on her toes, spins around, and falls back against me. I wrap my arms around her. She giggles. She says,

We should run away together.

Where would we go if we ran away?

We could sail this ship to Saint-Barth.

I don't speak French.

I'll teach you.

Tara kisses me. She presses her body against mine and I forget everything else. I scoop her up in my arms and carry her into the yacht. We bump into walls kissing. I kick the door open to the stateroom and lay her on the bed. I pull off my shirt. Then I drop my pants and step out of them. Tara removes her blouse, then her bra. She unbuttons her riding pants. I peel them off her long legs. I look at her perfect naked body stretched out on the bed.

I remember Paul telling me I could do anything except fuck her and as if she's reading my mind, Tara looks up at me and says,

Fuck me, Trevor!

I guide myself inside her. She arches and moans. I lean down, kiss her long, and slow. She digs her nails into my back and wraps her legs around me.

32 You Love Me?

Tara wakes me with her head beneath the sheets. When the last of my dreamy sleep is aroused away, I reach down, pull her into me, and feel the sweet flood of release. A wave of relaxation ripples down my legs to my toes and up through my torso to the tips of my fingers. I sink into the sheets and imagine the mattress, the boat, and the marina water absorbing my insignificant weight. It feels good to be right-sized.

Tara slides up next to me. She says,

I guess last night wasn't a dream.

I lean to the floor and fish through my piles of clothes for something to throw on. I grab a pair of slacks. Tara snatches them away. Oh, no you don't, she says. Who said I was done with you?

The photo of the boy that Evelyn gave me on the train falls out from the back pocket of my slacks. Tara picks it up. She looks from the photo to me. She says,

You have a child?

No, I don't have a child.

Is this you?

No, it's not me.

Well, who is it?

Just some photo an old woman gave me on a train.

He looks just like you, she says.

I kiss Tara on the forehead. I need a shower, I say, you can join me if you're not done with me.

When the shower works up a steam, I step in. Closing my eyes, I let the showerhead rain down on me. I know it was just the whiskey talking last night when Tara said we should run away together, but I imagine the shower water is tropical rain and that I'm in Saint-Barth with her anyway.

Tara steps in the shower and wraps her arms around me from behind. The shower is small but her naked body fits me like a puzzle piece. She says,

I'm divorcing Paul.

I turn around. Tara smiles. She says,

You're surprised.

A little.

Tara picks at the wet hair on my chest. She says,

I scheduled a meeting with our family attorney in Los Angeles tomorrow afternoon. I'm flying down there tonight. I want you to come with me.

You want me to come with you?

Tara lifts up on her toes and kisses me. She says,

I have a Malibu beach house in the Colony. I want you to live there with me.

I push Tara against the shower wall. I press my naked body against hers and kiss her neck. I say,

What would we do in Malibu?

Tara closes her eyes and rolls her head to the side exposing more neck. As I kiss my way around her throat, she says,

Watch movie stars jog by on our beach. Swim—the ocean's as warm as a bath. You'll work on your tan and I'll paint. Maybe you can plant us a little garden. I've always wanted a live-in gardener.

I pull my mouth away and laugh. Wait a minute, I say, you want me to be a live-in gardener?

Tara pulls me back to her neck. She says,

How about a live-in lover?

Mmm, that sounds better.

Her offer sounds like a dream. But if there is one thing I can't afford, it's to dream. What if she's screwing with me. I'm too close to making things happen for me. I pull away and search her face for the angle. I say,

But why me?

Because you're *innocent*, she says.

I'm *innocent*?

She reaches her hands between my legs. She says,

Okay, maybe you're not *that innocent*. But you have so much more potential than Paul does. You're a true prince, Trevor. Paul wants to be a king. I don't want a king.

What do you want?

I want kids.

With me?

Paul's sterile.

Does Paul know you're here?

He's sterile, not stupid.

I feel myself pulsing in Tara's hand and I remember Paul saying he'd castrate me if I fucked her. I did more than fuck her last night—I made love to her. And now Tara wants to leave Paul for me? What if Paul is on his way here now? A minute ago, the shower felt like a warm wet dream but now its walls are closing in on me. I wish I could slip down the drain, leak into the cold marina water outside, swim away and hide. I feel anesthetized, paralyzed, and powerless. Breathe, Trevor, breathe—God I need a drink.

I grab Tara's shoulders. I say,

What do I tell Paul?

She reaches up and touches my chin. She says,

Don't tell him anything, dear. Just come to Malibu with me.

I step from the shower, grab a towel and wrap it around myself. Tara stands in the shower looking out at me through the water-streaked door. I say,

Sorry, Tara. I'm late for our meeting with Benny Wilson.

I walk into the stateroom and dry my hair. We slept in—quarter past one already. I try to think up a story to tell Paul. Can I lie to him? I toss the towel on the bed and pull on my Armani suit pants, a clean shirt. I look down and see Paul's jeans lying on the floor where I peeled them off last night. I pick them up and dig my BlackBerry from the pocket—nine missed calls from Paul.

I look up in the dresser mirror and see Tara standing naked and dripping in the doorway behind me. She says,

I love you.

I turn around. She looks small and fragile with her wet hair hanging over her naked shoulders. I say,

You love me?

Yes. I love you, Trevor.

What do you love about me?

I love everything about you.

I want to tell her I love her too, that I've loved her since the moment my eyes landed on her photo in Paul's office. I take a deep breath. Tara searches me for a response. The BlackBerry vibrates in my hand—Paul calling. I say,

I need to think, Tara.

She snaps her wet hair behind her head and storms to the bed. She grabs my damp towel and wraps it around herself. She says,

Whatever, Trevor. You decide what you want and let me know.

I hunt for my Ferragamos. I can't find them. Then I remember they disappeared with my tuxedo when Paul sent the maid in with his boots. I dig in the closet for shoes and find a pair that will do. While I lace them, Tara says,

There's a restaurant at the Napa County Airport called Jonesy's Supper Club. Meet me there tonight if you decide you want to come with me—when you're done thinking, of course.

I see the photo of the boy looking up at me from the bed. I scoop up the photo and tuck it in my pocket. I grab my suit jacket and a tie. I grab my BlackBerry. Tara sits on the bed and I stand in front of her. When's your flight? I say.

She lifts her chin and says,

It's my jet, so whenever I tell it to take off.

Tara grips my wrist and pulls me down to her lips. She tastes sweet. Her hair smells like coconut. She moves her tongue up to my ear and I smell the wet, salty skin of her neck. I remember our sweat-dripping bodies wrapped around each other last night and I want to pick her up and slide her back in bed.

The BlackBerry vibrates in my hand—Paul.

I pull away from Tara's kiss. She sighs. She grabs the BlackBerry from my hand. Should I answer? she says.

I reach for the BlackBerry but she jerks it away. Relax, she says, I'm just putting my cell number in your phone. The airport Supper Club closes at 9 P.M. sharp. I'll wait for you until then. Only until then. So don't miss your flight.

When she finishes programming her number in the BlackBerry, she hands it back to me. Then she zips up my fly. She says,

Maybe when we're safe and up in the air together, you can fuck a baby into me!

33 Elevator Surfing

I check my messages in the car. Paul left the first one at 5:22 A.M. and he said to tell Tara that Ava birthed Conan's foal—he sounded drunk. He left another message at 11:53 A.M. reminding me to be at the office by one—he sounded sober but at least he didn't sound angry.

There's a fog rolling in as I cross the Golden Gate Bridge. The fog hasn't hit the city yet and I can see Fisherman's Wharf where Stephanie and I ate clam chowder that sunny Saturday afternoon only three weeks ago.

I rewind the last month. Images line up, hang in my mind like laundry on a clothesline, just as crisp and clear as the moment I first saw them. One after another, they roll across my mind and then fade into the fog—

Barbara meeting the train, her arms wrapping her shoulders.

Paul's red boot stepping on my résumé.

Blood-red wine dripping down Paul's chin.

The swollen vein snaking across Benny's forehead.

Stephanie tearing off the Tiffany necklace.

It's too late for Stephanie but now I have an offer from Tara— an offer that sounds too good to be true, an offer to run away with her to Malibu.

She said she loves me but can I trust her?

I think I love her but can I trust myself?

I grab the image of Tara and turn it over in my mind. I imagine myself in Malibu with her. I imagine long, drowsy days making love to the sound of ocean waves. I imagine more sharing, more kissing. But her image fades and I see myself sleeping in my car. Sneaking into the Y for showers. Doors slamming in my face. Pawning my mother's Porsche. Then I see Paul—

Paul gave me a job.

Gave me the keys to his yacht.

Gave me back my Porsche.

Gave me an envelope of cash.

Gave me a Rolex.

Even gave me his wife.

And Paul said when this CalTEARS money comes in,

He'll give me a million dollars.

THE VALOMBROSA BUILDING looks daunting as it scrapes the gray sky. Then the fog sweeps in and hides it.

I drive into the garage and park. I check my Rolex—1:55 P.M.— almost an hour late. I check my BlackBerry—no reception in the concrete bowels of the building.

Paul is 30-plus floors above me meeting with Benny Wilson and the CalTEARS CIO. For some reason, the thought of another person being at the meeting worries me. It's as if Paul, Benny, and I have been playing some kind of game, a game that we're all in on and this new person, an outsider, will somehow make it real and I'm not sure I want it to be real. I'm worried about Paul too. He mentioned Tara in his message and he must know I was with her last night.

I feel buried beneath 31 floors of concrete, glass, and steel. The crushing weight pushes against my chest. My heart races. What will I tell Paul? Maybe I'll tell him about last night and apologize. Maybe he'll forgive me. Maybe.

I walk to the elevators. In the elevator, the weight gets worse. The doors slide closed and I'm certain that when they open again something terrible will happen. I swipe my key-card. Push 30. The elevator rises. I sweat.

The doors open. Britney's not at her desk. I walk down the hall. Paul's doors are open and his office is empty. I check the conference room—it's dark. My office is as bare and white as the day I started. Everyone is gone. I missed the meeting.

I sink into my chair. I check my BlackBerry—there's one new message. I hit the voicemail button. A garbled message. Paul talking in the background. He pocket-dialed me again. I press the BlackBerry to my ear and listen. He must be talking with Mr. Chapel, his CFO who works on 31, because Paul says,

Quit with those fucking calf raises. They make me nervous.

Then I hear Mr. Chapel's squeaky voice. You're already nervous, he says, and so am I, that's why I do them.

I'm not nervous.

I didn't like that man's questions, Paul. Other people are asking questions too. I've held off on redemption requests as long as I can. We're out of money. It's time to talk to the attorneys.

I hear something slam down on a desk, a fist maybe. Paul says,

You talk to anyone and I'll cut your throat! You got that? Put the redemption requests on ice. CalTEARS will come through—

The message ends with a beep.

I hit the button and replay the message. What does Mr. Chapel mean we're out of money? People are asking questions? It's time to talk to the attorneys? It doesn't make any sense.

I walk down the hall in a daze. I push the button, step onto the elevator. The doors close. A minute passes before I realize I haven't swiped my key-card, haven't pushed the lobby button. What was I just thinking? Elevator surfing!

I remember elevator surfing at Sac State. My crazy roommate Tom wanted to take the party onto the roof of our dorm one night. He said the chicks would dig the view. The roof access was locked and that's when we learned how to elevator surf.

Tom was an engineering major. He figured that if we got in the elevator and pried the doors open mid-floor, the elevator would have to have a safety mechanism that stopped it. It did. Then we reached up and sprang the latch on the outer doors. They opened and the floor separation was waist high in front of us. Tom told me to jump out onto the floor above. I shook my head. I said,

What if the elevator drops when I'm half in, half out, Tom?

Tom laughed. Then you'll be on two floors at the same time, he said, and that's pretty cool.

Pretty cool? I said. You're the engineer, but I don't think being on two floors at the same time is compatible with life.

Tom called me chicken and jumped up himself. The elevator didn't drop and Tom stayed in one piece. Then he stepped onto the roof of the elevator. On top of the elevator, he found a service light and a control box. From the box, he switched the elevator into service mode and ran it up using the controls on the box. He found a vent and climbed onto the roof from the top of the elevator. Of course, the chicks had long since left. But we didn't care. We had discovered a new sport and we called it elevator surfing.

We tried it next on Solano Hall. It worked the same way there. All the elevators had similar setups. I don't think there's an elevator on the entire Sac State campus that we didn't surf.

~~~

I look at the panel in the Valombrosa elevator.

There's no reason it should be different.

I swipe my key-card and push 29.

The elevator drops and the doors open on the trading floor. It's the day after New Year's and the office is deserted.

I swipe my key-card again and push 30.

The elevator starts moving.

I pry the doors open—the elevator stops.

I crawl onto the 30th floor.

I roll onto my back and let out my breath. It's surreal to see Britney's empty desk from the carpet and then the open elevator jammed halfway between floors.

I stand up and step onto the roof of the elevator.

I find the safety panel.

Flip the light switch—a single bulb comes on.

I pull the doors to the 30th floor closed.

In the silence of the elevator shaft, I can hear the building shifting in the winds at 30 stories. The cables strain and creak. I can feel the hollow shaft dropping beneath me. A breeze blows through. I smell conditioned air and grease.

I press the safety panel up button.

The elevator rises to the 31st floor.

I release the safety latch.

Pull the outer doors open.

Step from the roof of the elevator onto the 31st floor.

The after-hours lights are on and the 31st floor is dim. Several offices line the windows but they're all empty. No chairs, no desks, no computers. At the far end of the hall, I find Mr. Chapel's office—the only office with a desk. The left side of his desk is stacked with Valombrosa Capital account statements waiting for envelopes. The right side has a postal box filled with sealed envelopes. Why would the Chief Financial Officer stuff and mail statements himself? Why would he need a floor to himself?

I hear a sound in an adjacent office.

I duck and listen—sounds like a printer.

I creep into the hall.

Slide against the wall.

Look in.

The office is empty except for a network of blinking computers stacked on shelves against one wall. On the other wall, a giant printer spits statements from its feeder. I step into the office and grab a stack of statements. I flip through them.

My arm hair stands up, my throat tightens. All the statements are the same. The shares traded, the options exercised, they're all the same. Only the amounts are different. Statement after statement of the same trades with different totals. And every account shows it was liquidated, parked in Treasury bills at year's end. That's impossible. It's too much money to liquidate. And why would you do it? Why would you pretend to do it? I guess it would show investors that their gains are safe. It would take the fear of loss away. It would make them leave the money in the account.

A vein of worry pulses in my mind. I grab hold of the thought and follow it deeper to its source. Why is Paul so desperate for the CalTEARS account? Because Valombrosa Capital is out of money. Why is Valombrosa Capital out of money?

The realization unfolds itself in my mind like a paper origami flower unfolding in a glass of water—

Valombrosa Capital is a Ponzi scheme!

I RUN TO THE ELEVATOR, step back on top.

I pull the outer doors closed.

Drop the elevator.

Stop halfway between 30 and 29.

Pull the outer doors open.

Switch back to Normal Operation.

Flip off the light.

Stepping down onto the 30th floor, I pull the inner doors closed to unfreeze the elevator. Then I close the outer doors. I press the elevator call button and stand in front of the doors like any other day waiting to leave the office.

The elevator rises, the doors open and I step on. Relieved, I lean against the wall and sigh. Now to get the hell out of here. I swipe my key-card and hit the lobby button.

As the elevator doors close, a hand reaches in and stops them. The doors open again and Paul is standing in front of me. He smiles at me. He says,

I've been looking for you.

PAUL PUNCHES the elevator garage button. You don't mind giving me a lift home, do you sport? he says.

What happened to Tony?

I fired the wop bastard.

We ride down in silence. The elevator opens on the garage, we walk to my Porsche. I grab the door handle, and Paul grabs my hand. Mind if I drive? he says. I shrug and hand him my keys.

I climb in the passenger seat. Paul starts the engine, revs it to redline. Then he backs the Porsche from its space and tears sideways out of the garage.

34 He Doesn't Belong

Paul pulls my Porsche up to the closed Valombrosa mansion gates. He lowers the jerky-power window, pushes the call button on the box. It rings several times until Tara's recorded voice picks up—

This is Tara and we're not in right now.

Paul slams the box. He looks over at me. I'm nervous. I say,

Don't you have a code that opens the gate?

Paul's glare burns through me and I sink back in the passenger seat hoping to hide in the shadows. Why should I need a code to my own fucking house? he says. I shake my head.

Paul throws his door open and says, Give me a boost.

Then he storms over to the stone wall next to the gates and raises his foot. I get out and walk over. Cupping my hands, I boost Paul up. He's heavier than he looks. He climbs on top of the wall. I head back to my car.

Where you going? Paul says.

I turn around.

Paul grins down on me. He's holding my keys. Wait there, sport. He disappears over the wall.

Not knowing what to do, I pace in front of the gates. It's almost nine. Even if I left now I might miss Tara. I pull out my BlackBerry and dial Tara's cell. The gates swing open. I hang up. Paul stands in the shadows on the other side. He says,

Sorry about being short with you, buddy. Been a rough day and I just need your help with a little something. Won't take long.

Relieved by his new demeanor, I force a smile. I say,

Sure. Anything, Paul.

He leads me to the stables. My BlackBerry vibrates. I check it on the sly, the caller ID says it's Tara.

Paul doesn't even look back, but he says,

Who's calling you?

Nobody. Just a friend.

Paul stops at the stable doors, turns to me and says,

A nervous friend?

Without waiting for an answer, he turns back and slides the stable doors open. He clicks a switch and starting from the door and running down the long hallway, the lights snap on. Horses whinny, hoofs scratch at hay.

I follow Paul down the hall to Conan's stall. He grabs a halter off the wall, throws the stall door open and loops the halter over Conan's head. Then he pulls Conan from the stall and hands me the lead rope. He says,

Follow me, kids.

Paul walks out the other side of the stables. I lead Conan clopping along behind me. The eerie, hollow sound of Conan's hoofs striking the concrete echoes in the silent hall and then disappears as we pass from the stable into the arena. Crossing the arena, we follow Paul into a field. The skies are clear in Napa tonight and the moon floods down washing everything in silver shades of gray. Paul says,

Ava birthed his foal this morning. Crooked legs. Son-of-a-bitch foal had crooked legs and this son-of-a-bitch cocksucker had crooked legs and that cocksucker Irish son-of-a-bitch had them straightened.

Where are we taking him?

Paul spins around.

I stop short and Conan's head bumps into my back. Paul flops his arm over my shoulder and leans in close. He lowers his voice to a whisper. He doesn't belong here, he says. Tara mothered him, but he doesn't belong here. Nobody can change DNA.

I can't tell if he's talking about Conan or me. I say,

What does that mean, Paul?

It means I should've kept my 11 grand and left the betraying cocksucker out in the cold.

Paul grips my wrist and pulls me farther into the field. Conan resists at first but then I feel the rope go slack in my other hand as he falls into step behind me. I remember the envelope with 11 grand in it—the envelope Paul gave me to blackmail Benny Wilson. Paul must be reading my mind because he looks back and drills me with a penetrating stare. Then he laughs and continues pulling me along.

Anyway, he says, Tara's bored with her baby. Or if she isn't yet, she will be soon. She's like that you know. Always falling for the flavor of the month.

Paul steps quick to the left. I catch myself just in time and pull my foot back from the edge of a black gaping hole in the middle of the field. The pit is deep, wide, 10 feet across. Grass roots hang from the ledge and then give way to red clay. On the far side of the pit, a compact excavator sits idle next to a six-foot pile of dark earth. I lean over the edge and look down. The moon shines into the hole like a searchlight and lands on the slick coat of a dead newborn foal.

When I look up, Paul is pointing a silver revolver at my belly. Its fat barrel glints in the moonlight and the jacketed-bullet tips shine in the cylinder like copper bees crouched in honeycomb. Paul cocks the revolver, the cylinder ratchets and then stops with a click. I gasp and hold my breath. Conan blows his lips and stomps his hoof in the grass behind me. Paul says,

You know what kind of gun this is?

What are you doing, Paul?

It's a Smith & Wesson revolver. Not just any Smith & Wesson revolver either. A Model 610. It's rare. Know why it's rare, sport?

Paul, don't do this.

This baby's rare because it chambers 10-millimeter Auto slugs. Not them pussy 40 shorts. They use these fuckers in Greenland to drop polar bears.

Paul, I don't know what—

Call me sir.

Yessir.

Paul releases his grip on the revolver—the handle drops, the barrel rotates up, the revolver hangs upright with Paul's finger in its trigger guard. Paul laughs. He says,

You shoulda seen your face right there, sport. You didn't think I was really gonna shoot ya, did ya, kid?

Paul turns the revolver and pushes the rubber grip to my chest. He nods to Conan. Kill him, he says.

Conan?

Shoot the fucker.

No way.

I'll pay you.

Not a chance, Paul.

I'll pay you $100,000.

I turn away from Paul. Conan blinks at me. Patting his head, I strengthen my grip on the rope and lead Conan toward the stables.

I take three steps—gunshot. I freeze. The lead rope strips from my hand. A thunderous thump, Conan hitting the ground.

I spin around. Conan lies on the ground in front of the pit. Blood spurts from a hole in his belly. Paul stands with the revolver dangling limp at his side. He leans his head back and lets out a lunatic laugh. Then Conan screams in pain and Paul laughs louder. Together they sound like hell's harmony.

Paul tosses the revolver on the grass. Then he tosses my keys next to the revolver. He says,

This horse is a broke-dick pussy. His foal is a broke-dick pussy. The guy who sold him to me is a broke-dick pussy. And you're a fucking broke-dick pussy.

Paul walks toward the house.

I watch him disappear into the shadows.

I bend over.

Pick up the revolver.

It's cold and heavy.

I grip the handle.

Slide my finger over the trigger.

Start after Paul.

Then Conan screams again. A haunting human scream that echoes back across the field. I turn around and look at his face. He wrinkles his nostrils. Stretches his lips. Wooden teeth glow in the moonlight. His upward eye rolls and spasms in its socket. He sucks at the air like a cribber. His legs kick. His muscles ripple with sweat. Blood pulses from the hole in his belly, pools in the trampled grass, runs over the clay edge and into the pit.

I approach Conan.

Hold the gun to his head.

His eye stares up at me.

He gets quiet.

His lips relax over his teeth.

I pull the hammer back.

Slide my finger over the trigger.

Turn my face away.

Squeeze back my tears.

Then I squeeze the trigger.

First gunshot—moan.

Second gunshot—whimper.

Third gunshot—silence.
Fourth gunshot.
Fifth gunshot.
Click.
Click.
Click.

35 Just Like Paul

My hands are still shaking and they smell like gunpowder. I've been replaying what Paul said about Tara always falling for the flavor of the month and I wonder if I'm just another in a long line of men Tara's offered to run away with to Malibu.

Runway lights flash outside the black windows of the empty airport Supper Club. A janitor is already vacuuming. I'm too late.

I turn for the door then stop—a man's laugh is coming from the far side of the restaurant. I follow the sound. An open door leads into a dim lounge. I stop in the doorway and take in the room.

Tara sits at the bar, a handsome man in a blue suit sits next to her. The bartender counts his till. Tara drains her martini glass. The handsome man waves a $100 bill at the bartender. He says,

We'll take two more.

I size up the handsome man. He's fit, his shoulders wider than mine. He moves smooth even though several empty martini glasses sit in front of him. He's well groomed, his suit athletic cut. It will take a nose shot to put him down. Better be a surprise nose shot too.

The bartender spots me in the doorway and nods. Tara follows his gaze and turns around. She says,

Hi, Trevor! What kept you?

Elevator trouble, I say, stepping up to the bar.

I'd given up on you.

Nodding to the handsome man, I say,

Yeah, looks like it. You didn't waste any time finding another stiff prick either, did you?

The handsome man straightens up on his stool. He says,

Hey, watch it, buddy.

I grab the back of his stool and strip it out from beneath him, forcing him to stand. I square up to him. I say,

I ain't your buddy, okay pal.

The bartender looks nervous. He sets two martinis on the bar—one in front of Tara, one in front of the handsome man. I grab the handsome man's martini, tip it back and throw the liquor down my throat. I slam the empty glass on the bar. Tara says,

What's gotten into you, Trevor?

I seize Tara and kiss her. She plants her hands on my chest and pushes free. I say,

What's the matter, Tara, bored with me? Already moved on to a new flavor of the month?

Then I grab her martini and gulp it down too. I set the glass back and wipe my mouth with my hand. I say,

You make me sick.

The handsome man grabs my shoulder from behind. I spin around and smash my fist into his nose. He backs away cupping his nose. He mutters from behind his hands. He says,

You're fucking crazy.

I laugh at him and say,

You're a broke-dick pussy!

Tara grabs my raised fist before I can hit him again. She says,

You're no different from Paul!

Oh, yeah, at least I'm not a fucking fraud!

Who's a fraud, Trevor?

You. Paul. Everyone.

What are you talking about?

Valombrosa Capital is a Ponzi scheme, Tara. And I think you know it. I think you've known it all along.

Did Paul tell you that?

What does it matter what Paul told me? I thought you were divorcing him. I thought you were flying me to Malibu tonight—or was that just another lie?

Tara's eyes widen. She puts her hands on her hips. She says,

I was flying tonight, until you smashed my pilot's nose.

I look over at the handsome man. He's Tara's pilot? How would I have known? Aren't they supposed to wear hats or something? Then I see silver wings pinned on his blue suit. He's holding a white bar towel to his nose. He pulls it away, inspects the thick, clotting blood, moans, and presses the towel back. I look at Tara. I say,

Well then, now you can go home and ask Paul about his billion-dollar fraud. And while you're at it, have him show you the new foal. Have him show you Conan.

What are you talking about, Trevor?

I'm talking about you and Paul. You two deserve each other.

Tara looks away from me. She takes a breath. Her jaw quivers. When she looks back, her eyes are welled up with tears. She says,

Damn you, Trevor. Just when I thought I'd found somebody different. I actually fell for you, you know. And I have changed. I really have. I wanted us to escape this shit. Find some peace together in Malibu. I wanted to have your baby. But you know what? You're not different at all. You're just like Paul.

Tara finishes and the bar is silent. She bites her lower lip and breaks my heart with a look. Then she turns and rushes from the bar. I listen to her heels clacking away across the empty restaurant.

Tara's pilot pulls the towel away from his face. He looks at the bartender and says,

Does my nose look okay?

The bartender inspects his nose, and then shrugs. He says,

Has it always been crooked?

The pilot turns to me. He says,

I'm gonna sue you for this!

I shrug too. I say,

Well that's what you get for drinking and flying.

The pilot flinches when I reach past him to grab a bottle of Stoli from behind the bar. I tell the bartender to put the bottle on his tab. Before I leave, I look back at the pilot and say,

Sue me for the Stoli too.

36 Get Yourself Together

No idea where I'm heading, I swig the Stoli as I drive. I need to tell someone what I know about Paul. My boss, my mentor, my friend—a fraud. Valombrosa Capital—nothing but a Ponzi scheme. But whom do I tell? The only person I can think of is Mr. Strawberry. He was nice to me and he set me up with the interview where I bumped into Paul. He needs to know that Mr. Feldman is just a shill feeding clients to a Ponzi scheme. But it's late. I have no idea where to find Strawberry. Maybe Mr. Charles has his number.

Then I remember that today is Tuesday. Mr. Charles meets the senior Edward & Bliss brokers in the Sus Barbatus chophouse bar in Sacramento on Tuesday nights. We met at Sus Barbatus rain or shine, even on market holidays.

Jameson Canyon Road dumps me onto I-80 and I burn gas blazing east to Sacramento.

I RIDE THE ESCALATOR from the parking lot up to the heavy chophouse doors. The captain recognizes me right away. He opens his mouth to say something but I walk right past him into the bar.

Pig-shaped pewter oil lamps cast glows on brown-leather club chairs and crystal snifters of amber booze and in the corner, just as if nothing in the world has changed, sits bossman Charles swelled up in his signature double-breasted suit and holding court over cognac with the Edward & Bliss guys.

I walk up. Mr. Charles sips his cognac, ignores me. He blathers on with some bullshit story about how he surmounted impossible odds, beat every competing broker, and landed a tomato farmer's fifty-million-dollar account. The brokers, some new, some familiar, notice me and, one by one, they stop listening to the story.

Mr. Charles sets his glass down and looks up at me. He says,

What do you want, Trevor?

I need to talk to you, Mr. Charles.

Call the office for an appointment.

You won't return my calls.

Mr. Charles laughs. He says,

Hey, I'm busy.

I step closer, lean down. I say,

Just three minutes.

You're drunk again, Trevor.

I'm not leaving until I get three minutes.

Mr. Charles heaves himself up from his chair. He grabs my arm and herds me through a wasteland of white-linen tables littered with cracked lobster carcasses, bloody bones of prime rib, and heaps of glistening oyster shells—

Heads turn.

Dripping mouths smirk.

Spoons dip, knives saw, teeth tear.

Moist hands pat swollen bellies.

Glasses rise into the air.

Mr. Charles pushes me through the bathroom doors. He grips my jacket lapels and slams me against the tile wall. He says,

You thought you could go over my head? Who'd you think Mr. Strawberry was gonna back, you skinny punk? You're pathetic. You always were. Now this is my place and if you come back here again, I'll kick your teeth in. You hear me?

I nod agreement. Mr. Charles stares at me, the folds of his face scrunched up like some sad sumo Shar-Pei. He sucks his teeth. His breath stinks, his fat chin wiggles. The bathroom is silent except for Tony Bennett crooning "Anything Goes" through the hidden ceiling speakers. Mr. Charles loosens his grip. I say,

It's just that I need Mr. Strawberry's number—

He slams my head against the wall—lights dim, Tony Bennett fades, and I slide to the floor. The music fades back in, the lights brighten, and Mr. Charles's shadow looms over me. A warm wet stream hits my face, my jacket, and my pants. Mr. Charles's voice echoes, seemingly from far away, and he says,

I vetoed your ass, punk. You're pissing up a dead tree.

Then he throws something at my face, some paper. Take this you sorry-fuck, he says. And get yourself together!

The bathroom door swings shut behind him. I pick myself up off the floor, wash my face in the sink, look in the mirror—my waxy skin is gray, my bloodshot eyes retreating into my thinning face.

I look at the floor and see the wad of money that Mr. Charles threw at me, three $100 bills soaked in piss. I look at my jacket, my pants—Mr. Charles pissed on me.

I pick the wet bills up off the floor and head back to the bar to shove them down his throat. When I get to the bar, Mr. Charles and the other brokers are already gone.

The captain grabs my arm and leads me out. His grip is soft and I can tell he's sorry to be doing it so I don't fight back. At the door, I stuff the 300 bucks in the captain's hand. He looks at the money, smells it, his face sours. What's this? he says. I smile and say,

It's a tip from cheap-ass Charles.

37 She Closes the Door

Redlining third, the party lights closing on me fast, the Stoli half empty, I knock back another swig. The lights hit me, I hit my blinker and ooze into the right lane. The CHP cruiser blazes past me. Relieved, I keep it under 60 the last five miles to Barbara's house.

Stephanie's Honda Civic is in the drive. I park across the street in the dark. I screw the cap on the Stoli and fish around in my glove box until I find some spearmint gum. I chew the flavor out of two pieces while I decide what to say. I'm hungry now.

~~~

Before the wheels fell off our relationship, Stephanie and I came here every Sunday for supper. Barbara always had a pot of hot mantapour soup ready on the stove. She served me lamb manti with sour cream and broth and I would dip those dumplings until I couldn't imagine ever needing to eat again.

On warm nights after dinner, we moved to the backyard and sat beneath the cherry trees sipping raki or mulberry vodka freezes. When Barbara switched our after-dinner drink to tarragon-flavored soda, I knew Stephanie had told her about my drinking. It wasn't long after that I started finding other things to do on Sundays.

~~~

I miss those Sundays now.

I take three deep breaths and get out of the car. I walk to the door. I knock. Someone pulls a curtain aside and a triangle of light lands at my feet. A moment later, the door opens and Barbara steps out. She pulls the door closed behind her. She says,

Hello, Trevor.

Hi, Barbara, is Stephanie here?

Trevor, you're drunk.

I know. I know. But is Stephanie here?

Barbara cups her hands together and bows her head as if she's praying. She looks up and her face is solemn. She says,

Trevor, I'm just gonna say it—she doesn't want to see you. And as long as you're drinking, neither do I.

Then Barbara opens the door and steps back inside the house. I jam my foot in the door. I say,

But, Barbara, I just need—

Barbara holds up her hand to stop me. She says,

You need help, Trevor. And you can't get it here.

I remove my foot.

She closes the door.

The deadbolt turns—clicks.

38 The Crash

The Doc is waiting for me at the yacht. I called him from the road. He didn't have any GHB but he suggested ecstasy instead. I told him to bring it along with a half-ounce of coke. Before we make the exchange, he looks at the bottle of Stoli in my hand—there's only a finger left.

Maybe you oughta slow down some, guy, he says.

I don't want to piss him off so I just nod and hand him the cash. He stuffs the drugs in my hand and walks away up the dock.

I unlock the door and stumble inside the yacht. Stripping off the piss-soaked Armani jacket, I throw it on the floor and fall back onto the couch. The coke is twisted into a ball at the end of a sandwich baggie and closed with a rubber band. The ecstasy is zip-sealed in a small baggie with a grinning cartoon face printed on it. I open the baggie, dump three purple pills into my hand—the words GET LOST stamped on their face. I wash the pills down with the last of the Stoli and toss the empty bottle in the corner. Then I spread the rest of my money on the table to see how long I can run. I must have four or five grand but my brain won't do the math.

I give up counting and grab my BlackBerry. I dial Kari. She answers on the second ring. Screw you, Trevor! she says, and then hangs up. I call back but she bounces me to voicemail.

I grab the baggie of coke.

Tear the bottom open with my teeth.

Dump the powder onto the coffee table.

Using my empty prepaid Visa, I carve out a nine-inch line. I snatch a $100 bill, roll it into a straw, and snort the entire rail. The coke burns my nose and drips into my throat, gagging me until it makes me numb.

I head to the galley to find a drink. One bottle of Pétrus left. I search the drawers. No corkscrew. I scoop up one of Paul's Mark Anthony boots from the floor. I slip the Pétrus in the boot shaft with the base of the bottle at the heel. Then I smash the boot against the counter. Five hard whacks force out the cork. I pull it free with my teeth. Spit the cork. Swig from the bottle.

I look at Paul's boot in my hand, his left boot, the same boot that stood on my résumé that day—the day I first met Paul. I look at Paul's portrait staring at me from the wall. His coiffed hair gloating above his shit-eating grin, his lips curling into a sneer, and I hear him say, You're a fucking broke-dick pussy.

I set the Pétrus down, kick off my left shoe, and tug Paul's boot on. I march to the portrait, pull it down, and lean it against the wall. I step up and kick the boot through Paul's pompous painted face.

I grab the Pétrus and Paul's other boot on my way out the door.

I COME TO, the Porsche spitting rocks in a shallow ditch.

I steer back onto 101 North. The Pétrus bottle rolls against my foot. Reaching to the floor, I nab it. A neck-width of wine didn't spill and I drain it down, my throat burning, and then closing one eye to navigate the lane, I rush north in a rage. The ecstasy pills kick in and the roof of the world lifts off.

The steering wheel turns to rubber in my hands and a hundred million stars burst through the windshield and the smells of leather and vanilla and red wine fill my nose and the hum of highway rolling by beneath me grows into a river of sound and floats me past wastelands of moonlit grapevines that blur behind me into blackness. I'm rising, higher, twisting, sinking down, and now I ratchet uphill, lift weightless to the crest, and slip over the summit rushing down the face of a dark wave toward the light of a golden V growing like the open mouth of an approaching sea creature.

The wheel jerks hard from my hand. I bump and bounce across a dark ocean. Waves swallow me. Something smashes against my face. My head rests on the wheel. A horn blasts into the blackness. A light blinks on somewhere far above. I sink down, down, down.

39 Do It Again

I'm lying on a bed in a green room. My eyes ache, my head throbs with pain. My mother leans over me brushing my sweaty hair away from my brow. I raise myself up to see her face—Tara smiles down on me. She says,

Your pupils are dilated, Trevor. Here, drink this, it'll help.

She holds a warm mug to my lips. I brace for more of Carlos's secret recipe but instead, honey-flavored tea spills from the edges of my mouth. I take the mug from Tara's hands and struggle onto my elbows to get a better angle. And there, sitting on the foot of the bed grinning at me, is Paul. He winks and says,

'Morning, killer.

I look back to Tara. My eyes fill with questions. She takes the mug of tea from my hand and sets it on the table beside the bed. Then she brushes my hair again. She says,

I'm flying to L.A. to see a man about a new horse. A prince of a horse too. Paul's taking me to the airport. Then he'll be coming back.

Tara leans down and kisses me on the forehead. Then she cups her hand under my chin and whispers in my ear. She says,

You are different. I'm sorry. Get out of here.

Paul holds the door open for Tara. She stops to look back one last time. Our eyes connect, an understanding between us, and then she smiles at me—a genuine smile. She turns and walks away from me into the hall. Paul flashes me a toothy-pretend grin before easing the door closed.

Lying back, I rest my head on the pillow and listen. The front door opens and closes. Feet on gravel. Car doors click open then slam shut. The car starts, rolls down the gravel drive, and then fades away. In the distance, I hear the rumble of a working tractor engine.

I stare at the ceiling above the bed. I'm going to get up and go, get out of here. But first, I'll just close my eyes for another sip of sleep. Just for a minute.

I BOLT UPRIGHT in a sweat. I listen—silence—nothing, not even the tractor working. Paul's red boots stand beside the bed again. For a moment, I imagine everything since the sex club to be a nightmare, a nightmare I'm just now waking up from, but then the moment is gone and I remember tugging on the boot and kicking in Paul's face last night on the yacht.

I part the shutters and peer down on the drive—it's empty. No tour bus, no horse carrier, just the pink-combed gravel leading down to the broken Valombrosa gates and then I see my Porsche. It's 20 feet off the drive smashed against the trunk of a live oak. I pat my pockets for my keys, search the bed, search the table next to the bed—no keys. I pull the boots on in a panic.

Dying for a drink, I stumble downstairs to Paul's study and search the liquor cabinet but it's empty and then I see the pig-hair sofa in the corner and I remember the wine in the woods and Paul holding the wineglass beneath my nose and saying, It's not like I'm asking you to marry me, Trevor.

I walk into the great room. I remember seeing Tara for the first time. I remember her standing here purring out directions to her workers as they hung Conan's portrait but now the room is dim and empty and when I raise my head to look—the portrait is gone.

I spiral downstairs to Paul's office and find the door ajar, a light on inside, the office empty. I remember Paul leaning over his ship-in-a-bottle and saying, Everything loses its magic when you realize it's just a trick.

The desk lamp shines on an open bottle of cognac. I rush to it, snatch it up—empty, and so is the glass sitting next to it. Then I see a memory book on the desk and I flip the cover open and see photos of Tara in bed with other young men, young men like me, young men wearing Rolexes just like the one Paul gave me. Page after page of young men with Tara and then I come to a photo of me in bed with Tara on Christmas Day. I turn the page again and see an 8x10 color photo of me passed out naked on the sex club floor-bed. Twisted with red ribbon next to the photo is a thick lock of my hair. My left hand jumps to my head and I slam the memory book closed.

I run to my Porsche where it sits crashed against the tree. I climb in and search for the keys. I search the glove box, center console, backseat, and floor—nothing. Frustrated, I sink into the seat and pound my fists against the steering wheel.

Then I notice the open stable doors, the lights on inside.

Walking to the stables, I poke my head in. Silent horse heads hang out from stalls as still and unblinking as mounted heads on a wall. A mechanical throbbing whirls from an open door. I walk to the door—the tack room. A refrigerator hums in the corner, a sign that says MEDICINES, a padlock. I grab a hoof-pick, break the clasp, open the fridge, search the vials and jars and then I find an amber bottle that says ADMINISTER ORALLY FOR PAIN. Fuck it.

I twist off the cap, dump fat horse pills into my hand, and toss them down my throat—the pills catch. I rush into the hall, turn on a hose, hold it to my mouth and choke the pills down. Then I notice Conan's stall. Staggering to it, I grip the bars and look in on its clean-swept floor. I remember Conan's scream last night, his staring eye, blood bubbling from his mouth, and I remember holding the gun to his head, I remember the white flash of rage when I pulled the trigger again and again wishing it were Paul I had been shooting.

I sprint from the stables into the field, the vast and haunting killing field of last night, but it looks simple and ordinary in the afternoon light. I tell myself it was all a dream, that it never happened and then I stumble on the mound of red earth, the new filled grave, and I drop to my knees and bury my hands in the dirt and scream—I scream until I can't scream anymore and when I stop, my scream echoes back across the field.

I COME TO, my face planted in the dirt, a beetle crawling across my lip. I spew out the decaying soil and roll on my back. The sky is darker, a storm blowing in, white puffs of clouds fleeing like sheep across the pastel sky.

I hear the sound of women's voices. Elbowing myself up, I peer over the grave. The breeze catches laughter and sends it rustling through the grass across the field. A red light glows from a dark grove of trees. The red light reminds me of summer camp when I was 10 and the bonfire and the prayer and the magic peaceful feeling and a sudden need to be back there again consumes me. I rise on wobbly legs and lock my eyes on the red light.

The horse drugs hitting, my feather hands lift, my concrete feet fall, and I wave and shuffle a lead-footed balloon-man floating toward the red light. Crossing the field is sleepwalking across the windy Sahara—heavy step after heavy step but no step brings me closer to the red light. No step will slake my dying thirst.

I see a tree stump. My goal. I measure my steps. When I reach the stump, I forget why and stand there in a daze. Then I hear the laughter, see the red light, and I set another goal, take another step.

At last, one more iron step and I lift my head and in front of me the grove of lashing trees, the red light shining through. A crack of blue lightening splits the sky, my arm hair rises transmitting invisible current. I measure my steps trunk to trunk through the whipping trees and when no more trees line the path, I stop and look up.

Rising against the dark dropping curtain sky, is a red Chinese pagoda with a black-copper roof—an exact replica of Grauman's Chinese Theatre. A long dragon stretches across the front and two Ming Heaven Dogs guard either side of the open door. The red light shines from inside.

I walk onto the wide forecourt and step on concrete squares imprinted with dates and names and shoes—dress shoes of the young men in the memory book. A dozen squares, a dozen names, a dozen pairs of shoes.

The red light from the open theatre door glistens on the dark surface of the last concrete square and when I step on it, my left boot sinks into the still wet concrete and there, scrawled next to an imprint of my size 12 Ferragamos are the words—

TREVOR ROBERTS, THE INNOCENT ONE.

I kick Paul's boots across the square erasing my name, erasing my Ferragamos. When I'm done, the boots are heavy with concrete and I'm standing in the gusting wind looking at the muddled square.

I step past the Ming Heaven Dogs and walk through the open doors into the silence of the theatre.

A dragon-print rug covers the floor and runs the entire width of the building. Red-lacquered columns support a silver-and-gold ceiling and hanging from the ceiling center is a giant bronze Chinese incense lantern. The burning lantern casts a red glow on the walls. The walls are covered with prints of animals and people piled together in gardens and cities like an ancient world map of orgies. At the far end of the lobby, in front of the inner theatre doors, a black 10-foot Imperial Bösendorfer grand piano sprawls across the carpet reflecting the blood-red light.

The lobby feels as expansive as the field I just crossed but my feet are no longer as heavy. I pass the lacquered wood of the grand piano, place my hand on the inner theatre door, and with nothing driving me on except the detached and empty curiosity the drugs allow, I push the door open.

Inside the dark theatre, an aisle lined with red-velvet seats dips down to the stage and meets the projection screen. And there, running on the silver screen, is the video from the sex club on New Year's Eve. I see myself lying naked on the red fur-covered bed, the models each projected twenty-feet long feasting on me, Tara on the bed kissing me.

I stand in the dark and watch.

The models finish and slither off the bed. Then a man's voice mumbles off-camera and Tara gets up from the bed. She kisses me, pulls on a robe, and walks off the screen.

On the screen, I lie alone on the bed. My eyes close. As I fall asleep, the worry leaves my face and I could be any carefree young man napping on a picnic blanket after skinny-dipping in a country lake. I sink into a velvet seat and watch myself sleep. I wonder if I'm up there, or down here, or if I'm even anywhere. I can't remember why I came here but now that I'm here, I'm exhausted.

A door opens. I open my eyes but I'm still sleeping. Movement on the silvery screen. I raise my head. Paul walks in. He sits on the edge of the bed. He watches me sleep. Then he reaches out and runs his fingers through my hair and I remember the memory book, the photo, my ribbon-tied lock of hair, and then Paul leans down and kisses me. I jump from my seat, step into the theatre aisle, turn for the door, and run into Paul.

He grabs the back of my head and forces his mouth onto mine. I shake him off and thrust him away from me. He falls into a seat, bounces up, comes after me. I race for the theatre door and burst into the red light. Paul grabs me. I slip free and run around the piano. Paul and I face each other across 10 feet of black, red-glowing wood. We're both panting like defeated boxers.

My eyes adjust to the red lobby light and I get a good look at Paul. His straggly wet hair hangs in his face. Puffy fat bags droop beneath his sleepless eyes. His skin is pale and waxy-white like someone who's been out in the cold. And the drugs must be screwing with my head because he's wearing my tuxedo—the made-to-measure tuxedo that Mr. Lussier cut for me. The jacket hangs on his smaller frame, sags open at the lapels. Then I see he is wearing my Ferragamos too and the Ferragamos have concrete on the edges of their soles. Paul stalks toward me. He says,

I said anything except fuck her.

I step away.

We circle each other around the Imperial Bösendorfer grand. Paul runs his hands through his hair, pulling it away from his face. You broke the rules, boy, he says. Now, I'm gonna break you.

Paul circles toward me. I circle away. I say,

Is that why you're wearing my tux? My shoes? You wanna be me, Paul? You wanna be me so Tara won't need other men? Well, it doesn't fit. I'm too big for you.

Paul stops. A disarming smile appears on his face and for a second, I almost feel like we're friends and this is all just another one of his jokes. Then he grabs his crotch and says,

I don't wanna be you, sport. I wanna be inside you. Just like you got inside Tara. You owe me.

Paul lunges for me. I dodge away and we circle each other again. Then Paul switches gears. He strolls around the piano slower and he drops his voice to a soft-sell tone. He says,

What's the matter, buddy, not attracted to me? You know, everyone's a little bisexual. Even the green-neck mallards in my pool fuck other drakes when the hens run off to lay their eggs. I watched one daffy bastard fly into our glass doors and die and his buddy fucked his corpse right there on the pool patio. Now, I'm not ruling it out, but I'd rather fuck you alive. Come on, I know you've thought

about it, sport. I think about it all the time. Think about me inside
you. Think about nothing between us anymore. You might enjoy it.
It's just sex.

I shake my head and ball my fists. I say,

This isn't about sex for you—it's about power, Paul.

Yeah, well, look around yourself, pal, he says. I have all the
fucking power here. I own you.

I'm not for sale.

I already bought your soul, slugger. I paid for it with my wife.

The drugs are taking hold, my feet are heavy, my fingers numb,
I can't hold a fist. As we circle the piano, Paul switches speeds again.

Listen, kid, he says. Let's make a deal. CalTEARS is moving the
first block of money over this week—five-hundred-million. I'll pay
you a half-point. That's 2.5 million dollars, sport! You can buy your
own yacht. Get rid of that ratty-old Porsche. Buy a new Porsche. Or
how about a Ferrari? And you know what? We can both fuck Tara. I
don't mind sharing.

I'm getting dizzy. Paul's words are smooth and soft and the
sound of 2.5 million dollars charms me like those flutes they use on
snakes. I'm tired of fighting, I'm tired of thinking, and I'm tired of
circling this fucking piano. I just want to rest.

Besides, Paul says, nobody will love you like I do.

I stop and the room continues to spin. Paul pushes me against
the piano and kisses me. I close my eyes letting the drugs take me.

I don't know where I am anymore.

I don't know who I am anymore.

I don't know who Paul is anymore.

I don't know anything anymore.

I hear the clink of Paul's belt buckle. His hands on my head
push me down. I smell his sweat. Instinct straightens my legs, but
they wobble and I sink to my knees in front of Paul. He grips the
back of my head and pulls me to him and my father's face flashes

before me—my father's drunk and sloppy face, his hands pulling me beneath the covers, pulling me down, again and again, night after night, and now I'm back in that dark room and a terrible taste fills my mouth and then the key turns, the lock opens, and a flood of fury rises from the hollowed hole in my gut—No!

I grab Paul's bowed head with both hands, snag his hanging hair, and hoist myself up and, cupping a hand behind his head, I smash his face into the edge of the piano.

Paul slaps at the piano. He raises his face. Blood trickles from his nose to his lips. He kisses me again. His blood tastes like metallic rot. I jerk him away by his hair and drive his face into the piano—his nose cracks, the piano twangs, and Paul falls limp to his knees.

I stand over him holding a handful of black hair ripped from his head. I press the hair into his bloody face. I say,

Press this in your book of memories!

His head lolls forward. He kneels like a head-bowed supplicant in front of the piano, his black hair hanging, my tuxedo pants around his ankles. The theatre is silent. I stand still wondering if I killed him.

I see my Porsche keys peeking out from his tuxedo trouser pocket. I reach down and grab the keys. As I pull my hand back, Paul grips my arm. He raises his face. His dead, black eyes look up at me through the hair and the blood. His red tongue darts from his mouth, licks the gushing blood, and he smiles at me and says,

Do it again!

I PLUNGE FROM the theatre into pouring rain. The rain rages down and I rush through it running for my life. I run a straight shot across the field without looking back and I can feel the dirt and the blood washing away.

I jump in my Porsche, fumble my keys, and turn the ignition—it starts. Reverse, clutch, gas—the tires spin in the grass, the car is stuck against the oak tree I hit last night.

I get out and look at the bumper jammed up on a thick vein of tree trunk. I squat, grab the bumper, and with a bone-breaking shrug, muscle my car free.

I fall behind the wheel panting.

Backing the Porsche from the lawn, I turn onto the gravel drive. I look in the rearview mirror expecting to see Paul limping after me, but the stable and the mansion sit quiet in the peaceful twilight rain. Searching the shadows at the far end of the empty field, I see the red light shining out from the dark grove of trees.

I ease down the drive. My wipers squeal, my tires rub against the fender. As I approach the broken gates hanging from their hinges, my one working headlight illuminates the bent and twisted golden V.

I pass through the open gates and the red light and Valombrosa mansion fade in my rearview mirror.

40 For the Road

Looking in my rearview mirror, I don't know whether to expect police cars, or Paul barreling down on me in his bus, or Conan's ghost galloping after me. My legs and arms are shaking and I can't keep a straight line on the road. Even horse tranquilizers are no match for the adrenalin pumping through my veins.

I drive down off Atlas Peak Road and watch the pulsing storm fade in the distance behind me where it clings to the top of the dark mountain. I drive into the soft orange light of the sun already slipped below the horizon. I drive in a trance, numb, and when I pull into the yacht club parking lot, the sky is ebony dark.

I trot across the parking lot, rush down the dock. I need to get my money, my clothes, and then get the hell away from here. I race past the yachts and at the end of the dock, I stop. The *Valombrosa II* is gone—black water—an empty slip.

I pull my BlackBerry from my pocket, turn it on—NO SERVICE. No service, no message. No message, no Ponzi-scheme proof. I pitch the BlackBerry in the water.

I storm into the yacht club. Francis leans back in his office chair facing away from the door and talking on the phone. He sips his brandy. He says,

I've been to Yugoslavia. Now that the bastards cut it into seven pieces, I don't know where I've been.

I twist my Porsche key off the ring and tuck it in my pocket. Then I throw the yacht keys on the desk. Francis jumps, sets down his brandy, hangs up the phone without saying goodbye. He looks at the keys on his desk. I say,

Where's the yacht?

I couldn't say, mate.

I pound my fist on the desk. How many times, Francis? How many times has Paul used you as his pimp desk clerk to lock out guys like me?

Francis plucks the yacht keys off his desk. He holds up the black dik-dik charm in its silver setting. I tried to warn you, kid, he says, but a dik-dik ain't no match for a lion.

Everything I have is on that boat, I say. My clothes. My wallet. My money. Everything!

Francis stands. Stuffs the keys in his pocket. He says,

I'm so, so sorry. My dad used to tell me just because there's a crack, doesn't mean you've got to put your finger in it.

What the fuck does that have to do with anything?

You know what, he says, I still don't know. Just something to say, I guess.

What am I supposed to do, Francis?

I don't know that either. I do know that hunters kill those little dik-diks just to silence them from warning bigger prey.

I'm lost.

You look like it, mate.

Francis grabs his jacket. He says,

It's late. I have to go home now. Let me have Charlie order you dinner and a drink on me. You look like you could use a drink.

Francis walks me to the bar. He whispers to Charlie, points to me, and then smiles and waves on his way out the door.

Charlie slides over. He sets a glass in front of me, pours me a stiff Jack and Coke. He says,

Hey, fella. What'll it be for dinner?

I don't care, I say, surprise me.

Charlie nods and walks off. I drain my Jack and Coke. My jaw loosens a little. I think over my situation. I remember rushing out stoned last night, leaving everything on the yacht—my money spread on the coffee table next to a pile of cocaine, my clothes in the stateroom closet, my jacket on the floor. All I have now is what I'm wearing, the clothes I put on the morning I left Tara on the yacht two days ago—no, it just seems like it—yesterday morning. A torn dress shirt, dirt-covered Armani slacks, and Paul's boots that are pinching my feet. I'm soggy, washed out, and back where I started—sleeping in my car. At least I have that.

A plate lands on the bar in front of me. That was fast. Prime rib, mashed potatoes, and wilted spinach. The potatoes are burnt around the edges from a heat lamp and the prime rib looks undercooked. Charlie refills my drink, but with straight Jack this time. He says,

You look like you need to relax a little, fella.

I cut a bite of prime rib. Blood oozes onto the plate. The meat is gristly. I'm coming down from the drugs. My teeth hurt. I look down at the prime rib and see Paul's bloody face. I see him grinning up at me through the blood. I see him mouthing, Do it again. I spit the half-chewed meat onto the plate and push it away. Charlie says,

Not hungry?

Nah, I gotta get goin' anyway.

Charlie grabs a bottle of Jack Daniel's. He stuffs it in a brown-paper sack. He hands the sack to me. He says,

This is for the road.

I thank Charlie and head for the exit. There's no reason for me to come back here and it's strange walking to the doors for the last time. I remember walking in these doors that afternoon Paul took me to meet Benny for lunch, that afternoon he gave me the keys to the yacht. I wonder if I'll miss this place.

I clutch the whiskey bag, push through the doors, and descend the steps. My Porsche is on the back of a flatbed tow truck heading for the street. I run after it—run with everything I have. The tow truck slows before pulling onto the main drag and I get close enough to see the license plate frame that reads SECOND CHANCES.

The driver guns it and tears off down the street. I bend over my knees to catch my breath. I watch my car disappear.

I trudge back to the yacht club. As I climb the entry stairs, Charlie locks the doors from inside. I grab the handle and rattle the doors. Charlie shakes his head from behind the glass. He turns and walks back to the bar. I watch him clear my plate and glass and wipe the counter with a rag.

41 Ferried Across

It takes 30 minutes to jog to the Tiburon Tennis Club, past its MEMBERS ONLY signs, and down to Pier 41. I'm rushing to make the last ferry of the night, the 7:45. I step on the boat just as a worker is pulling the dock plate.

The small ferry carries a sprinkling of quiet passengers. A red-headed 20-something girl with her arm sleeved in tattoos caresses the head of her sleeping boyfriend, a businessman plays solitaire on his cell phone, an old lady on the edge of her seat stares straight ahead with her hands folded in her lap. I walk past them to the farthest empty seat, slump down, and lean against the dripping window.

As we round Angel Island, the view opens up and the San Francisco skyline shimmers across the bay. Sea spray beads on the glass and paints the city lights distant and mysterious.

We head straight toward the Bay Bridge. From the water, it's just a band of red and white lights stretching across the dark bay—a Möbius strip of people pouring in, people draining out, and the throbbing city in its center pumping a perpetual dance of life and death until your song ends and you're yanked from circulation like a shot red blood cell.

I wish this boat were ferrying me out to distant seas, taking me to a land far away—somewhere I can sit alone, polish my memories into sad stones, and turn them over in my mind so that their lonely knocking against one another can comfort me.

The worker who pulled the dock plate walks through the cabin checking tickets. I fish in my pockets. I say,

I must have lost it.

He looks at my bottle of Jack in the brown-paper bag. He says,

You'll need to buy a ticket at the terminal when we dock.

As we approach the ferry terminal, I pretend its stone tower is Piazza San Marco in Venice and that I'm with Tara, gliding into Rio di Palazzo beneath the lover's Bridge of Sighs. I squint through the dripping window and it almost looks like pictures I've seen.

We dock. I step off last. As I pass the ticket window, the ferry worker calls—

Your ticket, sir!

Embarrassed, I pretend he's not a ferry worker but just another gondolier hustling tourists for fares.

I trudge up the hill to the industrial area where the Bay Bridge dumps its angry, sputtering trucks into the city. The short exit banks a hard right, and tire retreads torn from braking trucks coil beside the road like thick black snakes.

I pass the La Hacienda Motel. I remember huddling beneath my jacket and sleeping in my car that first night in the city. I remember pawning my car and renting a room. I remember moving into Paul's yacht. I laugh. I laugh at how stupid and naïve I was. I laugh because my life is a joke. And I laugh because here I am, right where I started, but worse—no car, no room, no money.

The truth stares down at me from every cornice, from every bridge, from every clear, raw memory. Dad abused me. Paul used me. Tara flew south without me. Stephanie walked away from me. And Barbara shut her door in my face.

It's drizzling—the kind of drizzle that penetrates your clothes and soaks into your bones. I'm shivering—a fugitive and nobody's even looking for me.

Not far past the motel, a boarded-up brick building leans into a chain-link fence wrapping an abandoned excavated lot. It looks like someone started building something once and gave up.

I'm wet and cold—my legs tired, my feet on fire. I step under the empty building's arched doorway grateful for the cover. Slumping down in front of the chained door, I scoot into the far corner and seesaw Paul's boots off my aching feet. Relieved, I rub my toes together through my socks to keep them warm.

I unscrew the cap from the bottle of Jack Daniel's and swig from the bag. Warmth spreads down my throat and into my gut, draping over me like a blanket from the inside.

The drizzle turns to rain and the thick drops bounce off the sidewalk outside my doorway. I'm glad to be tucked away in a cave. I raise the bottle to my lips again. I remember the day I left treatment. I remember the man in the trench coat stumbling down the street with a bottle of booze in a brown-paper bag. I laugh because he was better off than I am now—at least he had a coat.

I check my pockets for money and I find the photo of the boy Evelyn left for me on the train. I remember tucking it in my pocket when I took it from Tara the other morning, the morning she asked me to run away with her to the sunny shores of Malibu. Malibu feels a million miles away.

I start to take smaller slugs from the bottle—measuring my drinks, rationing them, making them last through the night.

I look at the photo of the boy. Orange streetlight cuts an angle across the doorway and when I turn the photo, it lights up his smile.

42 Surrender

Daylight funnels into my dark doorway and lands on the bristled scalp of a skinhead with his grinning vampire teeth filed to a point. Chains dangle from his clothes. He's struggling with my arm. I close my eyes then open them again. He's unclasping the Rolex from my wrist. The Rolex! I clamp my fist around the watch and jerk it back.

The skinhead's hand comes up with a blade. I grip his arm and pull him to the ground. I push myself up. He slashes at me, his blade just missing my belly. He lurches at me. I grab his arm and force him against the brick building. I let up and then tackle him against the wall. The blade clanks on the concrete. I release him, turn around, and pick up the blade—a butterfly knife.

I turn back. The skinhead is running down the street carrying Paul's red Michael Anthony boots. I look down at my sock-bare feet on the wet concrete and I don't know whether to cry or laugh.

I toss the knife over the fence into the vacant weed-covered lot. Stooping in the doorway, I retrieve my bottle of Jack. I unscrew the cap, raise it to my lips and take a long swig of whiskey. Every cell in my body screams against the poison and I spew the alcohol out in a violent mist. I screw the cap back on. I weigh the bottle in my hand. Then I hurl it against the brick wall where it smashes and falls to the ground in a twisted pile of glass and booze-soaked brown paper.

I rush to a garbage can at the curb and paw through it. My hands close on a half-eaten hamburger. I stuff the burger in my mouth and chew fast and frantic to drive the taste of liquor off my tongue. Sick, I drop to my knees and spit the chewed wad of meat onto the pavement.

The brutal pain of craving twists itself up in my gut, rises to a moan, and caterwauls from my open mouth echoing down the early morning street.

I crawl back to the broken bottle. Tearing a soaked piece of sack away, I suck the whiskey from the paper. The upturned cap lies next to the bag with a pool of whiskey in it. I pick away the glass shards and pinch the cap between my thumb and forefinger. I raise it to my trembling lips. I taste the alcohol with the tip of my tongue. I'm back in Paul's study, he's holding the wineglass beneath my nose, and I hear him say, What did God ever do for you?

The sun crests the building tops and shines on the photo of the boy lying in the shadowed doorway. Calm comes over me. The tiny puddle of whiskey shaking in the cap stills to a placid pool. I study my face in its amber reflection. I see the boy buried behind my disguise. I breathe deep and let go. The cap drops to the concrete sidewalk with an empty tinny clink.

43 You Win, Kid

The pawnbroker sits behind her counter watching FOX News. Her head pokes out from the neck hole of a colorful muumuu spreading beneath her like the flanks of Mt. Everest. She spies me walk in, but her head swivels back to her blasting TV where an animated panel of experts argues about an African American presidential candidate.

I reach past her and twist the TV off. She keeps her eyes on the blank screen. She says,

Poor nigger ain't got a frog's ass chance in hell.

Where's my Porsche? I say.

She snaps around to face me. She says,

That Valombrosa fella said you didn't pay him. He sold me back the note. Sorry, but you signed the title, kid.

Unclasping the Rolex from my wrist, I slip it off and hold in front of her fat face. I say,

This'll cover what you loaned me for the Porsche 10 times over. I'll take the difference in cash.

She snatches the Rolex from me, her greedy eyes searching the diamond bezel. Then she looks me over from head to toe. She sees my wet, socked feet and she narrows her bovine eyes into a smile.

I'll give you $1,500 for it, she says.

I reach my hand out for the Rolex. I say,

Sorry, lady, but you aren't gonna hustle me again. That watch you're holding is an $80,000 Day-Date Masterpiece.

She pulls the Rolex away from my hand. She picks up her phone. She says,

I'll call my Serbian. He'll know what it's worth.

She walks away as far as the stretched and knotted phone cord will allow and she mumbles into the mouthpiece. Then she lumbers back on her swollen legs and hangs up the phone. He'll be here in five minutes, she says.

I know she has long fingers, and I'd bet anything her Serbian does too, so I reach out and pry the Rolex from her hand. She grips it, her fleshy face falling into a wounded look, and she says,

You don't trust me?

I just smile and jerk the Rolex free.

I wander around the shop and look at all the dreams for sale beneath the glass counters and above on the dust-covered shelves. Guitars that never played the blues. Cameras that never developed into a photography career. Engagement rings that never heard vows. Grandma's jewelry that wouldn't sell. Knock-off art. Horn-handled knives. Rusty guns. Even a pair of bronzed-baby ballet slippers.

I inspect a dusty shelf of books. Maybe I'll pick up reading again. I know now that I stopped growing when I was 10. Inside, emotionally, I stopped growing and started surviving. It's all so clear from here. As if I've climbed out of the jungle and can look back on the path I cut through life.

Ambition led me to Edward & Bliss and when everything I ever wanted was mine—the house, the job, the woman—it didn't satisfy hungers hiding underneath, the hungers of a lost and lonely boy, a boy hungry for love and security.

The bells on the pawnshop door jingle and the Serbian walks in. He's short, sturdy, dressed sharp in a clean, black suit and he carries a matching black doctor's bag. He sets the bag on the counter. The pawnbroker points to me. The Serbian holds out his manicured hand for the Rolex. He's all business. He turns the Rolex over, front then back. He holds it an inch from his face. He reads the serial number as if he's decoding ancient Egyptian text. Then he pulls out a loupe, screws it in his eye, and inspects the bezel. Satisfied, he nods to the pawnbroker. She looks at me. She says,

Your Porsche plus $5,000.

Grabbing the Rolex from the Serbian, I head for the door. The pawnbroker says,

How much you want then?

I stop and look at the Rolex.

~~~

I remember La Spa Rouge du Soleil on Christmas Day. I remember finding the Rolex on the bed. I remember Paul with his camera. I remember Tara saying, You unwrapped your present, now it's time for me to unwrap mine. I remember Mr. Lussier measuring me for the tuxedo, looking at the Rolex, telling me I was living the dream. I remember seeing the same Rolex on the wrists of other men in Paul's memory book. I remember the shoes, the names.

~~~

I think about the hell I've been through and I'm tempted to just let it go for the five grand. I say,

Give me $20,000 plus my Porsche.

She shakes her massive head, swivels to face the TV, and turns FOX News back on. But I see her watching me from the corner of her eye—she's still negotiating, bluffing. Turning away, I grab the door. I hear the Serbian whisper to her behind me and then she says,

Hold on! Let us make a couple calls.

The Serbian steps behind the counter. They both disappear to the end of the knotted phone cord. Spotting a pair of varsity-red Nike sneakers in my size, I'm tempted to snatch them and walk out, but that feeling in my gut tells me not to do it and this time, I listen.

The TV chatters, they mumble into the phone, and I watch the cars passing by on the street. Where are they coming from? Where are they going? What are their stories, their hopes, their dreams? I remember driving down this street on a foggy day with nowhere left to go. I had empty pockets, an empty gas tank, and an empty hole in my gut. Not much has changed but everything is different.

The TV turns off behind me. The pawnbroker says,

You win, kid—$20,000 plus your car.

44 *Look What You've Done*

After the Serbian counted out $20,000 in 100s from his bag, I bought the varsity-red Nikes and put them on. Then the pawnbroker took me outside.

My banged-up Porsche was parked with a collection of broken cars and boats like a bruised body pulled from the delta and lined up on the coroner's slab to be identified. The pawnbroker wrestled off the rusty lock, slid the barbed-wire top gate aside, and handed me my title. The 20 grand was already tucked away in my pocket.

In Vacaville, I gas up the Porsche. Grab an orange juice. Two power bars. Wash my face in the bathroom. Jump back on the road. As I cross the Sacramento River into downtown, the sun flashes on the mirrored-glass CalTEARS building.

THE RECEPTIONIST takes one look at me and says,

I'm calling security.

I catch my reflection in the glass behind her and realize I'd call security on me too. Please don't, I say, I'm here to see Benny Wilson. He knows me. If you'd just call and tell him Trevor Roberts is here.

She picks up her phone, dials an extension, and turns her back to me. I hear her whispering into the phone. Then she turns around and hangs up. She says,

Mr. Wilson says he'll give you five minutes—

I sprint down the hall to Benny's office. I remember walking down this hall with those photos in my briefcase that day. That day I didn't listen to the ache in my gut. That day I made the wrong decision and let myself be Paul's blackmail errand boy. I stop and look down at the seal in front of the doors. Eureka!

I open the door. Benny sits behind his desk. He looks up, but he doesn't offer me a drink. I take a seat across from him. He frowns at me. He says,

You look like hell.

I've been there.

Paul fired you?

I quit.

Well, why are you here?

I came to warn you.

Warn me about what?

About Valombrosa Capital.

What about Valombrosa?

It's a Ponzi scheme.

A Ponzi scheme?

A fraud.

I know what a Ponzi scheme is, son. Are you drunk?

No, sir. I'm not drunk.

I know what you're up to, he says, and I'm not going to be part of your revenge.

I lean forward and grip Benny's desk. I say,

I've been to the 31st floor, Benny. The entire fund is a fraud. I've seen where they print account statements. I overheard Paul and Mr. Chapel talking after you and your CIO met with them in the city. Valombrosa Capital is out of money. A Ponzi scheme!

Benny leans forward, his tone warning, he says,

You're making dangerous allegations. I assume you have proof?

No, I don't.

No pictures this time?

I've seen it with my own eyes.

That's not proof.

Listen, Paul used me to blackmail you. I'd only been at the firm a week when he brought me to lunch. You said yourself he brought me because I'm young and attractive. You have to have suspicions, Benny. Deep down, you have to know. It's all a fraud.

How can it be? Paul's a rich man.

No, he's not. His wife is rich. Tara's rich. Paul built a swindle on her family's reputation.

Benny leans back in his chair, lets out a sigh. Well, it's too late, he says. We're moving money over now.

Paul rushed you. He's desperate for it.

The vein at Benny's temple swells again. His hands tremble. He loosens his tie. He says,

If this is true, you could be in trouble too.

I don't care anymore, I say.

Benny stands. He goes to the sideboard. He puts both hands on the counter and leans there with his back to me for several seconds and then he opens a bottle and pours himself a Scotch. He slugs it down. Then he turns back to me. He says,

I don't get it. First, you come here and blackmail me with my personal life to get our money, now you're telling me not to send it—make up your mind.

I just had to warn you.

If those photos get out, they cost me my job—my family!

You have to decide, Benny.

Benny walks to the window and looks out at the muddy river flowing by. I stand. Looking at his back, I say,

You'll have to excuse me if I don't feel sorry for you. You're all in bed fucking one another. And if you ask me, you deserve one another. But you said you cared about protecting your members, so I'm giving you a chance to prove it. I haven't told anyone else. And I won't tell anyone I was here. So it's up to you, Benny. You decide.

Benny doesn't turn around when I walk toward the door—he just keeps gazing out at the river running away from him. I grab the handle and open the door to leave. I can't tell if he's talking to me or to himself, but Benny says,

Look what you've done.

45 Is Jared Around?

On a tired street at the south edge of Stockton where weeds win the battle with asphalt, I slow to look at the addresses and spot a rusty building advertising muffler repair. Next to the building, lined against a fence, are beat-up cars with prices painted on their windshields.

I pull in and park. It's funny to see the Porsche fit in with the secondhand junkers—left fender twisted, headlight smashed, tan top layered with worn gray duct tape, white paint covered with dirt.

Inside an open shop-bay door, a man in grease-streaked white coveralls hunches beneath a hoisted car working with a welder. Blue sparks bounce off his mask. I stop at the edge of the door. I say,

Excuse me—hello!

The man pulls the lit torch away from the car, lifts his mask. His face is tough, bearded. I say,

Hi, I'm looking for Jared!

He turns off the torch. The hissing flame disappears and the garage gets quiet. He sets the welder down and takes a step toward me. He says,

You one of his goddamn drug buddies?

No, sir! Jared was my roommate—in Fresno—in treatment.

He pulls his mask off and lets it drop at his side.

Yeah, he says, Jared told me about you.

You're Mr. Luger.

Yeah, I'm Jared's dad.

Is Jared around?

He pauses, looks away. He says,

Sometimes I think so.

Then he looks back to me and his eyes are wet. He says,

Jared hung himself.

A million thoughts fight to get across my mind in that moment. I stand there gaping in shock. Mr. Luger points to a window in the back of the shop. He says,

In that trailer there.

I walk to the greasy window and look out on a dilapidated trailer sitting on wooden blocks behind the shop. Time stops. A fly bounces against the window. I sense Mr. Luger standing next to me. In a low voice, he says,

Christmas morning. Same as his mom.

I remember Jared on his bed the morning I left Brave Ascent. I remember asking him his own question—what would he do if he weren't afraid? He said he'd go be with his mom. I never bothered to ask him where his mom had gone. I look over at Mr. Luger. I say,

I'm sorry. I don't know what to say. I was sure if any of us was gonna stay clean, it was Jared.

Mr. Luger seems to stare a thousand miles past the little trailer. Sighing, he says,

He was sober when he done it. Strung a two-by-four across the skylight. Used the goddamn cord from my shop vac. What I'll never understand is the ceiling's low in there, real low. All he had to do was stand up. Just stand up.

After several seconds, he says,

That your little Porsche there, with the busted-up nose?

I nod yes. He says,

She's in bad shape.

I look back at my mother's Porsche. I say,

So was the driver.

Mr. Luger walks to the shop's other bay door and slides it open. Pull her in here, he says.

I walk to my car, get in, and start it. I can't believe Jared is gone. He called the number I gave him, he left me a message with Barbara. I never called him back. I was too busy fucking around with Paul.

I pull into the bay and drive onto the lift tracks. Climbing out, I place my keys in Mr. Luger's outstretched hand. I throw my arms around him. At first, he resists. Then I feel him wilt and he wraps his arms around me and he cries.

Mr. Luger pulls himself free. He wipes his eyes with the back of his hands. I look out the window at the trailer. I say,

Can I?

He pulls a shop rag from his pocket, dries his hands, and looks at the trailer. He stuffs the rag back in his pocket and says,

I don't lock it.

I STOOP INSIDE the trailer. A tarp drapes over the skylight and the sun filters through washing the cramped interior in a sad shade of blue. A guitar leans next to a small table. On the table is a lamp. Beneath the lamp is an ashtray heaped with cigarette butts. Next to the ashtray is the big blue sobriety book. I pick up the book and open the cover—Barbara's number is right where I wrote it. Beneath her number, Jared wrote—I'M NOT AFRAID ANYMORE.

Clutching the book to my chest, I lie back on Jared's bed.

I look up at the blue tarp-covered skylight.

See the two-by-four.

My throat hurts.

My belly shakes.

The blue blurs as tears fill my eyes.

I stop fighting and cry—

—I cry for Mr. Luger—I cry for Jared—I cry for my mom—I cry because I miss her—I cry for the life we might have had—I cry for her disease—and when I've cried five or maybe 50 minutes for my mom, I cry for the boy hiding inside me—I cry because that boy needs his mom—I cry for what his dad did to him—I cry because I couldn't help him—I cry 20 years' worth of tears onto that little trailer bed—I cry until my side aches, my throat swells, my eyes close.

And then I cry myself to sleep.

46 Clean Inside

Just as the sun was setting, I woke in Jared's bed after a long-needed sleep. Outside the shop, Mr. Luger had my Porsche patched up, tuned up, and gleaming fresh from a bath. He even peeled away my worn duct tape and patched the convertible top the right way—from the inside.

Now both headlights point me south on Highway 99. My fender no longer rubs. New wipers sweep away the misting rain.

The sign for the Modesto exit approaches. I remember pulling off here and driving under the Modesto Arch the day I got out of treatment, the day Dad floored that kid with his Bible. I floor the Porsche and speed past Modesto.

When Stephanie pulled me out of that hot tub, I was given a second chance. When Barbara paid to send me to treatment, I was given a new start. I blew it. Now, even though I don't deserve it, I've been given another second chance, another new start. This time I'm going to make something of it.

IT'S LATE WHEN I get to Fresno. I park across the street and look at the sign on the gate—BRAVE ASCENT RECOVERY CENTER.

Counting the bedroom windows, I find my old room. There's a light on. Never thought I'd be coming back here.

I open the gate, climb the steps, ring the bell. A woman's voice answers through the speaker—

Hello. May I help you?

I lean down and speak into the box. I say,

I need to talk to someone about getting treatment.

The door clicks, buzzes. I grab the handle and swing it open.

I walk down the shadowy hall to the admitting office and before I can knock, a woman opens the door and waves me into the bright room. She points me to a floral-print armchair. Then she sits across from me. I've never seen her before but she looks kind. She has red curly hair and freckles on the bridge of her nose. She's wearing white sneakers, blue hospital pants, and a maroon argyle sweater. She says,

I'm Leslie.

I lean forward, shake her warm hand. I say,

I'm Trevor Roberts.

She reaches over and grabs a clipboard off her desk. Then she pulls a pen from her ear, clicks it open, and writes my name on the admitting form. She says,

Now who sent you, Trevor?

Ah, nobody. Nobody sent me.

She smiles and clicks her pen a couple times. She says,

I'm sorry. It's just that you said you *needed* to talk to someone about treatment over the intercom, so I just assumed—

No, nobody sent me this time. This time I'm here for myself.

Her smile widens. She clicks her pen again, hovers it over the form. She says,

That's the right reason. Now, you've been here before, Trevor?

Yes. I was here in November.

Will your insurance cover another stay?

I don't have any insurance.

Well, how did you pay before?

A friend paid my way.

She clicks her pen closed and looks at me, her eyes filled with concern. She stands, opens a file cabinet, and retrieves a thick stack of forms. She sorts through them, engrossed, mumbling over her shoulder, she says,

There are government programs we might try. Medicaid if you qualify. An impossible long wait though. Private scholarship here. Only takes two weeks. It's a roll of the dice. Maybe your friend can—

I touch her elbow to get her attention. She stops, turns. I say,

How much is the treatment?

She sighs. Looks at the forms. Lets her hands fall at her side. She says,

For 28 days—$9,000.

I pull out the stack of hundreds. Her eyes bulge. She says,

You're paying cash?

Is that okay?

I don't see why not. It's just a little unusual, that's all. We take off 30 percent for private pay. We overbill the insurance companies because the insurance companies underpay.

She walks to her desk, opens a drawer and pulls out a calculator. Before she can punch it in, I say,

I figure 30 percent off $9,000 makes $6,300.

I peel off sixty-three $100 bills and slide the stack of cash across the desk. Leslie writes me a receipt. She locks the money in a safe.

We finish filling out my admittance form. She asks me when I had my last drink. I have to think. It was this morning, in the street— I sucked the booze from that paper sack. Seems like a lifetime ago.

When we complete the paperwork, Leslie says she can't admit me until tomorrow morning. She asks me where I'm staying. I tell her I'm camping in my car. Worry flickers across her face. She says,

You want me to call around? Find you a friendly bed?

No, thanks, I say, it's kind of you to offer, but I'll be fine.

She nods and shakes my hand. She says,

I believe you will be. We don't have patient parking here but Sam's Safe Storage is down the street. He cuts a deal for our people.

SIX BLOCKS from Brave Ascent, I find Sam's Safe Storage and park out front. An authentic taco stand glows across the dark street. Realizing I'm hungry, I walk over to buy myself a meal.

The building is a shack but the kitchen sparkles and so does the smile of the kid behind the counter. I order three fish tacos, ceviche, shrimp cocktail, and something called the Gobernador. The whole order is only $9.50 so I add a Coke, give the kid $20, and tell him to keep the change. I sip the Coke and wait on my order. The smells of frying fish and fresh salsa wafting out from the shack set my mouth watering. The kid hands me my food and the bag weighs five pounds. Carrying my dinner to a nearby picnic table, I eat beneath the stars. This is the first food I can remember tasting in a long time and it tastes good. When I finish eating, the bag is empty and I'm stuffed.

Now that I've made a decision—a decision for me and no one else—my mind is quiet and I feel clean inside.

I walk back to my car, fish through the cluttered boot and find an old jogging jacket. Then I settle back into my seat. Beneath the stars, beneath my patched canvas top, I huddle beneath my jacket and sleep without dreams.

47 He Ain't Lost

It's 28 days later and I'm standing at the same Brave Ascent window, looking out on the same Fresno street. I graduated again yesterday. Was free to leave at six this morning. This time there is no man in a trench coat and I'm not waiting on a cab. I'm not sure what I'm waiting for—

Maybe I'm waiting for Jared.

Waiting for him to roll over in his bed.

Waiting for him to ask me what I'm afraid of.

Wish I had been able to tell him.

I'm afraid to leave.

I'm scared as hell with no idea what to do.

A week into my treatment a bed freed up in my old room. I asked Mr. Shaw if I could move back. Mr. Shaw and I had already talked a lot about Jared, about my guilt around his suicide. Mr. Shaw never told me what to feel, or not feel, and I liked that about him. He did say the disease is a killer and that he's never surprised when one of us dies. He said he's surprised when one of us lives and decides to accept recovery.

I took Jared's bed. Another new guy is sleeping in my old bed now. He's older than I am, he snores, and he says he's not afraid of anything just like I did.

The staff encourages us to laugh about the trauma we've been through. Don't glamorize it they say. Don't make light of it they say. But, they say, do take the shame out of it. I don't talk about Paul and Tara. It's too shameful, too personal. I have been honest about my drinking and drug use though. And in private, I've talked with Mr. Shaw about my family. I even told him what my dad did to me. I've done a lot of work in here this time. I have a lot more to do.

A week ago at the breakfast table, Dave, an alcoholic minister, unfolded the Sunday paper. On the front page, above the fold, was a color photo of the Feds leading Paul from the Valombrosa Building in handcuffs. He was staring right into the camera and right off the page smirking at me. The headline read—

CALTEARS CEO EXPOSES $16 BILLION VC PONZI SCHEME!
FBI RAIDS SAN FRANCISCO HEDGE-FUND OFFICES
PAUL VALOMBROSA AND CFO ARRESTED

Dave folded the paper in half to read the sports page. I cut a hunk of bread, buttered it, and finished my oatmeal and eggs. I never filled out any paperwork at Valombrosa Capital. Nobody knows I exist. And as far as I'm concerned, Paul no longer exists.

I TURN AROUND, but Jared's not there—just his empty made bed with the big blue sobriety book resting on the pillow. I'm not much into the steps they preach here and I was planning to leave the book for the next guy, but on my way to the door, I change my mind and grab it.

I look at my snoring roommate. I hardly know him. I know he's not ready. I hope he lives long enough to find what he's looking for.

At the end of the hall, before I reach the exit, I stop and poke my head in to say goodbye to Mr. Shaw. He sits at his desk wearing his reading glasses and leaning over lamplit manila folders. I knock on the open door. He looks up. He says,

Leaving us now, Trevor?

Yeah, I just came to say goodbye.

Mr. Shaw gets up from his desk. He limps toward me on his fake leg. I stick my hand out to shake. He ignores my hand and wraps his arms around me. It feels good. He pulls away but keeps his hands on my shoulders. He says,

Remember to get connected out there this time, Trevor.

Okay, Mr. Shaw..

It's Ed now, he says, smiling. You're not a patient anymore. You're a fellow.

He pats my shoulder and then drops his hands. When I turn for the door, he says,

And, Trevor, remember to pray.

I look at the book in my hand. I say,

You know, I'm not sure I believe in a higher power.

He nods his head to tell me he understands. Then he says,

You know why God's so hard to find, Trevor?

No, Mr. Shaw, I say, why is God so hard to find?

God's so hard to find because he ain't lost!

Mr. Shaw chuckles at his joke and limps back to his desk.

I hesitate at the door. I look back. I say,

Hey, Mr. Shaw.

He looks up. I smile. I say,

Thanks, Ed.

THE CANVAS COVER slides easy off my car. I shake it, roll it up, and tuck it back in the boot. The Porsche, protected by the canvas, is still clean from Mr. Luger's wash job, but it shows the scars of what I've been through. The front bumper bent where it rested on the tree trunk at the Valombrosa mansion. The paint chipped away where I crashed through the gates. The canvas top sun-faded except for a dark spot where I used duct tape to patch the tear.

I climb in the driver's seat and slide my hands over the wheel. I take a deep breath, smell damp leather and the faded scent of Barbara's vanilla tree car-freshener beneath my seat. Reaching up, I run my finger along the new permanent patch covering the tear in the top. It's still a scar and always will be, but it's not leaking anymore.

I think about the hole in my guts, the hole I filled with booze and drugs and sex, the black hole that swallowed everything and still wanted more. I know that I tried to patch that hole from the outside. But it's an inside job.

I look in the mirror. My breath steams it, and then fades. My face is full and flush and smooth. My eyes are clear—the whites white, the irises blue-green, the pupils black and pure.

I turn the key halfway—the dashboard springs to life, the fuel gage climbs up to full. Just for kicks, I push the power button on the broken CD player—it turns on and "Silence" by Delerium plays mid-song, right where it stopped almost 10 years ago. I scroll forward to "Euphorian (Firefly)." Its lyrics fit the day.

I push the clutch.

I turn the key.

It starts.

48 Just Human

Barbara's backyard blooms with early bunches of yellow daffodils, clusters of red tulips, and Virginia bluebells hanging from a garden arbor. First week of February, spring already in the valley.

I'm sitting beneath a pink cherry tree watching lilacs sway in a gentle breeze. Barbara is inside brewing us more coffee. I've been here three hours telling her my story.

When I knocked on her door, Barbara was happy to see me. She told me that Stephanie had left for Istanbul, Turkey to spend her spring semester studying English language education there. I told her I wasn't here for Stephanie. She invited me in.

I told Barbara about Paul and Tara. What I left out, she guessed. Then I told her about my dad—what he did to me, how I repressed it. She looked sad, but she didn't say anything. She just let the birds sing in the trees and some time pass quiet between us. Then she asked me about my mother. I told her about our run for San Diego, about stopping north of Bixby Bridge. I told her about Mom's mastectomy. I told her about leaving for college, about Mom giving me her Porsche. I told her about the call, about my last weeks with her. Then I confessed to never visiting her grave, not once since the day we buried her.

Barbara said my mother was lucky to have me to love. She said my mother must be somewhere beaming down proud because of the man I've become.

You really think my mother would be proud? I said.

Barbara nodded and then she stood up, excused herself, and rushed in the house to brew us more coffee.

BARBARA RETURNS carrying two mugs of coffee.

She sits next to me, closer than before. She hands me a mug. You know, she says, it just occurred to me why I tried so desperately to keep you and Stephanie together . . .

Barbara chokes up and her voice trails off. She pats my knee, looks away. She says,

. . . I always wanted a son and I wanted him to be you.

I pull out the envelope and hand it to Barbara. She sees the money inside and her hand jumps to her mouth. She shakes her head, pushes the money back.

Barbara loved me enough to scrape together $6,300 for my treatment. I repaid her by blowing more than that on drugs and booze and bullshit and making her watch as I fell apart, but here is my chance to show that I love her too, to make it right, to pay what I owe. I force the envelope into her hand again. She takes it, she nods, she understands. She lays the envelope on the bench next to her. Then she says,

You know, I added you to my prayer list at church.

I sip my coffee and force a smile. I say,

That's nice, Barb, but I don't really believe in God.

Well, he believes in you, she says.

He never answered any of my prayers.

Barbara lifts an eyebrow at me. She says,

You sure about that? You're here. You survived. You know, Trevor, God hides himself pretty well in the world. If you want to find him, you might have to look left and right—not up. My mother could see things. She used to brew us girls Armenian coffee. Just like this we're drinking. When we finished a cup, she'd turn it over and let it cool. Then she'd turn it back and read our destinies in the grounds.

What did yours say?

I can't tell you that, she says, but when I read yours just now in the kitchen, it told me you're on the right path.

I did lots of bad things, Barbara.

So has everybody, Trevor.

I hurt lots of people.

Yourself most of all.

She's right. I think of that little boy and I want to go back, tell him what I know, tell him everything will be okay, spare him the 20 years of hell I've put myself through. But I can't wholly regret the wounds because they made me tough, they helped me survive, they taught me what I know—that I don't need anything from out there, that I've got everything I need right here inside me.

Barbara sighs. Sometimes I wonder if it's God's forgiveness we need, she says. Seems to me he forgives us before we even ask. It's forgiving ourselves that's long in coming.

Thinking about my dad, I look at Barbara and say,

I don't want to be like the Christians I know, Barbara.

Oh, Trevor, she says. You're already more Christian than most Christians I know.

No, I say. Just human.

Barbara smiles at me over her mug of coffee. She says,

Same thing, Trevor—same thing.

49 There'll Be Tomorrow

The cemetery rises against the blue sky in terraces from the parking lot at the river's edge. A stand of bigleaf maples, already flush with leaves, follows the river. Above the river on pylons, at the far end of the cemetery, an old-stone pump house with a great wooden waterwheel, pumps river water to the highest terrace where it drips down irrigating the entire cemetery.

The lower terraces are from a different time and the graves are a maze of broken-winged statues and towering stone crosses that cast long shadows on elaborate marble monuments all edge-worn and shaded by the maples and surrounded by lush, green sun-dappled lawns with tall tufts of headed grass in the corners where the mowers can't reach.

I slept at Barbara's house last night and this morning, she saw me off with a vase of fresh flowers from her garden. She didn't say it, but I think she knew I was going to see my mom.

Barbara's flowers are bright and fragrant in my hand, the vase cool and heavy as I climb the stone steps connecting the terraced levels. The higher I climb the drier the levels. The grass a lighter shade of green with each terrace. The higher I climb the more orderly the graves. The headstones more modest. And at the uppermost terrace, abutting the dry, rocky uphill end of the cemetery, a six-foot wall of blazing crepe myrtles spread their scarlet blooms in a long arc encircling perfect rows of flat stones flush with the grass.

I haven't been here in 10 years, but I count my way straight to Mom's grave. Seventeen stones south, nine stones north, and there she is—Mom.

Her small headstone is dirty and weathered, covered with dried winter moss. I remember going to see Dad, and I remember him saying it wasn't cheap keeping up Mom's flower service, and I remember him asking me for money and saying, You gotta honor your mother, son. All these years. All that money. It doesn't look like he or anyone has ever been here.

I set the vase of flowers down and strip off my jacket. I pull my T-shirt over my head, wad it up, tip the vase, and wet the shirt. Using the wet shirt, I scrub Mom's stone clean.

I position the vase of flowers next to the clean stone and stand back to look—

PATRICIA ROBERTS

1958–1997

"SMILE, AND THERE'LL BE TOMORROW."

I don't cry. I'm no longer holding back, I just don't have any tears left. It took everything to get me here to say goodbye.

In a way, cancer was the best thing that ever happened to my mom. After her mastectomy, she stopped letting Dad control her. She volunteered with a local mission and found some friends. Together they collected clothes and made lunches for the homeless, setting up every Thursday in the kitchen of the old Grange Hall. My mother never looked more alive.

I remember helping her one day. A stinky vagrant shuffled down the lunch line and when Mom asked him what he wanted on

his sandwich, he snarled at her and said he'd rather make it himself—
he said he didn't know where her filthy hands had been. I stepped
over to rescue her, but Mom just smiled, handed him a pair of latex
gloves and let him make his own sandwich.

My freshman year at Sac State, Mom started losing weight. She
went to the hospital for a checkup. I wheeled her out of the hospital
three weeks later to attend her own memorial service. We held it at
the Grange Hall and we called it a celebration of life. Her friends
gathered photos and put together a slideshow. There were no photos
of her from before the mastectomy except a few that I found stuck
together in a mildewed whiskey box in Dad's closet. It was as if her
life hadn't begun until the cancer told her life was ending.

Dad pulled himself off his barstool and came to the service but
he didn't speak. He just limped around telling everyone how hard it
was on him to see his wife suffer. How no one could imagine his
terrible grief. How God always has a plan and if it were God's plan
for him to outlive his wife, then he'd just have to call on the patience
of Job until he could join her in heaven.

Mom sat in her wheelchair and welcomed everything with a
halcyon smile. It must be a curious thing to be at your own memorial
service, even if it is called a celebration of life. I didn't know what to
say. I sat next to Mom holding her hand and whenever a photo of us
together flashed on the slideshow screen, she would squeeze my
hand and I'd look over and see tears in her eyes.

A week later, she was dead. I had expected the world to stop
spinning. It didn't. I saw most of the same people again at the funeral
but they were less approachable now that our connection was buried.

I never once visited Mom's grave. I wanted to remember her
alive, not cold and lonely buried beneath the dirt.

I would give anything to be reunited with my mom. Not in my
dad's heaven, but maybe in the paradise I saw that day through the
storm clouds South of Bixby Bridge.

A plump, red-breasted robin flutters to the ground behind Mom's headstone and pecks at the grass. The first robin of spring—my mom used to say whoever saw the first robin would have a year of good luck.

A lawn edger buzzes in the distance. I feel a cool breeze on my bare back, smell the fresh-cut grass. I look down the terraced hillside. The waterwheel turns. The silver river flows. The maples stir. I smile for my mom—the long and honest happy-to-see-you way she used to smile at me.

I love you, Mom.

50 Stay, Son

The open door pours a gold shaft of dusty daylight into the dim bar. A winter's worth of spilt beer and piss and puke rises in a shimmering stench from the floorboards. Hank watches a daytime soap on a small TV behind the bar. Dad sits on his personal stool under the yellow glow of the CARL'S BAR sign squinting to see who has come in. The door bangs shut. Dad recognizes me. He says,

Sonny boy, am I glad to see you. Hank! Get your head outta that trash TV and get us a round of Bourbon here to celebrate my son!

The kid here can have whatever he wants, Hank says, but your tab's no good, Carl.

I take a stool next to my dad. I say,

I'll buy a round, Hank, but just coffee for me.

Hank nods. He uncorks a bottle of Bourbon, slides a glass in front of Dad and fills it. Dad gulps the Bourbon down, slams the empty glass on the bar, nods in my direction and says,

I'll have his Bourbon too.

Hank sighs and refills Dad's glass. Then he pours two mugs of steaming black coffee, hands one to me. I hold out $20. Hank shakes his head and waves it away. He smiles. He says,

It's nice to see you, Trevor. You look different. You look good.

Hank takes his mug of coffee and returns to his soap. Dad blows a string of snot onto the floor and stares after him. He says,

Hank's got no right treating me this way in front of my son.

I'm sober now, Dad.

This whole place used to be mine.

It's been over a month since I had a drink, Dad.

My health ain't been none too good—

I went to see Mom, Dad.

I ain't seen no money for a while.

Some of that money I've been sending you all these years was for flower service, Dad. I didn't see any flowers, Dad.

Dad reaches for his Bible. He says,

Scripture says that the flower fadeth, but the word of our God shall stand forever.

I strip the Bible from his hands, slide it down the bar. I say,

You wanna know why you look so hard in that Bible but still can't find God?

Dad sips his Bourbon. His hands shake. I say,

You can't find him because God isn't lost.

His head snaps toward me. His soapy eyes narrow. His lips quiver. Goddamn church turned me out, son, he says. Turned me out in the goddamn cold!

I had planned to confront my dad about his abuse, planned to tell him that I remember what he did to me in that dark bedroom when Mom was working at the cannery. But now that I see him hunched over, cradling his precious glass of Bourbon, I wonder if he even knows what he did when he was drunk. He looks pathetic and powerless and impotent slumped on his ass-worn stool and in that instant, I forgive him. I forgive him and like water draining from the sand after a wave, the power he held over me disappears. A slow smile rises on my face. I look my dad right in the eye. I say,

I came to say goodbye, Dad.

I see the shock in my dad's face—the fear that appears there as I hold his stare—his eyes well up—he looks like he's about to cry. Pleading, he says,

Stay, Son. Just a little while. Play that old song? The one your mother liked. She sang it all the time. Even had us etch it on her stone. Remember? It's on the box over there. Play it, will ya? Please.

I walk to the jukebox and pump in a quarter. Flipping through the old list of records, I find Judy Garland and press the button. The album lifts onto the turntable and "Smile" plays.

All this time, I've been afraid of my dad but he's nothing to fear. He doesn't have any power over me I don't give him. Truth is he wouldn't have had any power over Mom either if she'd just been able to take it away—if she'd just kept driving and drove her Porsche over Bixby Bridge that day.

I walk back to the bar and sit down. I look at my dad and try to remember the good times. There were a few. He taught me to catch a football, throw a perfect spiral. He taught me to drive a stick and he didn't yell when I ran over my own bicycle. Most of all, without even knowing it, he taught me what I never want to become.

I lift my mug and stop short of taking a sip—I smell the liquid smoke and molasses of Bourbon. Dad poured Bourbon in my coffee while my back was turned to the jukebox. I set the mug down.

Standing, I reach out and press my hand on my dad's shoulder and when he looks away from me, I walk out of the bar.

51 The Other Side

The Pacific Coast Highway opens up before me at dawn. The big blue sobriety book sits on the seat next to me. I realize now that Jared was right—everyone is afraid of something.

When he wasn't afraid anymore, Jared died to be with his mom. Now that I'm not afraid anymore, I'm living for my mom.

Yes, something terrible happened to me when I was 10, and I got stuck right there, 10 years old, in my dad's dark bedroom living through it again and again until I could face what he did to me. When I did face it, I found that little boy hiding inside me. I found the dad that the boy needs hiding there too. Now it's time to move on.

I taped the photo of the boy who looks just like me to my rearview mirror because I never want to forget.

JUST AS SUNRISE touches the cliff tops, I pull the Porsche off the highway on the north side of Bixby Bridge.

I remember sitting in this same car, in this same spot, looking at this same sign 20 years ago—BIXBY BRIDGE 1932.

The canyon is deep, but not as deep as I remember. The narrow bridge is tall, but not as tall as I remember. And the south side of Bixby Bridge looks nothing like the paradise I remember.

I remember Mom crying, reaching over, touching my bruised cheek. I remember the apology in her eyes. I remember the rain that came flooding down. I look at the passenger seat and I know the boy is still there waiting to cross this bridge.

I don't know what lies South of Bixby Bridge for me, but I know I'm headed in the right direction. And I know next time I visit Mom, I'll be able to tell her I made it to San Diego at last. I don't know when that will be, the next time I'll be back—maybe not until it's time to bury Dad.

I turn 30 next month. I still can't picture the rest of my life without a drink, but I can picture the rest of today. I don't know where I'll live, I don't know what I'll do for work—I do know I'm done with the money business. Who knows, Highway 1 takes me right past Malibu on my way south—maybe Tara still needs a live-in gardener. Nah . . . I'm sure I'll just drive by without stopping. Maybe Stephanie will return from her trip to Turkey and call me one day.

I look in the rearview mirror at all that's behind me now. Releasing the convertible latch for the first time in 20 years, I press the top down. I pull back onto the highway and drive my mother's Porsche across the bridge.

South of Bixby Bridge, I thread the Pacific Coast Highway cliffs, between the towering redwoods of Big Sur and the big, blue Pacific.

I feel the wind in my hair and it feels good.

For the first time in my life, I'm not afraid anymore.

THE END

Descending Mount Rainier, July 2008
Photo by Todd Stone

About the Author

Ryan Winfield is a novelist, poet, and screenwriter.

When he's not climbing mountains or traveling in search of
new stories, he's writing in his downtown Seattle home.

South of Bixby Bridge is his first novel.

For more information go to:
www.RyanWinfield.com

I found a paper plane today.

I flew it home, across a sea of time
where morning mist glides
over old man Ikeard's pond,
climbs the willow where I hide
to hear his lonely rowing song
into shadows—
licked away by midday sun
wading now in shady shallows.
Run perch, run—fingerlings
memories swim beyond my grip
flare and fade forever from the tip
of my marshmallow stick—
when twilight oaks shiver
their fallen brothers burn the wind
distant campfires spark
the world mysterious again,
I hear mother's call
echo across pond and time
tuck me in—
my pillow smells of pine
fold the day up in goodnight.
Sleep son, sleep—dreams
paper planes sent to the night,
what any of it means
I'll forget by morning light.